THE
TRAGEDY
OF
ERRORS

MANFRED B. LEE AND FREDERIC DANNAY, 1943
(Photograph Eric Schall, *Life Magazine*, © Time Inc.; reproduction courtesy the Manfred B. Lee family)

THE TRAGEDY OF ERRORS

AND OTHERS

ELLERY QUEEN

**With Essays and Tributes to Recognize
Ellery Queen's Seventieth Anniversary**

Crippen & Landru Publishers
Norfolk, Virginia
1999

THE TRAGEDY OF ERRORS AND OTHERS

Cover design by Deborah Miller

Crippen & Landru logo by Eric D. Greene

ISBN (limited edition): 1-885941-35-8
ISBN (trade edition): 1-885941-36-6

FIRST EDITION

10 9 8 7 6 5 4 3 2 1

Crippen & Landru Publishers
P. O. Box 9315
Norfolk, VA 23505
USA

Email: CrippenL@Pilot.Infi.Net
Web: www.crippenlandru.com

TABLE OF CONTENTS

PUBLISHER'S PREFACE

Seventy years ago, two cousins, Frederic Dannay (1905-1982) and
Manfred B. Lee (1905-1971), chose "Ellery Queen" both as their joint
pseudonym and as the name of their detective, and their first novel, *The
Roman Hat Mystery*, was published. During the next decades Ellery
Queen became the most popular detective in America, and his creators
two of the most influential mystery writers. Queen appeared not only in
novels and short stories, but on the radio, in movies, on television, and
even in comic books. Queen as scholar and editor wrote a number of
critical books and articles on the detective story, and he assembled many
anthologies and founded *Ellery Queen's Mystery Magazine*, which has been
published for almost sixty years. *The Tragedy of Errors and Others*, the first
new Ellery Queen book since 1971, is published in honor of Queen's
seventieth anniversary.

A few words should be said about the contents and structure of this
book. The title story is a detailed plot synopsis for the final but never
completed Ellery Queen novel. As a general rule, Frederic Dannay
devised the complicated plots of each Queen novel and story, and
Manfred B. Lee did the actual writing—setting, character development,
and much of the dialogue. Dannay completed his work on "A Tragedy
of Errors," but Lee died before he could turn it into a full-length novel.
The second section of the book contains the six hitherto uncollected short
stories by Ellery Queen. "Terror Town," which many experts consider
one of Queen's finest tales, has never previously been published in a
Queen book probably because it does not feature the character Ellery
Queen. The remaining stories are lesser efforts, but include typical
Queen gimmicks especially dying messages and word play. The final
story, "The Reindeer Clue," was actually ghostwritten by Edward D.
Hoch, but since it was published during Frederic Dannay's lifetime and
approved by him, we have included it to complete the Queen saga.

The third section is made up of essays, tributes, and reminiscences
about Dannay and Lee and their contributions to the mystery story. The
essays begin and end with surveys from different viewpoints of the
cousins' accomplishments, and there is a rudimentary grouping of the

other essays around major topics, which the reader will quickly recognize. The reader will also note that because Frederic Dannay outlived Manfred B. Lee by more than a decade and, because as editor of *Ellery Queen's Mystery Magazine* he was a more public person, we have more essays about Dannay than about Lee. Manfred B. Lee was, however, just as important in the Queen story, and (as Jon L. Breen points out in his opening essay), it is time that a complete study be done of these two extraordinary men.

I would like to add a personal note. As someone who grew up reading and admiring the works of Ellery Queen, it is an honor to publish this book.

THE
TRAGEDY
OF
ERRORS

outline
of a new novel
by

ELLERY QUEEN

CONTENTS

ACT V

DRAMATIS PERSONAE

MORNA RICHMOND (née Mary Louise Ravich) was born on October 6, 1901. This story begins on April 3, 1967, so Morna is 65-plus. She was a superstar of the silent movies, world-famous throughout the decade of the 20s. She earned fabulous salaries and lived the fabulous Hollywood life of that era. When talkies came, in 1927-28, Morna was lucky—in fact, luck is really the keystone of her success. She was one of the most beautiful women in the world in the 20s, but she had almost no acting talent. Her voice proved to be sexy for the early talkies, so she easily made the transition from the silent screen to sound. But no director could change her stagey, exaggerated acting, which had been suited to the old silent pictures but was embarrassing in the new medium. Her beauty, reputation, and popularity carried her for the first few years of talkies, and then her career came to an almost abrupt end. She "retired."

Morna had been consistently lucky in financial matters. On the advice of her late business manager she had invested in Los Angeles real estate, and when the boom came, she sold out for huge profits. At the time this story begins, she is living in her castle known as Elsinore on a 100-acre hilltop overlooking Hollywood—a veritable castle with turrets, ramparts, an honest-to-goodness moat (in which swans still glide), a gatekeeper's lodge, and all modern conveniences including a swimming pool in the courtyard and an attached 8-car garage housing 4 autos— "his" and "her" sports cars (Morna's rarely used), a long black limousine (for "shopping"), and a long white Rolls-Royce (for "state occasions," which no longer occur). Morna bought the castle in the early 20s from an oil tycoon. In addition to Elsinore and a considerable fortune in jewelry, Morna, as of April 1967, has $10,000,000 in tax-exempt bonds which bring her about $500,000 a year in tax-free income, permitting her to continue living in the style to which she has become accustomed.

Morna is essentially a shallow person. She indulges herself emotionally, and nearly every upset sends her frantically to her psychiatrist, Dr. Rago, whom she often sees daily, and sometimes sees more than once a day. She has a sort of rough-diamond petty shrewdness or cunning that shows itself occasionally; but basically she is "temperamental," dramatic, sometimes imperious, suggestible, absent-minded and forgetful; she constantly protests her "impracticality"—she can't be bothered by business or household details; but she is keenly aware of every dollar coming in and going out. She is a mess of nerves and fears —emotionally disturbed about "getting old," about her faded beauty, about her lost fame.

BUCK (known socially as STUD) BURNSHAW (né Bernard Perkins) was born on July 6, 1937. When this story begins, he is nearly 30—one-half Morna's age. A small-part actor in low-budget Westerns, Buck is an ambitious, self-deluded, unscrupulous hustler who never made it in pictures, who blames his failure to be a star on bad luck instead of errors of judgment and actions, and who is willing to do anything to hit it big. Basically he is simple-minded, impulsive, often rash. He is easily influenced, gullible, unstable, always leaping before he looks and having no control of his vicious temper when things inevitably go wrong.

Morna and Buck first met in 1960, and quickly came to an arrangement. Morna needed a handsome, virile young man to satisfy her still-active physical desires and to feed her ego and vanity. Buck needed a situation that promised him a big score. There is no marriage—Morna would never even consider it—but they live together in Elsinore castle. For a year Elsinore rang with fabulous parties; news cameras caught the lovers' frequent personal appearances and gossip columns even hinted at Morna Richmond's "return" to films. But all attempts by Morna and her newly hired press agent to recapture the glamorous days of the 20s were doomed to failure. Neither Morna nor Buck has any real friends, and soon the hangers-on and freeloaders drifted away or were sent packing, leaving the two lovers alone in the Class-B-horror-film castle. (Morna is emotionally dependent on her psychiatrist, Dr. Rago; she confides everything to him, and in the sense that he helps her nearly every day, in a visit or by telephone, he is a friend.)

Morna's days have become routine: breakfast never earlier than noon; afternoons spent in perpetual cosmetizing and sunbathing at the pool— she is a sucker for any new lotion, cream, or whatnot, and a fanatical sun worshiper (vain attempts to halt the ravages of time—she is 65, insists she is 55, and looks 70); evenings glued to the television, which she says she detests, but really loves; sleepless nights watching late-late-late shows, especially old movies, hoping that some of her own will miraculously come to life; and nearly every day—bitter, recriminating quarrels with Buck, most of them followed by desperate visits to Dr. Rago.

Buck, who by now has invested seven years in this "main chance" and who will put up with anything to save his investment, hangs around, alternating between catering to Morna and treating her with bursts of contempt. Whenever he can't stand it any more, he drives off at reckless speed in "his" sports car to find solace with his girl friend, Cherry O'Hare. Morna's and Buck's lives are not ones of quiet desperation: their life together is violently loud and filled with cruelty and mutual hate.

CHERRY O'HARE is an ex-starlet reduced to B-girl, a go-go girl, or any other kind of girl who can make a fast or an easy buck. O'Hare is her real name, and she was christened Margaret. As a starlet she called herself Scarlett O'Hare, and when this didn't help she changed her first name to Cherry (suggested by Buck). She keeps turning up throughout the story like a bad penny—a frank opportunist constantly on the make.

DION PROCTOR is a young coal-black unproduced playwright. He wears a modified Afro-style haircut and conservative-style clothes. He seems to be passive and detached, interested only in his work; he is always cool, expressionless, self-protectively aloof, low-voiced, and he speaks only when he has to. Morna is his patroness: she gives him a monthly allowance and the use of the small renovated gatekeeper's lodge situated quite far from the castle, out of earshot, where the county road ends and the private road to the castle begins. Morna thinks Proctor is a second Shakespeare, and she has promised to finance the production of his first play, which he has been rewriting for years. Dion has no car— he gets around on his motorcycle. He never has visitors, and when he wants to socialize, he goes to an ethnic coffeehouse in L.A.

SERVANTS at Elsinore castle: cook, three maids, handyman-gardener, and chauffeur-butler.

THEODORE (Ted) CURTIS, JR. is an ambitious, aggressive lawyer. His father, Old Theodore, was also a lawyer, and in the 20s through the 50s he was a Hollywood character. Some of the most celebrated and/or notorious film people were the old man's clients. With a spectacular practice Old Theodore had lived like a motion-picture superstar. But this high living and a series of expensive wives (and even more expensive community-property settlements) and a string of careless investments finally brought the old man to suicide—in 1964. Ted inherited the remnants of his father's practice. Most of the old clients were dead, and those who weren't had little lucrative legal work left. One of the old clients is Morna Richmond, and Ted handles all her financial and business affairs, which really don't amount to much in actual legal fees. At the beginning of this story the once spectacular legal practice is reduced to a staff of two in a small suite of offices in a second-rate building, and for the past three years Ted has been scrounging and scratching for new clients.

DR. RAGO is in his early forties. His typical psychiatrist's (Freudian) beard almost makes him look older. He wears fashionably long hair, semi-mod clothes, and is a chain pipe smoker. His professional manner can be gently and compassionately persuasive, but usually he talks with authority, and always with a contemporary point of view.

ARNOLD KOLISHER is a publicity-minded criminal lawyer.

REED HARMON—see outline.

LIEUTENANT PEREZ is a lieutenant of Homicide, LAPD.

NOTE: The Prologue, the 5 acts, and the Epilogue—each to begin with an epigraph—a believe-it-or-not or shocking or incredible or really wild news story, in quotes and with source, from 1967. Also consider having a similar but much shorter quotation at the beginning of each scene.

PROLOGUE

Elsinore castle. "Sudden and quick in quarrel"

Monday, April 3, 1967: Morna and Buck have the most violent quarrel in their seven years of living together. It starts in the living room when Morna produces another woman's handkerchief, with the name Cherry stitched on it, which Morna found a week ago in one of Buck's twenty sports jackets. Morna demands to know who Cherry is. Buck says he knows nothing about the handkerchief or how it got into his pocket, and doesn't know anyone named Cherry. Morna laughs: does he think she's a fool? As soon as she found the handkerchief she hired a private detective to follow Buck. This morning she received the detective's report. She knows the girl's full name, Cherry O'Hare, where the tramp lives, how often Buck has visited her apartment, how long he stayed each time. Buck has broken his promise—he has been cheating on Morna.

Buck laughs: Cheating? He reminds Morna they are not married. And look who's talking about breaking promises? What about the large sum of money that Morna promised him seven years ago, or her promise to make out a will and name him her heir? The quarrel quickly degenerates to name calling and a double catalogue of all the complaints they have against each other.

Before the fight reaches its climax, there is a near-interruption. Dion Proctor has motorcycled from the gatekeeper's lodge to the terrace outside the living room. Morna and Buck are too deeply involved in their accusations and counter-accusations to hear the motorcycle. Dion is about to enter the living room when he hears the quarrel. He listens for a few moments, his face expressionless, then shrugs, starts his motorcycle—Morna and Buck are still oblivious of any outside noise— and drives back to the lodge.

Just after Dion's departure, Morna hits the peak of her rage and says the one unforgivable thing. Buck's left leg is slightly shorter than his right and he wears a special built-up shoe. Morna calls him a cripple. Buck loses his temper, seizes Morna by the throat, and begins to strangle her, yelling over and over again: "I'll kill you! I'll kill you!"

Morna's screams bring in the servants, who separate the two. When Morna recovers she goes to her bedroom and locks the door behind her. A little later, when Buck cools down, he tries to enter Morna's bedroom, but she calls out "Go away." Buck, desperately afraid he has gone too far this time, tells her through the door that he didn't mean it, that it will never happen again, to let him in to prove how sorry he is. He wheedles, cajoles, then slyly suggests, and finally Morna opens the door. Buck lifts her in his arms and carries her to the bed. He possesses one irresistible means of reconciliation. He whispers, caresses, excites . . .

An hour later, after Buck has left the bedroom certain that he has restored the status quo ante, Morna dresses slowly and thoughtfully. In the aftermath of lovemaking she realizes how close a call the interrupted strangling had been. She makes up elaborately and puts on one of her two dozen wigs. On the intercom she instructs the chauffeur to bring round the limousine—she'll be going out, first to see Dr. Rago, and then to visit Mr. Theodore Curtis (she is the only one who calls her lawyer Theodore; everyone else calls him Ted or Junior.)

ACT I. SCENE I.

Curtis' law office. "Let's choose executors and talk of wills"

Two days later, on April 5, in Curtis' law office: Curtis has prepared a will for Morna exactly the way she has instructed him to—with blank spaces for the name of the heir, for her signature and the date, and for the signatures of witnesses. Morna fills in the name of the heir on the two copies of the will, holding one hand over the paper so that no one, including the lawyer, can see what she is writing. Then she signs both copies, still concealing the chief provision of the will, and Curtis' two employees, his secretary and a receptionist, add their signatures as witnesses.

Morna takes one of the two copies and inserts it in an envelope labeled LAST WILL AND TESTAMENT OF MORNA RICHMOND, seals the envelope, and hands it to Curtis for safekeeping. She slips the other copy into a similarly labeled envelope, puts it in her bag, and makes a grand exit.

ACT I. SCENE II.

Elsinore castle. "Each thing's a thief"

Friday afternoon, April 7: While Morna is sunbathing at the pool Buck enters Morna's bedroom, pushes aside a picture on the wall, disclosing a safe, manipulates the dial four times, opens the safe, finds the envelope containing Morna's copy of the will, reads the will, then puts it in his pocket. Without saying anything to Morna, he gets into his sports car and drives to Cherry O'Hare's apartment where he hands the envelope, now sealed, to Cherry and tells her to keep it for him.

ACT I. SCENE III.

The same. "I needs must act alone"

Sunday, April 23: The servants at Elsinore have alternate Sundays off, staggering them so that half of the staff is present every Sunday. Today the cook, one maid, and the chauffeur are on duty. Shortly after dinner, while Morna is resting in her bedroom, Buck dismisses the three servants for the night. The chauffeur drives the cook and maid away.

ACT I. SCENE IV.

The same. "A necessary end"

The next morning, April 24: All the servants return early. Buck has breakfast at 10:00. At 12:15 Morna has still not rung for breakfast or come out of her bedroom. Buck sends one of the maids to inquire—and they all hear the maid scream.

Buck rushes to the bedroom, finds Morna dead on her bed, a bullet hole in her right temple, a gun lying on the floor under her dangling right hand. (Dead End Number One) The cook and chauffeur try to quiet the hysterical maid. Buck touches nothing. He phones Dr. Rago —Morna had no "family" doctor, she was in exceptional health for her age—and Rago tells Buck to call the police at once and he'll be over as quickly as he can.

ACT I. SCENE V.

Headquarters. "Upon a fearful summons"

Ellery is in Hollywood on an assignment—to write a screenplay for *Othello* treating it as a contemporary detective story. He is soaked in Shakespeare. On the morning of April 24 he has dropped in to renew his acquaintance with Lieutenant Perez of LAPD Homicide when the call comes in from Buck reporting the death by violence of Morna Richmond. Perez invites Ellery to tag along, and on the way to Elsinore castle Perez briefs Ellery on Morna's career and her relationships with Buck and Dion —all common knowledge in Hollywood.

ACT I. SCENE VI.

Elsinore castle. "Murder cannot be hid long"

Perez examines the body and the scene while Ellery watches. There are powder burns on Morna's right temple, indicating that the gun was held against her head or at most inches away. The gun on the floor had been fully loaded; only one shot had been fired.

Dr. Rago arrives in a hurry, followed almost immediately by the LAPD technicians. Perez motions Rago and Ellery to the living room, letting the (coroner)* and technicians go to work. The presence of the gun and the probability of a contact wound suggest that Morna may have committed suicide. She was right-handed and therefore could have shot herself in the right temple, and as she fell back on the bed the gun could have slipped from her hand and dropped to the floor.

Perez, to Dr. Rago: As the dead woman's psychiatrist, what do you think? Was Miss Richmond suicidal?

Dr. Rago hesitates. Then: Well, I suppose there is no reason to suppress it any longer. The truth is, she did try to commit suicide once.

It happened six years ago—on the most despondent day of the year for her. She was home alone, at midnight. She phoned him, told him

---

*Frederic Dannay put this word in parentheses to remind him or Manfred B. Lee to check whether this was the correct term in California.

hysterically that she couldn't go on, that she was going to end it all by taking an overdose of sleeping pills. He tried to talk her out of it, but she said goodbye and hung up. He rushed over, found her still alone, but unconscious, and saved her life. He told no one and never reported it to the police—there was enough of this sort of thing in Hollywood without adding another scandal unnecessarily. But—

Morna hadn't really intended to take her life. If she had, she wouldn't have phoned him. She was putting on one of her dramatic acts —she did that sort of thing all the time. Her call was a cry for help—she wanted him to save her. In Dr. Rago's professional opinion Morna was not at all suicidal.

Perez: You mean you think she was murdered?

Rago: I do.

Perez questions the servants. They tell how Morna and Buck hated each other, how they fought nearly every day, how Buck often threatened her. They describe the quarrel on April 3, three weeks ago—how it became so violent that they heard Morna scream; how they ran in and found Buck strangling her, yelling over and over that he'd kill her; how all of them had to pull him away from her by force. They are sure that if they had not been in the house, Buck would have murdered Morna.

Dion is called in. He has no alibi. He was alone in the gatekeeper's lodge, working on his play. No, he heard no sounds from the castle—the lodge is too far away. Yes, he heard the servants' car pass, heading for L.A. But no car passed the lodge heading for the castle, not while he was awake, and he worked till 2:00 a.m. Dion does not volunteer any information—he merely answers questions, succinctly, impassively, disinterestedly.

Perez summons Buck. The case against him grows more deadly with each question—but Buck is remarkably calm. Yes, he admits that Morna and he hated each other, that they quarreled incessantly, that he often threatened her—but he insists he did not kill her. He admits he sent the servants away last evening. Why? He wanted some privacy. Did Morna know the servants had been sent away for the night? N-n-no. Then he and Morna were alone in the house when she was shot? Yes—except for the murderer. Who would that be? A prowler, a tramp, a burglar—there were lots of them around. Anything stolen? No —maybe the thief was interrupted. Did Buck interrupt anyone? No.

Perez hammers away . . . Does Buck recognize the murder weapon? Yes, the gun is his, and he has a license for it; he bought it some years ago when there was an epidemic of prowlers and burglars in the neighborhood. Where did he keep the gun? In the drawer of the nightstand in his bedroom—yes, he and Morna had separate bedrooms. Was the gun loaded? Of course—otherwise what good is it? You mean the prowler entered the house, hunted for your gun, finally found it in your bedroom, then went to Morna's bedroom and killed her? Buck guesses it must have been that way. Why should a stranger look for *your* gun to kill Morna? How do I know, Buck says tightly, struggling to hold his temper; who knows? —maybe to frame me.

And the prowler found your gun in your bedroom without your hearing him? Buck wasn't in his bedroom—he was watching TV in the living room here until long past midnight. And you didn't hear a prowler enter the house? It's a big place and the TV was on pretty loud . . . altogether a flimsy, unconvincing story.

One of Perez's men interrupts. The coroner would like to see the lieutenant in Miss Richmond's bedroom. Perez and Ellery return to the scene of the crime. Morna's face has not yet been covered. Ellery gazes at it—he had not seen it clearly before. This hag, this crone—was this the face that launched a thousand sighs? That incredibly beautiful face of the 20s and 30s—in death it's the face of an old, old woman.

The coroner reports. He places the time of death at about 11:30 p.m. the night before. But even more important, there's something Perez and his men obviously missed—it's so small the coroner almost missed it himself.

Coroner: Look what I found clutched in her left fist—open her hand, Lieutenant, it's still there.

Perez can barely pry the fingers apart (rigor mortis). In Morna's left hand is a tiny metal pellet immediately recognizable as a BB, also called a BB shot.

Perez swears at himself and his men, then hurries back to the living room where he confronts Buck with the newly found evidence: This is the clincher—she's practically accused you of killing her. Buck Burnshaw—your initials, BB. She put the finger on you—"BB shot me."

Buck protests vehemently: I didn't do it! I didn't kill her!

Perez stares hard at Buck, then shrugs. There's no hurry, there's plenty of time. He dismisses Buck with the warning not to leave town, when Ellery speaks for the first time. Ellery understands that Buck and Morna were not married. Buck nods sullenly. Does Buck know if Morna had a will? Buck shakes his head—he doesn't know. Then Buck doesn't know if he gains by Morna's death? All that Buck knows is that seven years ago Morna promised to make him her heir or settle a large sum on him—that's one of the things they fought about, and Buck doesn't know if she ever kept her promise. So Buck would have no monetary reason to kill Morna? Buck's poise cracks for a moment, and he yells: "I tell you I didn't kill her!"

After Buck leaves the room, his left foot dragging, Perez says to Ellery: We'd better check on that will business right away.

ACT I. SCENE VII.

Curtis' office. "Wherefore are these things hid?"

Perez and Ellery question lawyer Curtis who has just returned from a business trip out of town and is shocked at the news of Morna's death. Yes, he has a copy of her will. He goes to his safe and comes back empty-handed and aghast. His copy of the will is missing!

There is no evidence of burglary. Who else has the combination of his office safe? Only his secretary. She is called in. It takes Perez only a few minutes to break her down. She admits she stole the sealed envelope containing the will. Someone called her on the phone in a disguised voice—no, she doesn't know if it was a man or a woman—and offered her $500 if she would steal the will. She had to do it—she is desperately in need of money because of family illness and hospital bills. The next morning—which day?—only a few days after Miss Richmond signed the will—the secretary received the money in the mail, small bills in an unmarked envelope. No, she no longer has the envelope—she burned it according to instructions given to her over the phone. She was also instructed to mail the will to a box number in General Post Office.

Perez calls headquarters and has one of his men go at once to the General Post Office. While waiting, Ellery asks the secretary if she read the will. The secretary shakes her head.

Perez, to Curtis: Do you want to press charges against her?

Curtis, shocked and bewildered: No, she has been in my employ, and in my father's, too long . . . and turning to his secretary, Curtis tells her to pack up and leave.

Ellery, to Curtis: Of course you know the provisions of the will. Who is the heir?

Ellery and Perez are bowled over when Curtis says he does not know, and explains how Morna kept the identity of her heir secret.

Perez's man phones from the Post Office. The box to which the will was mailed is now empty, and no one at the Post Office knows or remembers anything.

Curtis says there is a second copy, that Morna took it, that it is probably in Morna's safe in her bedroom—she once told him she kept her more important papers in the wall safe. No, he doesn't know the combination, but Buck probably knows it.

Perez and Ellery go back to Elsinore.

ACT I. SCENE VIII.

Elsinore castle. "The empty vessel makes the greatest sound"

In Morna's bedroom: Morna's body has been removed. With the old, old face gone, the shadows and wrinkles of age have also departed from the room. But the memory of one of the most beautiful women in the world lingers. The woman is dead, the legend is alive.

Buck shows them the safe. It has an unusual dial—not the ordinary dial with numbers and lines. Buck explains that Morna could never manage lining up the numbers accurately—the safe door would never open for her. So she had a special dial made—like a phone dial with letters, but with no numerals. The safe has a combination of four letters and all Morna had to do was pretend she was dialing a phone number.

Yes, Morna told Buck the combination. She was absent-minded, so she used a 4-letter word she couldn't possibly forget. Her outstanding triumph in films was an early hospital drama called "The House of Pain." She couldn't forget her greatest film success, so she chose the 4-letter word in its title. Buck remembers that she laughed when she told him the combination: she said PAIN was her little joke, but it would open the safe anyway.

Perez twirls the dial—the P in PRS, the A in ABC, the I in GHI, the N in MNO, and the safe door opens. The envelope containing the will is gone. (Dead End Number Two)

ACT 1. SCENE IX.

Dr. Rago's office. " 'Tis mad idolatry"

Monday, May 1: Ellery can't get back to his screenplay of *Othello*—the missing will gnaws at him. He decides to visit Dr. Rago—perhaps Morna's psychiatrist (he had said Morna confided everything in him) knows where her copy of the will is, or what the will specified.

But Dr. Rago doesn't have Morna's copy or know the terms of the will. Disappointed, Ellery is about to leave when he remembers something Dr. Rago said at the scene of the crime—that Morna's suicide attempt six years ago had occurred "on her most despondent day of the year." That was an odd statement—what did Dr. Rago mean by it?

The psychiatrist explains: Morna Richmond had one unfulfilled acting ambition—she had always wanted to be a Shakespearean actress. But she had never been given an opportunity, not even in stock or repertory. Morna had a passion for Shakespeare; she read the plays and poetry constantly. You understand, Mr. Queen, that she could love Shakespeare's work and yet understand very little of it—she didn't have the intellectual capacity to appreciate Shakespeare. Her passion for the greatest of all writers was not one of her affectations—and the Lord knows she had plenty of those! It may have started as an affectation, but it developed into a genuine love. She could declaim passage after passage, and hardly be aware of their meaning. Somehow the words, the rich imagery, the resonance brought her comfort, solace, support, and of course Dr. Rago encouraged her Shakespearean obsession—it was far better for her than drugs.

Ellery listens fascinated—Morna was quite a gal . . . In any event, Dr. Rago continues, April 23 was the most despondent day of the year for Morna. It is the anniversary of Shakespeare's death, and she spent every April 23 in deep mourning. That particular day six years ago—

Ellery: Just a moment, Doctor. April 23—I should have remembered the date of Shakespeare's death! She tried suicide six years ago, on April 23, and she was killed on April 23. Is it a coincidence that the attempted suicide and the actual killing occurred on the same date?

Dr. Rago doesn't think so. As he said, that date was her worst one every year. He recalls that six years ago Morna and Buck quarreled, Buck had left the house threatening he would never come back, and this had intensified her annual "mourning," her unhappiness about her faded beauty, her lost fame, her neglect by the public, her terrible loneliness—she really hadn't a friend in the world.

Ellery: But you said she really didn't mean to take her life?

Dr. Rago: I still believe that—she never stopped being an actress.
Ellery leaves. Morna's will remains a dead end.

The case is beginning to get to Ellery, beginning to be a hang-up.
There's something—what?—off-center, odd, elusive about it. Does
everything connected with Hollywood have a touch of the bizarre, a
suspicion of the irrational? (Where in the world did Morna find a BB
just before she died?) This mad, mad world of Hollywood—but is
Hollywood really any different from the rest of the world?

ACT I. SCENE X.

Headquarters. "Strict in his arrest"

Perez discusses the case against Buck with Ellery.

Motive: fully substantiated testimony of hate and threats, and most
damaging of all, at least one attempt by him to kill Morna—the attempt
actually witnessed by servants; also, Buck could have thought he would
gain a considerable sum by inheritance—although that missing will
business is puzzling.

Opportunity: Buck himself arranged for only two persons to be at
Elsinore the night of the murder—Morna, the victim, and Buck; so he
was the only one who had opportunity—and any red herring about a
prowler or burglar will sound so weak in court that it will hurt Buck
more than it will help him.

Means: Ballistics has proved that it was Buck's gun that killed
Morna. And that BB in Morna's hand! She was actually accusing Buck
of killing her—the D.A. will nail Buck's hide to the wall, the jury will eat
it up.

Ellery: Don't be so sure.

Perez: What do you mean? You know something?

Ellery: How did she happen to have a BB handy just before she died
of a bullet in the brain? A good lawyer could make hay out of that.

For a minute Perez is stopped cold. But he recovers quickly. The
point is she *did* have it—Ellery nods—and it points to one person and
one person only—Ellery nods—and besides, what else could it mean?
Ellery admits he has no other explanation that makes sense.

Perez makes up his mind. He recaps by ticking off the case against
Buck: first, no one else has such powerful motives to have killed Morna;
second, no one else had as good an opportunity; third, no one else had

easier access to the weapon; and fourth, no one else is pointed to by the BB clue.

So Buck is charged with Murder One, warned of his legal rights, arrested, booked, jailed. He can't raise ten cents worth of bail.

Ellery should be satisfied. It's a clear-cut case. As Perez so cogently argued, motive, opportunity, and means can be proved beyond the shadow of a doubt. But is any case of murder, without an eyewitness, ever so clear-cut? Murder as the solution to a problem is always an act of insanity. But Morna's murder—was it a clear-cut act of insanity? Or did its almost naive simplicity make it an act of—what?

ACT II. SCENE I.

A prison cell. "There is a tide in the affairs of men, which, taken at the flood, leads on to fortune"

May 19: Cherry O'Hare visits Buck in jail. Buck is surprisingly un-worried, even cheerful.

Buck: That envelope I gave you—it's safe?

Cherry nods.

Then Buck has a burst of euphoria—as in a drug experience. He once had a small part in a remake of the Count of Monte Cristo story— he played Edmond Dante's cellmate in the Chateau d'If. Remember it, Cherry?—the guy in prison, how he escaped and became a rich and powerful man. That's me, baby!

Cherry: You mean you're going to escape from here?

Buck: In my own way, yes. And when I get out I'm going to be rich and powerful. Then we're going to live, baby, really live!

ACT II. SCENE II.

A courtroom. "Reserve thy judgment"

Ellery finishes his writing assignment on *Othello* and returns to New York. But he comes back to Hollywood for the trial—irresistibly drawn to whatever it is in the case that is still bugging him.

Buck's trial begins on Monday, September 18. Because of Morna's background and the "wondrous strange" elements the trial quickly becomes a *cause célèbre*—front-page stories in every edition. And inexorably the prosecution builds its case—motive, opportunity, means, and the BB. The clue of the BB catches the imagination of the press and public, and the case is dubbed The BB Murder.

Arnold Kolisher, a publicity-minded criminal lawyer, has undertaken Buck's defense—not for a fat fee (Buck hasn't a dime) but for the national communications exposure. Kolisher has one field day after another, enhancing his notoriety, but his defense of Buck is inept. Buck appears unconcerned.

Dion Proctor attends the trial. Every day he takes a seat in the rear of the courtroom and listens intently to the testimony, making copious notes in a loose-leaf book. His face is a black mask.

ACT II. SCENE III.

Ellery's hotel room. "Help me, Cassius, or I sink!"

Near the end of the trial, when the case against Buck becomes more hopeless with each passing hour, Kolisher calls on Ellery. It is Sunday night, October 8. The lawyer says he has checked on Ellery, learned how many rabbits Ellery has pulled out of hats. That's what Buck, needs now —a rabbit. Would Ellery look into the case before it's too late?

Ellery tells Kolisher he has been in the case from the beginning, knows all about it. There's nothing he can do—the evidence against Buck is overwhelming.

Kolisher: But you've done it before, Mr. Queen! I know all the miracles you've pulled!

Ellery: By the way, what do you hear from Wrightsville?

Kolisher: Wrightsville? Never heard of it. Where is it?

Ellery: You haven't checked on me, you don't know anything about me. Who suggested that you ask me to intervene?

Kolisher hesitates, then: My client, Buck Burnshaw.

Ellery: Now, that's odd.

He phones Lieutenant Perez who has no objection to Ellery looking into the case again—but he's wasting his time.

ACT II. SCENE IV.

Elsinore castle. "They say miracles are past"

The next morning, Monday, October 9, Ellery goes back to the scene of the crime, Morna's bedroom. The room out of the past is, surprisingly, not dead. Something alive hovers there—the spirit of that once beautiful woman still haunts Elsinore castle.

Ellery's eyes swivel round the room. He doesn't know what he is looking for or what he expects to find. Then he recalls Morna's passion for Shakespeare, how she read the Bard constantly. Now that he thinks of it, why wasn't there a copy of Shakespeare in her bedroom where she did most of her reading? He doesn't remember seeing one.

On the bottom shelf of Morna's nightstand, in full view, he finds a thick volume, nearly 1500 pages, *The Complete Shakespeare.* He riffles through the pages, idly, almost absent-mindedly, and a single sheet of paper falls out. He reads it and is staggered.

When he recovers, he phones Perez to come to Elsinore at once.

Again that strange feeling comes over Ellery: this weird anachronism of Elsinore castle—who can believe it in 1967? This oddball murder case —is it sane or insane? Ellery tries to clear his head. He feels as if he is watching a motion picture that is curiously fluid on the screen, its focus constantly changing.

ACT II. SCENE V.

A courtroom. "The jury, passing on the prisoner's life"

At the request of defense attorney Kolisher the trial is adjourned for two days, to permit full investigation of the new evidence found by Ellery. When the trial reconvenes, Kolisher galvanizes and goes to work.

First he re-establishes the date of Morna Richmond's death—April 23, 1967.

Then he puts Ellery on the stand. Ellery describes finding the paper in Morna's bedroom copy of Shakespeare. The paper is a sheet of Morna's personal stationery. Ellery reads aloud what is written on it.

At the top: the date, April 23, 1967—the day Morna was killed.

Then: To my beloved fans all over the world . . . and Morna tells of her great personal troubles and how she can no longer bear them and how she hopes her fans will understand and forgive her for taking her own life . . . signed Morna Richmond.

There is a furor in the courtroom. The prosecution is glum. Kolisher calls Lieutenant Perez who admits that the police have thoroughly checked the handwriting of Morna's suicide letter and there is absolutely no question of its authenticity—Morna Richmond wrote it.

Kolisher, now pressing his case from every angle, calls Dr. Rago to the stand. He reminds the psychiatrist that he had previously stated Morna was not suicidal, that he was sure Morna would not use a gun. Dr. Rago tries to defend himself: he says he is still sure. Kolisher pounds at him: the suicide letter—does Dr. Rago doubt its genuineness? N-n-no . . . and finally he is forced to admit that in the circumstances he cannot be positive that Morna did not commit suicide using a gun—yes, she might have.

The case against Buck has collapsed. True, he still had motive—but motive alone is not proof of guilt. True, he was still the only other person in the house at the time of Morna's death—but the only other person can be present innocently if the victim has committed suicide. True, the gun was his—but Morna herself could have taken the gun from Buck's nightstand. True, the BB accusing Buck was found in Morna's hand—but Kolisher comes up with an explanation: Morna committed suicide and tried to frame Buck for murder—her last act of revenge and hatred!

The defense rests.

The jury is out exactly seventeen minutes.

Verdict: Not Guilty.

Buck is free. As he walks out of the courtroom, with Cherry on his arm, he pauses in front of Ellery. They don't speak to each other—they just stare. Then, with a grin, Buck leaves. There is no sign of his left foot dragging.

Dion Proctor, sitting in the rear of the courtroom, watches Buck and Cherry pass. Dion's face is emotionless.

Ellery sits there, slumped in his chair. He is terribly uneasy. What is bothering him? Is it only what Perez has kept repeating the past two days? Perez and his men had searched the bedroom on the morning of April 24 and had not found the letter. How could they possibly have overlooked it? But then they had overlooked the BB in Morna's hand.

Ellery knows his anxiety has a deeper source. What? Why is he so disturbed?

ACT III. SCENE I.

Curtis' office. "Plays such fantastic tricks"

The very next day, Friday, before they have recovered from Buck's acquittal, the first bombshell explodes. Before the day is over, they are in a state of almost total shock.

Buck asks for a meeting in Curtis' office. Present are Buck, Curtis, Perez, and Ellery.

Buck calmly announces that it was he who bribed Curtis' former secretary to steal Curtis' copy of Morna's will, that it was he who stole Morna's copy from her bedroom safe and gave both copies to Cherry to hold for him—no, the terms of the will can wait another few minutes, they've waited this long.

Then, turning to Curtis, Buck asks: Isn't it true that if a person is tried for murder and acquitted he can't be tried again, that he can't be put into double jeopardy?

Curtis admits that is substantially true.

Buck looks to Perez for confirmation, and Perez nods.

Then, still calm but with gloating in his eyes, Buck announces that he did murder Morna.

Shock, confusion, even horror . . . But the suicide letter? It was dated the day she died and established incontrovertibly to be in Morna's handwriting.

Buck explains: The suicide letter is absolutely genuine, except for one almost infinitesimal change—a most careful penstroke less than one-sixteenth of an inch long. Buck was sure it would be missed, and it was. The suicide letter *is* genuine—it was written by Morna—but it was written by her exactly six years before! It was a suicide letter she wrote the time she attempted to take her life on April 23, 1961. Buck says he found it and kept it—he knew he'd have a use for it some day. All he had to do, using the same color of ink and the same type of pen, was to put a tiny horizontal stroke at the top of the second 1 in 1961, changing it to 1967, and then to kill Morna on that date, April 23, 1967.

But why did Buck do all this? Why did he suppress the will, deliberately build the case against himself (establishing motive, arranging opportunity, using his own gun, putting the BB in Morna's hand), deliberately plan to be tried for murder, deliberately alter the old suicide letter so that it could be produced dramatically at the last minute and prove his innocence—why this fantastic and dangerous course of action?

Buck: So that I could qualify for Morna's estate under the terms of her will.

And then comes the second shocker of the day. Buck shows them the will. Morna had written in the blank space that she gave everything she possessed *to the person who murdered her.*

Oh, Buck knows why Morna did it. It was her last joke on him—a joke meant to be played from beyond the grave. All the seven years they had lived together she had tantalized him with promises of a big settlement—at least $1,000,000—even sometimes promising she would make out a will and give him everything. But she never meant a word of it. And when she became afraid that he might really kill her before she could protect herself or get rid of him, she made out a will that would give her the last laugh. Somehow Morna had learned that the law does not permit a murderer to benefit from his crime. So if she willed everything to her murderer, and if Buck did kill her, he'd have to prove he killed her, and if he did that to qualify under the terms of the will, the law would deprive him of any benefit . . . But Buck outwitted the old bitch.

Oh, he outwitted her all right. Her will gives everything to Morna's murderer. Buck is Morna's murderer. Therefore Buck inherits.

Curtis protests: But you admit you know that a murderer can't benefit from his crime!

Buck is triumphant: That's why I arranged to be tried and acquitted. Legally I'm *not* a murderer! And you've admitted I can't be tried again! So I qualify as the murderer and I inherit as the acquitted murderer!

It is absolutely fantastic. No, not fantastic—mad. Again Ellery's mind reels: insane sanity or sane insanity? Where does one draw the line? For a while there is dead silence, the enormity of Buck's plan sinking in. Curtis and Perez sit there, as dumfounded as Ellery. Then Ellery pulls himself together and asks Buck where he found out about all this—about double jeopardy and a murderer not benefitting from his crime.

Oh, he read up on it—in law books at the library.

Ellery throws the ball to lawyer Curtis who says that Buck should have read up more carefully—better still, he should have consulted a lawyer. Didn't he learn in his "reading up" that Morna's will hasn't a snowball's chance of standing up in court, that it will be thrown out as against the public interest. Does Buck think, for example, that someone can will a fortune to the person who assassinates the President of the United States, and that such a will would be accepted as valid?

Buck has gone pale. He starts to object, and irritation, frustration creep into his voice.

Curtis: Even your double jeopardy protection is doubtful—you really should have consulted a lawyer, you should have come to me. You were acquitted on falsified evidence. In my opinion, if the state wishes, you could be retried.

Buck is stunned. His far-out plan didn't make it. Doing his thing has turned into a bad trip.

Curtis: You've gone through this insane rigamarole for nothing. In my opinion you haven't got any claim on Morna's estate—not for a dime!

Buck comes out of it. His temper erupts. It's a conspiracy—they're depriving him of his rights, they're robbing him. He threatens them, he'll appeal to the courts, and finally he storms out, leaving Curtis, Perez, and Ellery exhausted.

Ellery notices that Buck dragged his left foot when he went out. Ellery had never noticed any dragging before. Shouldn't he have noticed it? Ellery has the sinking feeling that he is not sharp, he is not clicking, that he is enmeshed in a net of errors—surely he should have realized the BB was a plant, should have seen through Buck's manipulating and maneuvering—or should he have?

Curtis and Perez discuss the legal aspects. There's no doubt the fantastic will is invalid. That means Morna died intestate. Who will inherit? Morna had often told Curtis she didn't have a relative in the world, and Curtis remembers that his father's file on Morna confirms that. Of course they will have to search for a relative, just to make sure; but if no relative is found, the entire estate—well over $10,000,000, including Elsinore and the jewelry—will go to the state of California.

Ellery rouses himself and asks: Do you know what day it is?

Perez: Friday—

Ellery: —the 13th. Buck's unlucky day.

Ellery shakes his head, but it won't clear. Maybe it's everybody's unlucky day. Maybe every day is unlucky. Only one thing is sure: something is wrong in this case—he feels it in his mind, in his heart, in his bones. Something is rotten in the state of California.

ACT III. SCENE II.

The same. "Nature's infinite book of secrecy"

The very next day, Saturday, October 14, before they have had a chance to recover from Buck's revelations, the second bombshell explodes.

Curtis hurriedly summons Perez, Ellery, and Buck to his office. Buck brings Cherry with him. A new figure has suddenly appeared in the case —Reed Harmon, a seedy, dissipated-looking man in his sixties. Curtis asks Harmon to tell the others the story he has told Curtis.

Harmon is an oldtime bit-part Western actor. For the past 40 years he has been living in Paloma Beach, a small oceanside town south of L.A. Back in 1930 he and Morna Richmond met and were secretly married— Morna always had a weakness, it seems, for bit-part Western actors. The marriage lasted exactly ten days and then Morna regretted it. She told Harmon she was going to divorce him, and if he would keep their marriage a secret (she was afraid the publicity would hurt her career, which was still successful, though fading), she would set up a trust fund of $200,000 the income of which, about $10,000 a year, would go to him for life—or until their marriage became known.

Harmon had agreed, and he has been living on that income ever since. Morna told him she got a secret divorce in Mexico, and he hasn't heard from her or seen her since.

Harmon doesn't read newspapers or listen to news on radio or TV (who needs it, with what's going on in the world?), and he's just learned from an acquaintance of Morna's death. What he wants to know now is: has he any claim to Morna's estate? And will his trust-fund income continue now that Morna's dead? Harmon is a pathetic figure, frightened to death that his livelihood will be cut off.

Perez, Ellery, and Buck stare at Curtis. What does this mean? Curtis, nervous and worried, asks Harmon to step out of the office and wait in the reception room. Then Curtis tells the others that since phoning them to come to his office he has examined his father's old file on Morna, to see if there is any record of the secret marriage, and he did find confirmation. Harmon's story is true. But Curtis found something that Harmon doesn't know. Harmon thinks Morna divorced him. But

Morna was so afraid of the marriage becoming known and ruining her career that she only told Harmon she had obtained a divorce. She must have thought that even a secret divorce would double the chances of a leak, so she did nothing, certain that Harmon would never reveal the secret and lose his life income.

Which means? That Reed Harmon was still legally married to Morna when she died, and with no relatives and with Buck having no claim (not even a possible claim of common-law marriage), Reed Harmon, the husband of the deceased, is the sole heir to Morna's estate!

Buck has another tantrum. He spent seven years of hell with that old woman, and now everything goes to a—to a stranger! He'll contest it, right up to the Supreme Court if necessary!

No one answers Buck—they know it's bluster, empty threat. Buck leaves, his left foot dragging again, with Cherry following him and casting a speculative look back at Reed Harmon.

And something strange has happened to Reed Harmon now that he has realized his incredibly good luck—heir to more than $10,000,000. A transformation has taken place before their eyes. His clothes are still seedy-looking, his face still shows lines of dissipation; but he has straightened to a dignified, erect posture, and an air of importance now emanates from him. It is not the clothes that make the man; money makes the man.

Ellery sits there silent and depressed. Things are happening too fast, and yet he can't put his finger on anything wrong. But there *is* something wrong . . . He decides he will start all over again in this case, start at the beginning—if he can find the beginning, the right beginning.

ACT III. SCENE III.

Paloma Beach. "Speak the truth"

The next day, Sunday, October 15, Ellery drives to the small fishing village where Reed Harmon lives and finds Harmon's dilapidated shack on the beach—a shack and Harmon now a multimillionaire. Harmon has company—Cherry O'Hare is brazenly with him and Harmon is beaming. Obviously, Buck is washed up in Cherry's eyes and Reed Harmon, old as he is, is a hot prospect. Ellery shrugs: he has more serious problems on his mind.

No, Harmon has no objection to answering Ellery's questions—he

has nothing to conceal. Where was he the night of April 23, the night
of Morna's death? Harmon doesn't remember—that's nearly six months
ago. What day was April 23? Sunday? Well, he can make a good
guess. For years now he has been going on a bender every weekend, so
he was probably on one that weekend. He usually winds up in jail early
every Sunday morning on a "drunk and disorderly"—he's a weekend
fixture in the local jug. Ellery can check it easily enough if he sees the
Chief of Police.

Which Ellery does, and learns that Reed Harmon was in jail from
1:07 a.m Sunday morning, April 23, until 9:45 a.m. Monday morning,
April 24. Morna's death was placed at about 11:30 p.m. Sunday night,
April 23. If Ellery had any notion that Harmon could possibly have
killed Morna, the answer is definitely no—Harmon's alibi is incon-
trovertible. (Dead End Number Three) Wrong beginning. Have to
make another start. But where?

ACT III. SCENE IV.

Elsinore castle. "Like an icicle"

Buck is still living in Morna's house—he has been given until the end
of the month to move out and then Harmon will move in. Ellery decides
to begin again with Buck, and the next day, Monday, October 16, he
goes back to Elsinore.

As Ellery approaches the gatehouse he remembers Dion Proctor.
What has happened to him? Is he still living in the lodge? Ellery stops,
gets out of his car, and is about to knock on the front door when he hears
the sudden clattering of a typewriter. Ellery looks through a window and
sees Dion working. Apparently no one has asked Dion to leave, or if
anyone has, Dion has coolly stayed on. Probably no one has even remembered Dion . . . Ellery gets back into his car and continues up the
road to the castle.

Elsinore is empty. Strange, supernaturally strange, but even in this
emptiness Ellery senses the presence of Morna Richmond. The old star
still lives in this dying castle. Her aura, her spell, inhabits every silent,
empty room, even the terrace and the sleeping pool.

Returning to his car, Ellery passes the open row of garages and is
startled out of his reverie to hear sobbing. He looks in and sees Cherry
sitting on the floor, hunched over, shaking. And then he sees why.

Buck, fully clothed in his old Western costume, is hanging from an open beam in the garage ceiling. He has hanged himself with his own rope. Ellery cuts him down, but Buck is dead. Ellery lifts Cherry, leads her into the house, and phones Perez.

Cherry takes a stiff drink and regains some of her composure. She had come to the house to tell Buck she was finished with him, that she was hooking up with Harmon. She hated to do it—she really cared for Buck, loved him in a way, but there was no future with Buck—and found him hanging in the garage.

Ellery: Just what was your cut for helping Buck? You're smart enough to know that he never would have married you. What did he promise you?

Cherry: All of Morna's jewelry.

Ellery: Worth half a million at least.

Cherry: Buck said it was worth a million.

Poor Buck. His future had not been bleak, it had been totally barren. A confessed murderer, publicly disgraced, broke, no chance for a job or a career, aware that Cherry would probably desert him, aware that he couldn't prey on women any more—they would be frightened of him now, wouldn't let him come within a mile of them. Oh, he wouldn't have cared about any of that if he had got his hands on the $10,000,000 in tax-exempt bonds. But with the last possible chance of inheriting gone now that Reed Harmon has turned up . . . Wealth is a snare: Buck's life has been a tragedy of errors. (Dead End Number Four)

ACT III. SCENE V.

Headquarters. "Goes out sighing"

Ellery and Perez have a talk before Ellery goes back to New York. With the self-confessed murderer dead, the case is over, the file is closed. Harmon will inherit Morna's estate, move into Elsinore, and *l'affaire Morna* will be ancient history in a week. There is nothing more for Ellery to do—no need for a new beginning, nothing to look for. He is left with a gnawing inside of him that something strange has passed him by, that he has missed something . . . but what? Those two bombshells—Buck's revelations and Harmon's appearance—coming directly after Buck's acquittal and before they could recover from the successive shocks blew up the case, leaving not even threads to pursue . . .

At the door of Perez's office, after having shaken hands and said goodbye, Ellery turns—a last-minute thought. Probably nothing will come of it—but then, what harm can it do? He suggests that Perez keep track of Reed Harmon, especially of how he acts, what he does.

Perez: Have something in mind? Expect something?

Ellery shakes his head—no, nothing really. But let me know of any development.

Perez hesitates, then nods.

Ellery sighs and goes out . . . wondering if he'll ever see Perez again, if he'll ever hear of Reed Harmon again—if he'll ever investigate a case again. (Dead End Number Five)

ACT IV. SCENE I.

Ellery's apartment. "What news on the Rialto?"

Two months later, on Monday, December 18, Ellery receives a long-distance call from Perez. The Lieutenant had promised to keep Ellery informed about Harmon. Well, this probably doesn't mean anything, but Harmon is dickering for a whopping big loan from a Los Angeles bank—millions, plus future financing; Harmon wants to go into the movie business, wants to buy a studio that is up for sale.

Ellery: Doesn't sound promising . . . but look, I've never been happy about the Morna Richmond case—there was a kind of insanity about it, or crazy sanity, never could figure out which. Millions, you say . . . I'll catch the first plane out.

Perez: Another piece of news that may interest you. Cherry O'Hare got married last month. She's now Mrs. Reed Harmon.

Ellery: I *will* catch the next plane out.

ACT IV. SCENE II.

Banker's office. "Seeking the bubble"

Wednesday, December 20, in a banker's office: Yes, the bank is considering a loan to Harmon to buy a movie studio. But there is a hitch. The loan and the subsequent financing commitments are so large that Harmon does not have enough collateral. He's willing to put up every cent he has—$5,000,000 in tax-exempt bonds—

Ellery's nose twitches: Every cent he has?

Banker: Yes, and he's offered his house and his wife's jewelry too. He's so anxious to get the loan and purchase the studio that I think he'd put his gold fillings into the pot if we asked him to.

Ellery: $5,000,000 in tax-exempt bonds?

Banker: He swore that's all he has for collateral.

Ellery and Perez look at each other.

ACT IV. SCENE III.

Curtis' office. "That searches to the bottom"

They go to see Curtis who now has a new address—swankier offices and a large staff in a prestige building. Ellery inquires about this new prosperity. Curtis laughs: ever since his connection with the Morna Richmond murder case his business has improved—you know Hollywood: notoriety brings more business than integrity.

It was Curtis who arranged for the transfer of the tax-exempt bonds from Morna's estate to Harmon—Curtis handled all the legal matters arising out of Morna's death, and has continued to act as Harmon's attorney.

Perez: How much in tax-exempt bonds?

Curtis: Why, you remember—$10,000,000.

Perez: Harmon claims all he has now is $5,000,000—not a cent more. What happened to the other $5,000,00?

Curtis looks puzzled, then worried. Is Perez sure? Curtis doesn't know what happened—and as Harmon's lawyer, he should know. But he is positive that Harmon inherited $10,000,000 in bonds.

Perez phones Harmon, now living at Elsinore. Yes, Harmon will see Perez. What is it about? The Lieutenant says that something has come up about Harmon's inheritance—a little problem about the tax-exempt bonds.

Harmon: Make it after lunch—say, at 2:30. I'll be expecting you.

ACT IV. SCENE IV.

En route to Elsinore castle. "Road of casualty"

On the way to Elsinore, on one of the ascending hairpin turns, Perez's car is stopped at a roadblock. The police are there, investigating an accident. A car had plunged off the turn into a deep canyon. The body of the driver is being brought up. Perez and Ellery take a look. It's Reed Harmon—dead. There is a bullet hole in his head. (Dead End Number Six)

A motorcycle roars up and is stopped by the police. The rider takes off his helmet and they see it is Dion Proctor. The police wave Dion on as the body of Reed Harmon is pushed into the back of the ambulance. Dion is incurious—he pays no attention, doesn't even glance at the dead man's face.

Ellery, to Perez: Is Proctor still living in the gatehouse?

Perez: Yes—Harmon said he could. But now—I guess no one will mind if he stays there. He doesn't bother anybody.

Ellery: In the Morna Richmond investigation did you—

Perez: Check out Proctor? Yes—he was clean. We checked out everybody connected with the case. They were all clean—except Buck.

Ellery and Perez do no go on to Elsinore. They return to L.A. Ellery is sure the castle is dead at long last and that he'll never set eyes on it again.

ACT IV. SCENE V.

Headquarters. "Something rotten"

Perez investigates the missing $5,000,000. The broker who converted the bonds into cash and paid Harmon in bills of large denomination is found—and the trail ends there. The $5,000,000 in cash is not in Harmon's estate; there is no record of what Harmon did with the money —not a trace of the missing $5,000,000. (Dead End Number Seven)

Ellery's old disquiet has come back full blast. There are too many loose ends, too many dead ends. He feels as if there is some sane explanation to all this insanity—but the saneness hovers just beyond his mental grasp. He reaches for the solution that will make the crazy pattern rational, but it dances away. There is still something rotten . . .

ACT IV. SCENE VI.

Ellery's hotel room. "Something in the wind"

Friday morning, December 22: Ellery phones Perez. Ellery has been up all night, has gone over the case from the very first day he became involved, that morning of April 24 when he accompanied Perez to Elsinore to examine the dead body of Morna Richmond—eight long months ago. And now the spell is broken: they have come to the finale, the curtain.

Ellery: Today is showdown.

Perez: Where?

Ellery: Meet in Curtis' office.

Perez: Who will be there?

Ellery: You, me—and Curtis.

Perez: No one else?

Ellery: No one else.

Perez: So that's the way the wind blows.

ACT IV. SCENE VII.

Curtis' office. "Seeking light"

In Curtis' private office, behind closed doors: Ellery has solved the case, and he gives the solution step by step.

Examine and analyze what Buck did—the suppression of Morna's will, the deliberate building of the murder case against himself, the saving of himself at the last minute by the appearance of the suicide letter with the falsified date—the whole wild crazy plan to circumvent the terms of Morna's will and to outwit the law. Did Buck have the mentality to conceive and execute this far-out plot? No. Buck was essentially a simple-minded gullible person. Someone in the background was pulling the strings like a master puppeteer.

Examine and analyze what Morna did—the far-out terms of her will, her attempt to have the last laugh on Buck by twisting legalities. Did Morna have the mentality to plan this? No. Morna was essentially the same as Buck—a simple-minded gullible person. So she too was manipulated. Someone in the background was suggesting to Morna and Buck exactly what they should do, giving them precise, detailed instructions.

Now, what was the result of this manipulation of Morna and Buck? Buck killed Morna. And what was the result of Buck's killing of Morna? $10,000,000 was inherited—by Reed Harmon. Question: Was Reed Harmon the manipulator of Morna and Buck for the purpose of becoming the heir to Morna's estate?

No, Harmon was not the master puppeteer. For two unassailable reasons: first, he too was murdered—proving there is still someone in the background; and second, Harmon gave away one-half of the $10,000,000. That missing $5,000,000 sounds like a fifty-fifty split of the loot, a payoff to the person behind it all.

Look at the pattern. Three deaths: first, Morna murdered—victim; second, Buck a suicide—instrument of Morna's murder and victim himself; third, Harmon murdered—beneficiary of the first two deaths and then victim himself. So we have the manipulator of Morna, Buck, and Harmon still at large. Who is this manipulator, this person behind everything that has happened? The real murderer.

Ellery has written out a list of the seven qualifications of the real murderer. Some persons in the case have some of the qualifications—but only one person in the case has all seven qualifications.

The tension is growing unbearable. Perez watches Ellery closely, but he keeps shifting his gaze to Curtis, who is becoming more and more nervous and worried-looking.

Qualification Number 1: the murderer had to know the terms of Morna's will.

Qualification Number 2: the murderer had to know of Morna's attempted suicide six years ago.

Qualification Number 3: the murderer had to possess the old suicide letter to be able to plan Morna's murder for April 23, 1967, and to plant the letter in Morna's bedroom while Buck was in prison.

Qualification Number 4: the murderer had to be responsible for the disappearance of both copies of Morna's will.

Qualification Number 5: the murderer had to know of Morna's secret marriage to Reed Harmon and that there never was a divorce.

Qualification Number 6: the murderer had to know that Perez was going to question Harmon about the missing $5,000,000, so that Harmon could be killed before he could talk.

Now, who in the case meets all these qualifications? Just one person —Theodore Curtis, Jr.

Curtis could have known the terms of Morna's will by simply opening the envelope containing his copy.

He could have known of Morna's attempted suicide—from notes and records in his father's file on Morna.

He could have had possession of the suicide letter—also from his father's file.

He could have been the one really responsible for the disappearance of his copy of Morna's will and for the stealing of Morna's copy—true, Buck claimed he was responsible for both, but remember that the real murderer was manipulating Buck, telling him what to do and say.

He could have known of Morna's secret marriage to Harmon and her false story to Harmon about a divorce—again from his father's file which, he admitted, contained the information.

And most damning of all, he could have known—*he was the only person other than Perez, Ellery, and Harmon who knew*—that Perez was going to question Harmon about the missing $5,000,000; Curtis could have arranged by phone (after Perez and Ellery left his office) to meet Harmon, then shoot him and drive his car off the hairpin curve, before the 2:30 appointment.

There is dead silence. Curtis tries to talk but he can't get a word out. Perez watches the accused man, alert for any move. And finally Curtis manages to speak: You're crazy! I don't care what qualifications you say I have. I didn't manipulate anyone. I didn't kill anyone. This whole analysis of yours is a tissue of lies and stupidities. It's all theory and conjecture and circumstantial nonsense. What proof do you have? What shred of proof?

Perez, softly: Yes, Ellery, what proof? . . . And besides, you said there are seven qualifications. You've only given us six. What is the seventh?

Ellery: The clincher, the proof. Qualification Number 7: the murderer has to have possession of the missing $5,000,000.

Curtis explodes: I have no $5,000,000! I don't have five million cents!

Ellery: That is our final problem—to locate the missing money.

Curtis, sarcastically: Would you care to search my office safe?

Ellery, still confident: Not likely to be there—too risky if any of your employees know the combination. No, more likely you've cached the money in safe-deposit boxes in a bank. Do you have any safe-deposit boxes?

Curtis hesitates. Perez catches it.

Curtis: Yes, I do have safe-deposit boxes. But—

Ellery: I suggest you take us to them—now.

Curtis: Now just a minute! Those boxes contain some of my clients' personal papers. Letting you search them would be an invasion of their privacy.

Perez, quickly: Any hesitation on your part to permit me to search those boxes would be highly suspicious. Besides, you know I can get a court order.

Ellery: What's the telephone number of your bank? I'll call and make the arrangements.

Curtis: Palmyra 4-2000. But I tell you—

Ellery goes to the phone and begins to dial the number—but he never finishes. After two spins his finger stops and his whole body stiffens. He sits in front of the phone, a statue.

Minutes pass. Curtis starts to say something, but Perez gestures him to be quiet—the lieutenant knows Ellery. The minutes continue, Perez and Curtis watching the silent, immobile Ellery.

Finally the spell is broken, and Ellery moans softly.

He turns to Perez, a stricken look on his face: Tragedy of errors . . . When you look back over the case, it was a tragedy of errors for nearly everyone involved. The whole world is a tragedy of errors . . . Lieutenant, we begin again—this time "the true beginning of our end."

ACT V. SCENE I.

A safe-deposit vault. "Light in darkness"

Later that day, in the safe-deposit vault of a bank: Perez, Ellery, and another person are given three extra-large boxes, ushered into a private room, and left there.

Perez and Ellery open the boxes, the third person watching. The boxes are stuffed with packets of currency—bills of high denomination. The packets are marked with amounts, and Perez makes a quick calculation of the grand total.

Perez, grimly: You were right, Ellery—$5,000,000 on the nose.

He turns to the third person: How do you explain this $5,000,000 in safe-deposit boxes in your name?

The third person stares at Perez, then crumples and buries his head in his hands.

Perez: How do you explain it, Dr. Rago?

ACT V. SCENE II.

Headquarters. "Full of light"

Sunday, December 24: Ellery puts it all together for Perez. Then Ellery has one more visit to make, and the next day he will fly home to New York.

The final revelation began when Ellery started to dial the number of Curtis' bank. He had commenced to dial the exchange, PALMYRA, and had got through P-A. Suddenly the sight of the phone dial reminded him of the similar dial on Morna's bedroom safe—the same kind of dial except that Morna's had only letters, no numbers. Morna's dial combination had been P-A-I-N. P-A . . . and then Ellery remembered Morna had told Buck that PAIN was her little joke, but if you dialed it the safe would open *anyway*.

So P-A-I-N was not the real combination even though it opened the safe.

What other word, what other combination, would the dialing of P-A-I-N spell out? And then it hit him. P̲R̲S—P. A̲BC—A. G̲H̲I—I. M̲N̲O—N. P-A-I-N. But also P̲R̲S—R. A̲BC—A. G̲HI—G. MN̲O̲ —O. R-A-G-O. Rago! That was the real combination, the word Morna could not possibly forget.

That was only the spark of the revelation—the flame of it started a conflagration in Ellery's brain. Rago. What have we been looking for? The real murderer, the manipulator of Morna, Buck, and Harmon. The background of the case—Shakespeare—Morna's secret passion, Elsinore castle, protégé and playwright Dion a second Shakespeare, the volume of Shakespeare containing the suicide letter, Ellery's working on *Othello* . . . Who was the greatest manipulator in Shakespeare? Iago in *Othello*.

Iago. Change one letter. I to R. Rago. What a magnificent trick of fate! What a magnificent Shakespearean jest!

Could Rago have been the manipulator of Morna, Buck, and Harmon? Did Rago satisfy all seven qualifications of the real murderer? Surely he could have manipulated Morna—she was utterly dependent on him, she confided everything to him, she may even have thought she was in love with him. Rago must have been planning his fantastically mad scheme for some time. When Morna came to him after Buck had almost strangled her, for comfort and reassurance and for advice about a will,

Rago was ready to put his plan into motion. He told Morna exactly what to write in the will so that she would protect herself against Buck's murderous temper and at the end have the last laugh. This ironic revenge on Buck— which Rago probably characterized as Shakespearean —appealed to Morna's theatrical sense and she followed Rago's instructions without question.

Rago then communicated with Buck, told him the terms of Morna's will, and showed him how to circumvent them. Could Rago have manipulated Buck? Of course. Buck was greedy, unscrupulous, suggestible; he would believe anything and do anything to get his hands on Morna's fortune. He too followed Rago's instructions to the letter: bribed Curtis' secretary to steal Curtis' copy of the will, stole Morna's copy, suppressed both wills (having Cherry keep them for him), built the case against himself for the murder of Morna—doing precisely what Rago told him to do at every step of the way—including sending the servants away, planting the BB (suggested by Buck's name), and later, getting Kolisher to persuade Ellery to intervene so that the suicide letter could be found in the nick of time, and the big confession scene in Curtis' office—the whole fantastic, far-out, crazy sequence of events.

And when Buck had done his part of Rago's plot, finally washing out, Rago then produced Reed Harmon, Morna's secret husband. Rago knew all about Harmon—Morna confided everything to him. Could Rago have manipulated Harmon? Indeed he could—by dangling the bait of inheriting Morna's estate—provided, after Harmon inherited, that he give one-half of the $10,000,000 in bonds to Rago.

Perez: One thing puzzles me. Why didn't Harmon rat on Rago? Once Harmon inherited everything, why didn't he simply refuse to pay Rago off? He could have kept the whole schmear, and what could Rago have done about it without acknowledging that he was behind it all?

Ellery: I've thought that out. Remember, Harmon believed he was divorced and therefore had no legal claim to Morna's estate. I think Rago convinced Harmon that he really was divorced, but that he, Rago, had managed to suppress all the divorce records so that Harmon could be accepted as Morna's husband and heir. Harmon believed Rago—he was no less credulous that Morna and Buck. "Lord, what fools these mortals be! . . . and all our yesterdays have lighted fools the way to dusty death."

If Harmon had refused to give Rago one-half of the $10,000,000, Rago would simply have threatened to make the divorce known and then, according to Rago, Harmon would inherit nothing. $5,000,000 versus nothing—Harmon was not only eager but perfectly willing to keep his end of the bargain.

Ellery continues: When we learned of the missing $5,000,000 and when you phoned Harmon that you wanted to question him about it, Harmon, you'll recall, asked you to come to see him after lunch, at 2:30. He was stalling for time. He realized the significance of what you wanted to ask him, and he was frightened—he may even have panicked. He phoned Rago and told him what was going to happen—and Rago saw the danger at once. Rago asked Harmon to meet him for instructions before you could question him. Rago no longer had any choice: he could not be the background manipulator any more, having others do the dirty work. This time Rago had to bloody his own hands. Harmon alive was no longer safe—so Rago shot him and sent the car over into the canyon.

Perez: Just a minute, Ellery. You said you had dialed P-A in Curtis' office and then the whole thing opened up. But how did you *know?* Iago, Rago—that was only a flashing light—though I admit I never would have seen it myself. Morna's phone-dial, her real combination, all the manipulations of Morna, Buck, and Harmon—none of them *proved* that Rago was the one behind it all. You had to have more than "it could have been Rago."

Ellery did have more. He remembered what Rago himself had told them, and Rago's own words convicted him. Qualification Number 2: the murderer had to know of Morna's attempted suicide six years ago. Qualification Number 3: the murderer had to possess the old suicide letter to be able to plan Morna's murder for April 23, 1967, and to plant the letter in Morna's bedroom. Remember what Rago told us about that 1961 suicide attempt? Morna was home alone that night. She phoned Rago, and he rushed to the house, found her still alone but unconscious, and saved her life. He said *he told no one* about her attempt to commit suicide, didn't even report it to the police.

Therefore, *only Rago* knew of Morna's attempted suicide six years ago —*only Rago* could meet the second qualification for the murderer.

Who could have found Morna's suicide letter? Only Rago.

Therefore, *only Rago* could have had possession of that letter and planted it, with the date falsified, in Morna's bedroom copy of Shakespeare—*only Rago* could meet the third qualification for the murderer.

(If only we had thought of questioning Rago about the suicide letter directly after Buck's acquittal we might have seized the truth, but the two bombshells—Buck's revelations and Harmon's appearance—came so fast, and with such numbing developments, that we were shocked out of our wits.)

I've already shown how Rago met the other qualifications: he knew the terms of Morna's will because it was he who suggested them; he used Buck to steal both copies of the will; he knew all about Morna's secret marriage—she confided in him; he didn't have to be present when you phoned Harmon—Harmon phoned him.

Therefore, only one person could have been the manipulator, the real murderer—only Dr. Rago.   And his possession of the missing $5,000,000 was final positive proof.

Ellery and Perez wish each other a Merry Christmas—no, Ellery won't stay over and have Christmas dinner with the Perez family, maybe next year—but thanks anyway and give Mrs. Perez a big hug and all the little Perezes a kiss each . . . and Ellery leaves.

EPILOGUE

A prison cell. "Truth will come to light"

and Ellery leaves . . . to make his last visit in L.A. before he takes a plane back to New York.

It is late Christmas Eve when, through special permission arranged by Perez, Ellery enters Dr. Rago's cell.

Ellery is startled to see Dion Proctor in the cell talking to Rago. At Ellery's entrance Dion nods goodbye to Rago, and leaves. He passes Ellery without any acknowledgment—still aloof, still inaccessible.

Ellery notices that Rago has changed considerably in the last 48 hours. He no longer needs his professional-looking beard to make him look older. His whole face looks old now. Is it agony that Ellery sees in Dr. Rago's eyes?

Ellery, gently: I'm still puzzled about one thing. Help me to understand, Doctor. It's about the motive. Oh, I know you wanted the money—$5,000,000 is a big stake even in these days of inflation. It's enough to make a man plan and do anything—even to be responsible for four deaths—the murders of Morna and Harmon, the suicide of Buck, and your own death, Doctor. But money was only the practical motive, the realistic motive, what one might call the *civilized* motive. I've watched you, listened to you. I think I know you, Doctor, and I believe —something deep inside of me tells me—that it was not the money alone. It must have been something more . . . Were you playing God, Dr. Rago?

Rago is silent. Ellery waits patiently for him to answer. Then the barest smile flickers on Rago's lips, the ghost of a smile, and he shakes his head.

Ellery: But there was another reason?

After another silence Rago says softly: Have you ever heard of a Scottish psychiatrist named Ronald D. Laing? Of course you have—I shouldn't have asked. You know everything, don't you, young man?— no, don't shake your head. That young black man who was just here— he knows everything too.

Ellery is taken aback.

Rago lapses into introspective silence. Ellery waits, almost trembling, as if on the verge, the very edge, of a great revelation.

Then Rago says, even more softly: Dr. Laing once suggested that insanity may be a sane reaction to an insane world . . . He's right, you know. The world's insane . . . It's Christmas Eve, isn't it? And on earth peace, good will toward men . . . Oh, yes, my reason, my real reason. Dion Proctor asked about that too. What I did, Mr. Queen, was my sane reaction to an insane world. I could say to you: young man, go thou and do likewise. But I won't. Instead, I'll tell you something I once read —words written by Walter Lippmann many years ago, in 1940, I think: "There is no use looking into the blank future for some new and fancy revelation of what man needs in order to live"— today it would be, "in order to survive" . . . and he reminded us that "truth, justice, and righteousness—and the grace of love and charity—are the things which have made man free . . . These are the terms stipulated in the nature of things for the salvation of men on this earth" . . . But you know these things, don't you, Mr. Queen? That is why you do what you do . . . So I say to you: go, young man, and tell the others—tell them before it is too late.

Dr. Rago closes his eyes and Ellery is almost sure he has fallen asleep.

Ellery tiptoes out of the prison cell, and outdoors he looks around for Dion Proctor—but there is no sign of the black man. And suddenly it is midnight and Ellery hears the church bells announce that it is Christmas Day.

LETTER FROM FREDERIC DANNAY
TO MANFRED B. LEE

Man,

Now that you have read the outline, which you will have to read more than once—

1. *The Tragedy of Errors* is intended to reflect, within the strict framework of the detective novel, the insanity of today's world.

2. The good man, the very good man, even the very best man, can be corrupted by the insanity of today's world.

3. The final scene reveals, among other things, a double motive for murder—the oldest one and the newest.

Dan

SHORT STORIES

TERROR TOWN

Young Susan Marsh, red-haired librarian of the Flora G. Sloan Library, Northfield's cultural pride, steered the old wreck of a Buick around the Stanchion blinker in the center of town and headed up Hill street toward the red-brick Town Hall, coughing as the smoke came through the floorboards. Susan did not mind. She had discovered that the 1940 sedan only smoked going up steep grades, and the road between town and her little cottage in Burry's Hollow three miles out of Northfield, her usual route, was mostly as level as a barn floor.

The vintage Buick had been given to Susan a few weeks before, in October, by Miss Flora Sloan, Northfield's undisputed autocrat and, to hear some tell it, a lineal descendant of Ebenezer Scrooge.

"But Miss Flora," Susan had exclaimed, her ponytail flying, "why me?"

" 'Cause all that robber Will Pease offered me on her was a measly thirty-five dollars," Miss Flora had said grimly. "I'd rather you had her for nothing."

"Well, I don't know what to say, Miss Flora. She's beautiful."

"Fiddle-de-sticks," the old lady had said. "She needs a ring job, her tires are patchy, one headlight's broken, the paint's scrofulous, and she's stove in on the left side. But the short time I had her she took me where I wanted to go, Susan, and she'll take you, too. It's better than pedaling a bike six miles a day to the library and back, the way you've had to do since your father passed on." And Miss Flora had added a pinch of pepper: "It isn't as if girls wore bloomers like they used to when *I* was twenty-two."

What Miss Flora had failed to mention was that the heater didn't work, either, and with November nipping up and winter only weeks away it was going to be a Hobson's choice between keeping the windows open and freezing or shutting them and dying of asphyxiation. But right now, struggling up Hill Street in a smelly blue haze, Susan had a much more worrisome problem. Tom Cooley was missing.

Tommy was the son of a truck farmer in the Valley, a towhead with red hands, big and slow-moving like John Cooley, and sorrow-eyed as his mother Sarah, who had died of pneumonia the winter before. Tommy had a hunger for reading, rare in Northfield, and Susan dreamed dreams for him.

"There's not an earthly reason why you shouldn't go on to college, Tommy," Susan had told him. "You're one of the few boys in town who really deserves the chance."

Tommy had said, "Even if Pa could afford it, I can't leave him alone."

"But sooner or later you've got to leave anyway. In a year or so you'll be going into the Army."

"I don't know what Pa'll do." And he had quietly switched the subject to books.

There was a sadness about Tommy Cooley, a premature loss of joy, that made Susan want to mother him, high as he towered above her. She looked forward to his visits and their snatches of talk about Hemingway and Thomas Wolfe. Tommy's chores kept him close to the farm; but on the first Monday of every month, rain, snow, or good New England sunshine, he showed up at Susan's desk to return the armful of books she had recommended and go off eagerly with a fresh supply.

On the first Monday in November there had been no Tommy. When he failed to appear by the end of that week, Susan was sure something was wrong, and on Friday evening she had driven out to the Cooley place. She found the weather-beaten farmhouse locked, a tractor rusting in a furrow, the pumpkins and potatoes unharvested, and no sign of Tommy. Or of his father.

So on Saturday afternoon she had closed the library early, and here she was, bound up Hill Street for Deputy Sheriff Linc Pearce's office on an unhappy mission.

It had to be the county officer, because Northfield's police department was Rollie Fawcett. Old Rollie's policing had been limited for a generation to chalking tires along Main and Hill Streets and writing out overtime parking tickets for the one-dollar fines that paid his salary. There was simply no one in Northfield but Linc Pearce to turn to.

Susan wasn't happy about that, either.

The trouble was, to Linc Pearce she was still the female Peter Pan who used to dig the rock salt out of his bottom when old Mr. Burry caught them in his apples. Lengthening her skirts and having to wear bras hadn't changed Linc's attitude one bit. It wasn't as if he were immune to feminine charms; the way he carried on with that overblown Marie Fullerton just before he went into the Army, for instance, had been proof enough of *that*. Linc came home quieter, more settled, and he was doing a fine job as Sheriff Howland's deputy in the Northfield district. But he went right back to treating Susan as if they were still swimming raw together in Burry's Creek.

She parked the rattletrap in the space reserved for "Official Cars Only" and marched into Town Hall with her little jaw set for anything.

Linc went to work on her right off. "Well, if it isn't Snubby Sue," he chuckled, uncoiling all six-foot-three of him from behind his paper-piled desk. "Leave your specs home?"

"What specs?" Susan could see the twitch of a squirrel's whisker at two hundred yards.

"Last time I passed you on the street you didn't see me at all."

"I saw you, all right," Susan said coldly, and drew back like a snake. "Linc Pearce, if you start chucking me under the chin again— "

"Why, Susie," Linc said, "I'm just setting you a chair."

"Well," Susan sniffed, off guard. "Is it possible you're developing some manners?"

"Yes, ma'am," Linc said respectfully, and he swung her off the floor with one long arm and dropped her into the chair.

"Some day . . ." Susan choked.

"Now, now," Linc said gently. "What's on your mind?"

"Tom Cooley!"

"The silk purse you're working on?" He grinned. "What's Plowboy done now, swiped a library book?"

"He's disappeared," Susan snapped. And she told Linc about Tommy's failure to show up at the library and her visit to the Cooley farm.

Of course, Linc looked indulgent. "There's no mystery about John. He's been away over a month looking to buy another farm as far from Northfield as he can find. John took Sarah's death last winter hard. But Tommy's s'posed to be looking after the place."

"Well, he's not there."

"Probably took off on a toot."

"Leaving a four-thousand-dollar tractor to rust in a half-plowed lot?" Susan's ponytail whisked about like a red flag in a high wind. "Tommy's got too much farmer in him for that, Linc."

"He's seventeen, isn't he?"

"I tell you, I know Tommy Cooley, and you don't!"

Deputy Sheriff Lincoln Pearce looked at her. Then he reached to the costumer for his hat and sheep-lined jacket. "S'pose I'll never hear the end of it if I don't take a look."

Out in the parking space Linc walked all around Susan's recent acquisition. "I know," he said gravely. "It's John Wilkes Booth's getaway car. Where'd you get her?"

"Miss Flora Sloan *presented* her to me three weeks ago when she won that Chevrolet coupé at the bazaar drawing."

Linc whistled. Then he jackknifed himself and got in. "Is it safe? The chances I have to take on this job!"

He went on like that all the way into the valley. Susan drove stiffly, silently.

But as they turned into the Cooley yard Linc said in an altogether different kind of voice, "John's home. There's his jeep."

They found John Cooley crouched in a Morris chair in his parlor, enormous shoulders at a beaten-down slope. The family Bible lay on his massive knees, and he was staring into space over it.

"Hi, John," Linc said from the doorway.

The farmer's head came about. The bleached gray eyes were dazed.

"My boy's gone, Lincoln." The voice that rumbled from his chest had trouble in it, deep trouble.

"Just heard, John."

"Ain't been home for weeks, looks like." He peered through the dimness of the parlor. "Where's Tommy at, Sue Marsh?"

"I don't know, Mr. Cooley." Susan tried to keep her voice casual. "I was hoping you did."

The farmer rose, looking around as if for a place to put the Bible. He was almost as tall as Linc and half again as broad, a tree of a man struck by lightning.

"When did you see Tom last, John?"

"October the second, when I went off to look for a new place." John Cooley swallowed. "Found me one down in York State, too. Figured to give Tommy a new start, maybe change our luck. But now I'll have to let it go."

"You hold your horses, John," Linc said cheerfully. "Didn't the boy leave you a note?"

"No." The farmer's breathing became noisy. He set the Bible down on the Morris chair, as if its weight were suddenly too much.

"We'll find him. Sue, you saw Tom last on the first Monday in October?"

Susan nodded. "It was October the third, I think, the day after Mr. Cooley says he left. Tommy came into the library to return some books and take out others. He had the farm truck, I remember."

"Truck still here, John?"

"Aya."

"Anything of Tom's missing?"

"His .22."

Linc looked relieved. "Well, that's it. He's gone off into the hills. He'll show up any minute with a fat buck and forty-two kinds of alibis. I wouldn't worry."

"Well, I would," Susan said. She was furious with Linc. "Tommy'd never have left on an extended trip without bringing my library books back first."

"There's female reasoning for you." Linc grinned. But he went over to Cooley and touched the old man's shoulder. "John, you want me to organize a search?"

The shoulder quivered. But all the farmer said, was, "Aya."

Overnight, Linc had three search parties formed and the state police alerted. On Sunday morning one party, in charge of old Sanford Brown, Northfield's first selectman, headed west with instructions to stop at every farm and gas station. Rollie Fawcett took the second, going east with identical instructions. The third Linc took charge of himself, including in his party Frenchy Lafont, and Lafont's two hound dogs. Frenchy owned the Northfield Bar and Grill across Hill Street from Town Hall. He was the ace tracker of the county.

"You take her easy, John," Lafont said to John Cooley before they set out. "Me, my dogs, we find the boy. Why you want to go along?"

But the farmer went ahead as if he were deaf, packing a rucksack.

Linc's party disappeared into the heavily timbered country to the north, and they were gone two weeks. They came back bearded, hollow-cheeked, and silent. John Cooley and Frenchy Lafont and his two hounds did not return with them. They showed up ten days later, when the first snowfall made further search useless. Even the dogs looked defeated.

Meanwhile, Linc had furnished police of nearby states with handbills struck off by the Northfield *Times* job press, giving a description of Tommy Cooley and reproducing his latest photograph, the one taken from his high-school yearbook. Newspaper, radio and TV stations co-operated. Linc sent an official request to Washington; the enlistment files of the Army, Navy, Marine Corps, and Air Force were combed. Registrars of colleges all over the country were circularized. The FBI was notified.

But no trace of Tommy Cooley—or his hunting rifle—turned up.

Linc and Susan quarreled.

"It's one of those things, I tell you." The cleft between Linc's eyes was biting deep these days. "We haven't been able to fix even the approximate time of his disappearance. It could have been any time between October third and the early part of November. Nobody saw him leave, and apparently no one's seen him since."

"But a grown boy doesn't go up in smoke!" Susan protested. "He's got to be *somewhere*, Linc. He didn't just run away from home. Tommy isn't irresponsible, and if you were half the sheriff's white-haired boy you think you are you'd find out what happened to him."

This was unreasonable, and Susan knew it. For a thrilling moment she thought Linc was going to get mad at her. But, as usual, he let her down. All he said was, "How about you taking my badge, half-pint, and me handing out library books?"

"Do you think you could locate the right one in the stacks?"

Susan stalked out. After the door banged, Linc got up and gently kicked it.

Once, in mid-December, Susan drove out to the Cooley farm. The rumors about John Cooley were disturbing. He was said to be letting the farm go to seed, mumbling to himself, always poring over his Bible.

She found the rumors exaggerated. The house was dirty and the kitchen piled with unwashed dishes, but the farm itself seemed in good order, considering the season, and the farmer talked lucidly enough. Only his appearance shocked Susan. His ruddy skin had grayed and loosened, his hair had white streaks in it, and his coveralls flapped on his frame.

"I've fetched you a blueberry pie I had in my freezer, Mr. Cooley," she said brightly. "I remember Tommy's saying blueberry's your favorite."

"Aya." Cooley looked down at the pie in his lap, but not as if he saw it. "My Tom's a good boy."

Susan tried to think of something to say. Finally she said, "We've missed you at Grange meetings and church . . . Isn't it lonesome for you here, Mr. Cooley?"

"Have to wait for the boy," John Cooley explained patiently. "The Lord would never take him from me without a sign. I've had no sign, Susan. He'll come home."

Tommy Cooley was found in the spring.

The rains that year were Biblical. They destroyed the early plantings, overflowed ponds and creeks, and sent the Northfield River over its banks to flood thousands of acres of pasture and bottom-land. The main highway, between Northfield and the Valley, was under water for several miles.

When the waters sank they exposed a shallow hole not two miles from the Cooley farm, just off the highway. In the hole lay the remains of John Cooley's son. A county crew repairing the road found him.

Susan heard the tragic news as she was locking the library for the day.

Frenchy Lafont, racing past in his new Ford convertible, slowed down long enough to yell, "They find the Cooley boy's body, Miss Marsh! Ever'body's goin' out!"

How Susan got the aged Buick started in the damp twilight, how she knew where to go, she never remembered. She supposed it was instinct, a blind following of the herd of vehicles stampeding from town onto the Valley road, most of them as undirected as her jalopy. All Susan could think of was the look on John Cooley's gray face when he had said the Lord had given him no sign.

She saw the farmer's face at last, and her heart sank. Cooley was on his knees in the roadside grave, clawing in the muck, his eyes blank and terrible, while all around him people trampled the mud-slimed brush like a nest of aroused ants. Linc Pearce and some state troopers were holding the crowd back, trying to give the bereaved man a decent grieving space; but they need not have wrestled so. The farmer might have been alone in one of his cornfields. His big hands alternately caressed and mauled the grave's mud, as if he would coax and batter it into submission to his frenzy. Once he found a button rotted off his son's leather jacket sleeve, and Linc came over and tried to take it from him, but the big hand became a fist, a mallet, and Linc turned away. The big man put it into the pocket of his coat along with a pebble, a chunk of glass, a clump of grass roots—these were his son, the covenant between them, Mizpah. . .

Afterward, when the heap under the canvas had been taken away by Art Ormsby's hearse, and most of the crowd had crawled off in their cars,

Susan was able to come close. They had John Cooley sitting on a stump near the grave now, while men hunted through the brush. They were merely going through the motions, Susan knew; time, the ebbing waters, and the feet of the crowd would have obliterated any clue.

She waited while Linc conferred with a state trooper lieutenant, and Dr. Buxton, who was the coroner's physician for Northfield. She saw Dr. Buxton glance at John Cooley, shake his gray head, and get into his car to drive back to town. Then she noticed that the lieutenant was carefully holding a rusty, mud-caked rifle.

When the trooper went off with the rifle Susan walked up to Linc and said, "Well?" They had spoken hardly a word to each other all winter.

Linc squinted briefly down at her and said, "Hello, Sue." Then he looked over at the motionless man on the stump, as if the two were painfully connected in his mind.

"That rifle," Susan said. "Tommy's?"

Linc nodded. "Tossed into the hole with the body. They're going to give it the once-over at the state police lab in Gurleytown, but they won't find anything after all this time."

"How long?"

"Hard to say." Linc's firm lips set tight. "Doc Buxton thinks offhand he's been dead five or six months."

Susan's chest rose, and stayed there. "Linc . . . was it murder?"

"The whole back of his head is smashed in. What else there is we won't know till Doc does the autopsy."

Susan swallowed the raw wind. It was impossible to associate that canvas-shrouded lump with Tommy Cooley's big, sad, eager self, to realize that it had been crumbling in the earth here since last October or early November.

"Who'd want to kill him?" Susan said fiercely. "And why, Linc? Why?"

"That's what I have to find out."

She had never seen him so humorless, his mouth so much like a sprung trap. A wave of warmth washed over her. For the moment Susan felt very close to him.

"Linc, let me help," she said breathlessly.

"How?" Linc said.

The wave recoiled. There was no approaching him on an adult level, in the case of Tommy Cooley as in anything else. Susan almost expected

Linc to pat her shoulder.

"It's a man's job," Linc was mumbling. "Thanks all the same."

"And are you the man for it, do you think?" Susan heard herself cry.

"Maybe not. But I'll sure give it a try." Linc took her hand, but she snatched it away. "Now, Susie," he said. "You're all upset. Let me do the sweating on this. With the trail five-six months old . . ."

Susan sloshed away, trembling with fury.

In the weeks that followed, Susan kept tabs on Linc's frustration almost with satisfaction. She got most of her inside information from Dr. Buxton, who was a habitué of the library's mystery shelves, old Flora Sloan, and Frenchy Lafont. Miss Flora's all-seeing eye encompassed events practically before they took place, and Frenchy's strategic location opposite Town Hall gave him the best-informed clientele in town.

"Linc Pearce is bellowing around like a heifer in her first season," Miss Flora remarked one day, in the library. "But that boy's all fenced in, Susan. There's some things the Almighty doesn't mean for us to know. I guess the mystery of poor Tommy Cooley's one of 'em."

"I can't believe that, Miss Flora," Susan said. "If Linc is fenced in, it's only because it's a very difficult case."

The old lady cocked an eye at her. "Appears to me, Susan, you take a might personal interest in it."

"Well, of course! Tommy—"

"Tommy, my foot. You can fool the men folks with your straight-out talk and your red-hair tempers, Susan Marsh, but you don't fool an old woman. You've been in love with Lincoln Pearce ever since *I* can remember, and I go back to bustles. Why don't you stop this fiddling and marry him?"

"Marry him!" Susan laughed. "Of all the notions, Miss Flora! Naturally, I'm interested in Linc—we grew up together. This is an important case to him—"

"Garbage," Miss Flora said distinctly, and walked out.

Frenchy Lafont said to Susan in mid-May, when she stopped in his café for lunch, "That Linc, he's a fool for dam-sure. You know what, Miss Marsh? Everbody but him know he's licked."

"He's *not* licked, Mr. Lafont!"

The fact was, there was nothing for Linc Pearce or anyone else to grab hold of. The dead boy's skull had been crushed from behind by a blow of considerable force, according to Dr. Buxton. His shoulders and back showed evidences of assault, too; apparently there had been a savage series of blows. But the weapon was not found.

Linc went back to the shallow grave site time after time to nose around in a great circle, studying the road and the brush foot by foot, long after Tommy Cooley was buried in the old Northfield cemetery beside his mother. But it was time wasted. Nor were the state police technicians more successful. They could detect no clue in the dead boy's clothing or rifle. All they could say was that the rifle had not been fired —"Old Aunty Laura's blind cow could see that!" Susan had snapped— so that presumably the boy had been killed without warning or a chance to defend himself. Tommy's rifle had been returned to his father, along with the meaningless contents of his pockets.

No one remembered seeing Tommy after October third. So even the date of the murder was a mystery.

Motive was the darkest mystery of all. It had not been robbery; Tommy's wallet, containing most of the hundred dollars his father had left with him, had been intact in the grave. Linc went into the boy's life and through his effects, questioned and requestioned his friends, his old high-school teachers, canvassed every farmer and field hand within miles of the Cooley place. But the killing remained unexplained. The boy had had no enemies, it seemed, he had crossed no one, he had been involved with no girl or woman.

"John," Linc had pleaded with Cooley, "can't you think of anything that might tell why Tommy was murdered? Anything?"

But the farmer had shaken his head and turned away, big fingers gripping his Bible. The Book was now never far from his hand. He plodded about his farm aimlessly in the spring, doing no planting, letting the machinery rust. Once a week or so he drove into Northfield to shop in the supermarket. But he spoke to no one.

One night toward the end of May, as Susan was sitting on her porch after supper, rocking in the mild moonlight and listening to the serenade of the peepers in the pond, the headlights of a car swung into her yard and a tall figure got out.

It couldn't be! But it was. Linc Pearce come to Burry's Hollow. The mountain to Mohamet.

"Susie?"

"Well, if it isn't Lanky Linc," Susan heard herself say calmly. Her heart was thumping like an old well pump.

Linc hesitated at the foot of the porch steps, fumbling with his hat. "Took a chance you'd be home. If you're busy—"

"I'll put my dollies away," Susan said. "For you."

"What?" Linc sounded puzzled.

Susan smiled. "Sit down, stranger."

Linc sat down on the bottom step awkwardly, facing the moon. There were lines in his lean face that Susan had never noticed before.

"How've you been?" Susan said.

"All right," he said impatiently, and turned around. "See here, Susie, it's asinine going on like this. I mean, you and me. Why, you're acting just like a kid."

Susan felt the flames spread from her hair right down to her toes. "*I'm* acting like a kid!" she cried. "Is that what you came here to say, Linc? If it is—"

He shook his head. "I never seem to say the right thing to you. Why can't we be like we used to be, Susie? I mean, I miss that funny little pan of yours, and that carrot top. But ever since this Cooley business started—"

"It started a long time before that," Susan retorted. "And I'd rather not discuss it, Linc, *or* my funny pan, *or* the color of my hair. What about the Cooley case?"

"Susie—"

"The Cooley case," Susan said. "Or do I go to bed?"

"Hopeless. It'll never be solved."

"Because you haven't been able to solve it?"

"Me or anybody else," Linc said, shrugging. "One of those crimes that makes no sense because it never had any. Our theory now is that the Cooley boy was attacked on the road by some psychopathic tramp, who buried him in a hurry and lit out for other parts."

"In other words, the most convenient theory possible."

Linc said with elaborate indifference, "It happens all the time."

"And suppose it wasn't a psychopathic tramp?"

"What do you mean?"

"I think it was somebody in Northfield."

"Who?"

"I don't know."

Linc laughed.

"I think you'd better go, Linc Pearce," Susan said distinctly. "I don't like you any more."

"Now, Susie. . ."

The phone rang in the house. It was three rings—Susan's signal, and she stamped inside.

"It's for you, Linc," she said coolly. "The bartender over at Frenchy Lafont's."

"Bib Hadley? Should have known better than to tell Bib I was stopping in here on my way home," Linc growled, unfolding himself from the step. "Some drunk acting up, I s'pose. . . What is it, Bib?"

Discussing me in a bar! Susan thought. She turned away in cold rage.

But then she heard Linc say, "I'll get right on out there, Bib," and hang up.

Something in the way he said it made her turn back.

"What's the matter?" Susan said quickly.

"Another murder."

An icy hand seized her heart.

"Who, Linc? Where?"

"Frenchy Lafont." Linc's voice sounded thick. "Some kids out in a hot rod found his body just off the Valley road. Whole back of his head caved in."

"Like Tommy Cooley," Susan whispered.

"I'll say like Tommy Cooley." Linc waived his long arms futilely. "Bib says they found Frenchy lying in the exact spot where we dug up Tommy's body!"

The Valley road was a wild mess of private cars and jeeps and farm trucks.

Susan wormed past. In one car Susan saw Miss Flora Sloan. The withered despot of Northfield was driving her new Chevrolet like a demon, the daisies in her straw hat bobbing crazily.

Linc kept his siren going all the way.

We're scared witless, Susan thought.

Two state police cars had set up roadblocks near the site of the new horror. Linc plowed onto the soft shoulder and skidded around into the cleared space. The road in both directions was a double string of lights. Everywhere Susan looked, people were jumping out of cars and running along the road and the shoulders. In a twinkling the fifty feet of highway between the roadblocks was rimmed with eyes.

Susan almost trod on Linc's heels.

She peeped around his long torso at what lay just off the road on the north side. It sprang at her, brutally detailed, in the police flares. Susan jerked back, hiding her eyes.

She was to remember that photographic flash for the rest of her life. The mound of sandy earth where the grave had been refilled after the removal of Tommy Cooley's body, pebbled, flint-spangled, scabby with weeds; and across it, as on one of Art Ormsby's biers, the flung remains of what had been Frenchy Lafont.

Susan could not see his wound; she could only imagine what it looked like. They had turned him over, so that his face was tilted sharply back to the stars. It did not look the least bit like Frenchy Lafont's face. Frenchy Lafont's face had been dark and vivid, lively with mischief, with beautiful lips over white teeth and a line of vain black mustache. This face looked like old suet. The mouth was a gaping black cavern; the eyes stared like dusty pieces of glass.

"Just like the Cooley kid," one of the troopers was saying.

His voice raised a deep echo, like a far-off growl of thunder. There was more than fear in the growl; there was anger, and under the anger, hate. The troopers and Linc looked around, startled.

"Sounds like trouble, Pearce," one of the older troopers muttered to Linc. "They're your people. Better do something."

Linc walked off toward one of the police cars. For a moment Susan almost ran after him; she felt as if she had been left standing naked in the flares.

But the eyes were not on her.

Linc vaulted to the hood of the car and flung his arms wide. The rumble choked and died.

"Neighbors, I knew Frenchy Lafont all my life," Linc said in a quiet way. "Most of you did, too. There isn't a man or woman in Northfield wants more to identify the one who did this and see that he gets what's coming to him. But we can't do it this way. We'll find Frenchy's killer if you'll only go home and give us a chance."

"Like you found the killer of my boy?"

It was John Cooley's hoarse bass voice. He was near the west roadblock, standing tall in his jeep, his thick arm with the flail of fist at the end like a wrathful judgment. Linc turned to face him.

"Go home, John," Linc said gently.

"Yeah, John, go home!" a shrill voice yelled from behind the other barrier. "Go home and get yourself murdered like Tommy was!"

"That's not helping, Wes Bartlett," Linc said. "Use your head, man—"

But his voice went down under a tidal wave.

"We want protection!"

"Aya!"

"Who's next on the list?"

"Long as *he's* deputy . . ."

"Resign!"

"New sheriff's what we need!"

"Aya! Resign!"

In the roar of the crowd the clatter of Linc's badge on the hood of the police car was surprisingly loud.

"All right, there's my badge!" Linc shouted. "Now who's the miracle man thinks he can do the job better? I'll recommend him to Sheriff Howland myself. Come on, don't be bashful! Speak up."

He gave them glare for glare. The glares dimmed; the answering silence became uneasy. Something embarrassed invaded the night air.

"Well?" Linc jeered.

Somewhere down the line a car engine started . . .

Ten minutes later the highway was empty and dark.

Linc jumped off the police car, reached for his badge, and went over to the troopers.

"Nice going, Sheriff," Susan murmured.

But he strode past her to the edge of the burial mound, rock-hard and bitter.

"Let's get to it," he said.

At first they thought it had been a murder in the course of a robbery. Frenchy Lafont's wallet was found untouched on the body, but an envelope with the day's café receipts, which he had been known to have on him earlier in the evening, was missing. The robbery theory collapsed overnight. The envelope of money was found in the night depository box of the First National Bank of Northfield on Main Street when the box was unlocked in the morning.

The weapon was not found. It was the Tommy Cooley case all over again.

Everything about the café owner's murder was baffling. He was a bachelor who lived with his aged mother on the old Lafont place off the Valley road, a mile out of town. His elder brother, a prosperous merchant of Quebec, had not heard from him in months. The brother, in town to make the funeral arrangements and take charge of the mother, could shed no light on the mystery. Old Mrs. Lafont knew nothing.

On the evening of his murder Lafont had left the café shortly before nine, alone, taking the day's receipts with him. He drove off in his new Ford. An hour or so later he was dead some six miles out of town, on the site of the Cooley tragedy. His car was found near the mound. It was towed into the police garage at the Gurley town barracks and gone over by experts. It yielded nothing but Frenchy Lafont's fingerprints. No blood, no indication of a struggle, no clue of any kind. The fuel tank was almost full.

"He dropped the envelope into the slot at the bank," Linc told Susan, "stopped in at Howie Grebe's gas station to fill up, and drove off west on the Valley road. He must have gone straight to his death. Nothing to show that he was waylaid and held up—nothing was taken, and Frenchy didn't touch the pistol he carried in his glove compartment. Bib Hadley says he was his usual wisecracking self when he left the café."

"You think he had a date with somebody he knew?" Susan asked.

"Well, Hadley says he got a phone call at the café," Linc said slowly, "about eight o'clock that night."

"I hadn't heard that! Who phoned him, Linc?"

"Bib doesn't know. Frenchy answered the call himself."

"Did Bib Hadley overhear anything?"

"No."

"Was Frenchy excited? There must have been something, Linc!"

"Bib didn't notice anything unusual. The call might have had nothing to do with the case."

"Maybe it was some woman Frenchy was fooling with. I've heard stories about him and Logan Street."

Susan colored. Logan Street was a part of Northfield no respectable girl ever mentioned to the opposite sex.

"So far all alibis have stood up." Linc passed his hand over his eyes like an old man. "It's no good thinking, theorizing. I have to *know*, Sue, and there's not a fact I can sink my teeth into."

"But there's got to be a reason for a man's getting the back of his head knocked in!" Susan cried. "*Why* was Frenchy murdered? *Why* was his body dumped on the spot where the murderer had buried Tommy? You can hardly say it was another psychopathic tramp, Linc."

Linc looked at her in a persecuted way. He was glassy-eyed with exhaustion. But he merely said, "Maybe not. Only there doesn't seem to be any more sense in Frenchy's death than in Tom Cooley's. Look,

Susie, I've got work to do, and talk won't help me do it even with you.
If you'll excuse me . . ."

"Certainly," Susan said frigidly. "But let me tell you, Linc Pearce,
when these murders are solved it'll be talk and theories and *thinking* that
solve them!" And she swept out, thoroughly miserable.

Susan tossed night after night, asking herself unanswerable questions.
Why had Tommy Cooley been killed? Why had Frenchy Lafont followed
him in death? What was the connection between the two? And—the
most frightening question of all—who was going to be the next victim?

A week after Lafont's murder Susan was waiting at the café entrance
when Bib Hadley came to open up.

"You must hanker after a cup of my coffee real bad, Miss Marsh," the
fat bartender said, unlocking the door. "Come on in. I'll have the urn
going in a jiffy."

"What I want, Bib, is information," Susan said grimly. "I'm sick and
tired of moping around, waiting to get my head bashed in."

The bartender tied a clean apron around his ample middle. "Seems
like every Tom, Dick, and Mary between Northfield and Boston's been
in for the same reason. Even had a newspaperman in yesterday from one
of the city wire services. Made a special trip just to pump ol' Bib. So get
your list in now, Miss Marsh, while Frenchy's brother makes up his mind
what to do with this place. What do you want to know?"

"The connection between Tommy Cooley and Frenchy Lafont," Susan
said.

"Wasn't any," Bib Hadley said. "Next?"

"But there must have been, Bib! Did Tommy ever work for Mr.
Lafont?"

"Nope."

"Did Tommy ever come in here?"

"Tell you the truth, Miss Marsh," the bartender said, lighting the gas
under the urn, "I don't believe Frenchy would have known young Tom
Cooley if he'd tripped over him in broad daylight. You know how
Frenchy was about teen-agers. He'd stand 'em all treat over at Tracy's
ice cream parlor, but he wouldn't let 'em come into his own place even
for coffee. Gave a good bar a bad name, Frenchy used to say."

"Well, there was a connection between Tommy and Frenchy Lafont,"
Susan said positively, "and these murders won't ever be solved till it's
found."

"And you're going to find it, I s'pose?"

Susan jumped. There he was, in the café doorway, jaws working away like Gary Cooper's in an emotional moment.

"I saw you ambush Bib from my office window," Linc said bitterly. "Don't you trust me to ask the right questions, either?"

I don't know why I'm feeling guilty, Susan thought furiously. *This is a free country!*

Linc jammed his big foot on the rim of the tub holding the dusty palm. "You want my badge, too, Sue? Don't you think I've asked Bib every question you have, and a whole lot more? This is a tough case. Do you have to make it tougher for me by getting under foot?"

"Thanks!" Susan said. "People who won't accept help when they're stuck from people trying to unstick them are just—just perambulating *pigheads*."

"We stopped playing tag in you dad's cow barn long ago, Sue," Linc said. "When are you going to grow up?"

"I've *grown* up! Oh, how I've grown up, Linc Pearce—and everybody knows it but you!" Susan screamed. "And do we have to stand here screaming in front of people?"

"I'm not people," Bib Hadley said. "I ain't even here."

"Nobody's screaming but you." Linc drew himself up so tall Susan's neck began to hurt. "I thought we knew each other pretty well, Susie. Maybe we don't know each other at all."

"I'm sure of it!" Susan tried to say it with dignity, but it came out so choky-sounding she fled past Linc to her jalopy and drove off down Hill Street with the gas pedal to the floor.

Two nights later the body of Flora Sloan, autocrat of Northfield, was found by a motorcycle trooper just off the Valley highway. The back of her head had been battered in.

As in the case of Frenchy Lafont, the old lady's body had been tossed onto Tommy Cooley's winter grave . . .

Flora Sloan had attended a vestry meeting in Christ Church, at which certain parish and financial problems had been argued. As usual, Miss Flora dominated the debate; as usual, she got her way. She had left the meeting in lively spirits when it broke up just before ten o'clock, climbed into her Chevrolet, waved triumphantly at Sanford Brown, who had been her chief antagonist of the evening, and driven off. Presumably she had been bound for the big Sloan house on the western edge of town. But she never reached it; or rather, she had by-passed it, for the Valley road ran by her property.

When her body was found shortly after midnight by the motorcycle trooper, she had been dead about an hour.

Had Flora Sloan picked someone up, who had forced her to drive to the lonely spot six miles from town and there murdered her? But the old lady had been famous for her dislike of tramps and her suspicion of hitchhikers. She had never been known to give a stranger a lift.

Her purse, money untouched, was found beside her body. A valuable ruby brooch, a Sloan family heirloom, was still pinned to her blue lace dress. The Chevrolet was parked near the grave in almost the identical spot on which Frenchy Lafont's Ford had been abandoned. There were no fingerprints in the car except her own, no clues in the car or anywhere around.

Three nights after Flora Sloan's murder, Sanford Brown, first selectman of Northfield, called a special town meeting. The city fathers, lean old Yankee farmers and businessmen, sat down behind the scarred chestnut table in the Town Hall meeting room under an American flag like a panel of hanging judges; and among them—Susan thought they looked dismally like prisoners—sat County Sheriff Howland and his local deputy, Lincoln Pearce.

It was an oppressive night, and the overflow crowd made the room suffocating. She saw everyone she knew, and some faces she had forgotten.

Old Sanford Brown rapped his gavel hard on the table. A profound silence greeted him.

"Under the authority vested in me," old Brown said rapidly through his nose, "I call this town meetin' to order. As this is special, we will dispense with the usual order of business and get right to it. Sheriff Howland's come down from the county seat at the selectmen's request. Floor's yours, Sheriff."

Sheriff Howland was a large, perspiring man in a smart city suit and black string tie. He got to his feet, drying his bald head with a sodden handkerchief.

"Friends, when I was elected to office in this county I looked for the best man I could find to be my deputy in your district. I asked 'round and about and was told there wasn't finer deputy material in Northfield than young Lincoln Pearce. I want you and him to know I have every confidence in his ability to discharge the duties of his office. Linc, you tell these good folks what you told me today."

The buck having been deftly passed to him, Linc rose. His blue eyes were mourning-edged and he was so pale Susan bled for him.

"I'm no expert on murder, never claimed to be one," Linc began in a matter-of-fact voice, but Susan could see his knuckles whiten on the edge of the table. "However, I've had the help of the best technical men of the state police. And they're as high up a tree as the 'coon of this piece. And that's me."

An old lady chuckled, and several men grinned. *Humility, Linc?* Susan thought in a sort of pain. *Maybe one of these days you'll get around to me . . .*

"Three people have been beaten to death," Linc said. "One was a boy of seventeen, son of a dirt farmer—quiet boy, Congregationalist, never in trouble. One was a bar-and-grill owner—French-Canadian descent, Roman Catholic, one of the most popular men in town. The third was the last survivor of the family that founded Northfield—rich woman, tight-fisted, some said, but we all know her many generosities. She just about ran Northfield all her life. She was a pillar of Christ Episcopal Church, on every important committee, with her finger in every community pie."

He thinks he has them, Susan thought, glancing about her at the long bony faces. *Linc, Linc . . .*

"The bodies of these three were found in the same spot. So their deaths have to be connected some way. But how? There doesn't seem to be any answer. At least, we haven't been able to find one so far.

"We know nothing about Tommy Cooley's death because of the months that passed before we found his body. Frenchy Lafont was probably lured to his death by a phone call from somebody he knew and wasn't afraid of. Flora Sloan probably picked her killer up as she left the church meeting, which she wouldn't have done unless it was someone she knew. Tommy Cooley's clothing was too far gone to tell us anything, and the rains this spring wiped out any clues that might have been left in his case. But we found dirt on the knees of Frenchy's trousers and Flora Sloan's skirt, so maybe Tommy was made to kneel on that spot just like Frenchy and Miss Flora afterward, and hit a killing blow from behind."

You can talk and talk, Linc, they won't let you alone any more, Susan thought. *They won't do anything to you—they'll just ignore you from now on . . .*

"That's all we have," Linc said. "No connection among the three victims—not one. No motive. No gain—nothing was taken in any of the three cases as far as we know. Tommy Cooley had nothing to leave anybody, Frenchy Lafont's business and house he left to his eighty-one-year-old mother, and now we're told that Flora Sloan willed her entire estate to charity. No motive—no woman or other man in the case, no jealous husband, wife, or sweetheart. *No motive.*"

Linc stopped, looking down. Susan shut her eyes.

"When someone kills for no reason, he's insane. Three people died because a maniac is loose in our town. It's the only answer that makes sense. If anyone here has a better, for God's sake, let all of us hear it."

Now the noise came back like a rising wind, and Sanford Brown banged it back to silence. But it was still there, waiting.

"I want to say one more thing."

Susan heard Linc's pride take stubborn voice again. *Linc, Linc, don't you know you've had it? Old Sanford, the selectmen, Sheriff Howland—they all know it. Don't you?*

"I'm not going to hand over my badge unless Sheriff Howland asks for it," Linc went on. "Want it, Sheriff?"

The politician squirmed. "No, Linc, course not—unless the good folks of Northfield feel—"

Poor Linc. Here it comes.

"Let Linc Pearce keep his badge!" a burly farmer shouted from the floor. "The boy's doin' his best. But he's just a boy, that's the trouble. What we need's a Committee o' Safety. Men with guns to stand watch near the grave site . . . patrol the roads!"

"Mr. Chairman . . ."

Susan slipped out of the meeting room as motions and resolutions winged toward the table from every corner. She caught up with Linc on the steps of the Town Hall.

" 'Lo, Susie," Linc said with a stiffish grin. "Come after me to watch me digest crow?"

"Committee of Safety, men guarding the grave," Susan said bitterly. "What do they expect him to do—walk into their arms? Linc, *please* let me help. You're not beaten yet. Let's you and I talk it over. There must be something you missed! Maybe if we put our heads together—"

"You know something?" Linc put his big hands about her waist and lifted her to his level like a doll. "All of a sudden I want to kiss you."

"Linc, put me down. Don't treat me as if I were a child. Please, Linc."

"My little old Susie."

"And *don't* call me Susie! I loathe it! I've loathed it all my life! Linc, put me down, I say!"

"Sorry." Linc looked genuinely surprised. He deposited her quietly on the step. "As far as the other thing is concerned, my answer's got to be the same, Sue. They can make up all the committees and posses they want—this is my job and I'll do it by myself or go bust. Can I drive you home?"

"Not *ever!*" And Susan fled to the safety of the old Buick Flora Sloan had given her, where she could burst into tears in decent privacy.

Linc sat in his office long after the last selectman had gone and Rollie Fawcett had darkened the building. He was blackly conscious of the thunderstorm that had sprung up. The rain lashing his windows seemed fitting and proper.

There must be something you missed . . .

Linc was irritated more by the source of the phrase going round in his head than by its persistence. That little fire-eater! She'd singed his tail from the start. Talk about your one-track minds . . .

Suppose she's right?

The thought was like his collar, chafing him raw.

What could he have missed? What? What hadn't he followed up? He'd been over the three cases a hundred times. He couldn't possibly have missed anything. Or had he?

Linc Pearce finally saw it—appropriately enough, during a flash of lightning. The bare office with its whitewashed walls for an instant became bright as day, and in that flash of illumination Linc remembered what he had missed.

It had happened on that first night of the long nightmare. The night Tommy Cooley's body had been found, washed out of its roadside grave by the receding waters of the spring flood. John Cooley had been kneeling in the grave, his hands scrabbling in the mud for some remnant of his son. The pitiful little things he had found and tucked away in the pocket of his checkered red mackinaw . . . *Suppose one of those things, unknown to Cooley, had been a clue?*

Linc grabbed a slicker and ran.

The Cooley farmhouse was dark. Linc turned off his lights and ignition, skin prickling at some danger he could not exactly define.

The rain had turned into a tropical downpour. Lightning tore the sky open in quick bursts, like cannon salvoes, lighting up the shade-drawn windows, the porch with the rickety rocking chairs turned to the wall, the open door of the nearby garage . . .

Cooley's jeep was not in the garage.

Linc reached for a flashlight and jumped out of his car. He splashed over to the garage and swung his light about. Yes, the farm truck was here, but the jeep was out.

Linc relaxed. He had not noticed John Cooley at the town meeting, but he must have been there. If he was, with a committee of safety forming, he'd surely be one of the men to be staked out in the brush near Tommy's grave.

Linc went up on the porch and tried the door. It was not locked, and he opened it and stepped into the hall.

"John?" He could be wrong. There might be a dozen explanations for the missing jeep. "John?"

No one answered. Linc went upstairs and looked into the bedrooms. They were empty.

He went back to John Cooley's old-fashioned bedroom and played his flash about. Of course, the chifforobe. He opened the doors. It was filled with winter garments.

And there was the red mackinaw.

Linc breathed a prayer and put his hand into the right pocket.

They were still there, all right.

He took them out one by one, carefully, turning them over in his fingers. The button from young Tom's rotted leather jacket. A pebble. A chunk of dirt-crusted glass . . .

The piece of glass!

It was thick, ridged glass with a curve to it, a roughly triangular piece cracked off from something larger. It was . . . it was . . .

My God! Linc thought.

He went over it again and again, refusing to believe. It couldn't be that simple. The answer to the murders that had happened. The warning of the murder that was going to happen. *The murder of Susan Marsh.*

For a moment of sheer horror Linc saw her flying red hair, the familiar little face, the snub nose he used to tweak, the brook-water eyes, the impudent mouth that had tormented him all his life.

He saw them all, soiled and still.

A world without Sue . . .

Linc never knew how he got out of the house.

Susan had gone to bed swollen-eyed. But she had been unable to sleep. The mugginess, the storm, the thunder crashes, the lightning bolts bouncing off her pond, made the night hideous. She had never felt so alone.

She crept out of bed, got into a wrapper, and pattered about, clicking switches. She put on every light in the house. Then she went into her tiny parlor and sat there, rigidly listening to the storm.

Oh, Linc, Linc . . .

Her first thought when the crash came and the curtains began blowing about and a cold spray hit her bare feet was that the gale had blown the front door loose.

She looked up.

John Cooley stood in her splintered doorway. He had Tommy's hunting rifle cradled in his arm. In the farmer's eyes Susan saw her death.

"They're watching at the grave," John Cooley said. His voice was all cracked and high, not like his bass at all. "So I can't take you there, Susan Marsh."

"You killed them," Susan said stiffly.

"Get down on your knees, and pray."

He was insane. She saw that now. He had been tottering on the brink every since Tommy's disappearance, his only son, the child of his beloved Sarah. And he had toppled over when the body was found. Only no one had seen it—not Linc, not she, not anyone.

Linc, Linc.

"Not Tommy," Susan whispered. "You loved Tommy, Mr. Cooley. You wouldn't—couldn't have killed Tommy."

The farmer's twitching face, with its distended eyes, softened into something vaguely human. Tears filled the eyes. The heavy shoulders began to shake.

Oh, dear God, let me find a way to keep him from killing me as he killed Frenchy Lafont and Miss Flora . . .

"I know you didn't kill Tommy, Mr. Cooley."

With the metal-sheathed butt of Tommy's hunting rifle. That was the weapon that had crushed out their lives . . . *Dear God . . . I mustn't faint, mustn't . . . those dark smears on the butt . . . get him talking . . . maybe the phone . . . No, no, that would be fatal . . . What can I do! Linc . . .*

"Not Tommy. Somebody else killed Tommy, Mr. Cooley. Who was it? Why don't you tell me?"

The farmer sank into the tapestried chair near the door. The rain beat in on him, mixing with his tears.

"You killed him, Susan Marsh," he wept.

"Oh, no!" Susan cried faintly.

"You, or the Frenchy, or the old woman. I knew from the hunk of glass in the boy's grave. A hunk of headlight glass. Headlight from an old auto. He was run over on the road, hit by an auto from the back . . . from the back. You killed him with an auto and you put him in a dirty hole and piled it on him and you ran away. You, or the Frenchy, or the old woman."

Susan wet her lips. "The Buick," she said. "My old Buick."

John Cooley looked up, suddenly cunning. "I found it! Didn't think I would, hey? I looked all over Northfield and I found the auto it come from. I looked for a smashed headlight, and the auto the old woman gave you was the one the hunk of glass fitted. Was it you run Tommy over? Or the old woman, who run the car before you? Or the Frenchy, who owned the Buick before the old woman bought it?"

"Frenchy Lafont sold that car to Flora Sloan—in October?" Susan gasped.

"Didn't think I'd track that down, hey?" John Cooley said with a sly chuckle. "Aya! Lafont sold it to the old woman when he bought his new Ford. And she gave it to you a couple weeks later when she won a Chevrolet in the Grange bazaar. Oh, I tracked it all down. I was careful to do proper justice." The eyes began to stare again; he whimpered. "But which one, which one? I didn't know which one of you killed Tommy in October, 'cause nobody knows what day in October he was run over. So I got to kill you all. That way the Lord's vengeance is mine. The Wrath. With the boy's gun. I phoned that Lafont and I says meet me at the grave, I have to talk to you . . . I walked into the town and I waited for the old woman to come out of the church, and I stopped her and made her drive out to the grave. 'Pray, Flora Sloan,' I says. 'Get down on your murdering knees, sinner, and pray for your damned soul,'

I says. And then I used the Lord's gun butt on her."

The room was shimmering.

John Cooley was on his feet, the great eyes shining.

"Pray, Susan Marsh," he thundered. "Down on your knees, girl, and pray for your soul."

Now the steel hand was at the back of her neck, forcing her to her knees.

Dear God . . . Linc, you're the one I love, the only one I've ever . . .

The last thing Susan saw as she strained against the paralyzing clutch on her neck was that exultant face, terrible in triumph, and the rusty blood-caked butt of the rifle held high above it.

She fainted just as Linc Pearce plunged into the room and hurled himself at the madman.

Susan opened her eyes. She was in her own bed. Linc's long face was close to hers.

"I thought I heard you say something, Linc, a million years ago," Susan murmured. "Or maybe it was just now. Didn't you say something, oh, so nice?"

"I said I love you, Susie—Susan," Linc muttered. "And something about will you marry me."

Susan closed her eyes again. "That's what I thought you said," she said contentedly.

They never did find out which one had accidentally run over Tommy Cooley, whether Frenchy Lafont or old Miss Flora. They argued about it for years.

UNCLE FROM AUSTRALIA

"How did you happen to call me, Mr. Hall?" asked Ellery. He had been annoyed at first, because it was half-past ten and he was about to bed down with his favorite book, the dictionary, when his phone rang.

"The security hofficer at the 'otel 'ere gave it to me," said the man on the line. His salty cockney accent savored of London, but the man said he was from Australia.

"What's your problem?"

It turned out that Herbert Peachtree Hall was not merely from Australia, he was somebody's uncle from Australia. Uncles from Australia were graybeard standards of the mystery story, and here was one, if not exactly in the flesh, at least in the voice. So Ellery's ears began to itch.

It appeared that Mr. Hall was all of three somebodies' uncle from Australia, a niece and two nephews. A migrant from England of thirty years' exile, Hall said he had made his pile on the nether continent, liquidated it, and was now prepared—ah, that classic tradition!—to give it all away in a will. The young niece and the two young nephews being his only kin (if he had any kith, they were apparently undeserving of his largess), and all three being New York residents, Hall had journeyed to the United States to make their acquaintance and decide which of them deserved to be his heir. Their names were Millicent, Preston, and James, and they were all Halls, being the children of his only brother, deceased.

Ever the voice of caution, Ellery asked, "Why don't you simply divide your estate among the three?"

"Because I don't want to," said Hall, which seemed a reasonable reason. He had a horror, it seemed, of cutting up capital into bits and pieces.

He had spent two months getting to know Millicent, Preston, and James; and this evening he had invited them to dinner to announce the great decision.

"I told 'em, 'Old 'erbert,' I says, 'old 'erbert 'as taken a fancy to one of you. No 'ard feelings, you hunderstand, boys, but it's Millie gets my money. I've signed a will naming 'er my heir.' " Preston and James had taken his pronouncement with what Hall said he considered ruddy good sportsmanship, and they had even toasted their sister Millie's good fortune in champagne.

But after the departure of the trio, back in his hotel room, the uncle from Australia had afterthoughts.

"I never 'ad trouble making money, Mr. Queen, but maybe by giving it away I'm asking for some. I'm sixty, you know, but the doctors tell me I'm fit as one of your dollars—can live another fifteen years. Suppose Millie decides she won't wait that long?"

"Then make another will," said Ellery, "restoring the *status quo ante*."

"Mightn't be fair to the girl," protested Hall. "I 'aven't real grounds for suspicion, Mr. Queen. That's why I want the services of a hinvestigator, to muck through Millie's life, find out if she's the sort to bash in 'er poor rich uncle's 'ead. Can you come 'ere right now, so I can tell you what I know about 'er?"

"Tonight? That seems hardly necessary! Won't tomorrow morning do, Mr. Hall?"

"Tomorrow morning," said Herbert Peachtree Hall stubbornly, "could be too late."

So for some reason obscure to him—although his ears were itching like mad—Ellery decided to humor the Australian. The hour of 11 p.m. plus six minutes found him outside Hall's suite in the midtown hotel, knocking. His knock went unanswered. Whereupon Ellery tried the door, found it opened to his hand, and walked in.

And there was a bone-thin little man with a white thatch and a bush tan stretched out on the carpet, face down, with a brassy-looking Oriental paperknife in his back.

Ellery leaped for the phone, told the hotel operator to send up the house doctor and call the police, and got down on one knee beside the prone figure. He had seen an eyelid flicker.

"Mr. Hall!" he said urgently. "Who did it? Which one?"

The already cyanosed lips trembled. At first nothing came out, but then Ellery heard, quite distinctly, one word.

"Hall," the dying man whispered.

"Hall? Which Hall? Millie? One of your nephews? Mr. Hall, you have to tell me—"

But Mr. Hall was not telling anything more to anybody. The man from down under was down, down under, and Ellery knew he was not going to come up again, ever.

The following day Ellery was an inquisitive audience of one in his father's office at police headquarters. The director was, of course, Inspector Queen; the cast were the three Halls—Millicent, Preston, and James. The banty Inspector put them through their paces peevishly.

"All your uncle was able to get out before he died," snapped the Inspector, "was the name Hall, which tells us it was one of you, but not which one.

"This is an off-beat case, God help me," the old man went on. "Murders have three ingredients—motive, means, opportunity. You three match up to them pretty remarkably. Motive? Only one of you benefits from Herbert P. Hall's death—and that's you, Miss Hall."

Millicent Hall had a large bottom, and a large face with a large nose in the middle of it. She was plain enough, Ellery concluded, to have grasped at the nettle murder in order to achieve that luscious legacy.

"I didn't kill him," the girl protested.

"So say they all, Miss Hall. Means? Well, there are no prints on the knife that did the job—because of the chasework on the handle and blade—but it's an unusual piece, and establishing its ownership has been a cinch. Mr. Preston Hall, the knife that killed your uncle belongs to you."

"Belonged to me," coughed Preston Hall, a long lean shipping clerk with the fangs of a famished ocelot. "I presented it to Uncle Herbert just last week. Father left it to me, and I thought Uncle Herbert might like to have a memento of his only brother. He actually cried when I gave it to him."

"I'm touched," snarled the Inspector. "Opportunity? One of you was actually seen and identified loitering about the hotel last night after the dinner party broke up—and that was you, James Hall."

James Hall was a bibulous fellow, full of spirits of both sorts; he worked, when one of the spirits moved him, in the sports department of a tabloid.

"Sure it was me," James Hall laughed. "Hell, I stayed around to have a few belts, that's all, before tootling on home. Does that mean I am the big bad slayer?"

"This is like coming down the stretch in a three-horse race," complained Inspector Queen. "Millicent Hall is leading on motive—though I'd like to point out that you, Preston, or you, James, could have knocked the old boy over to teach him a lesson for not leaving his money to *you*. Preston's leading on means; I have only your uncorroborated word that you gave the letter knife to Herbert Hall; what I *do* know is that it's yours. Though, again, even if you did give Hall the knife, you, Millie, or you, James, could have used it in that hotel room. And James, you're leading on opportunity—though your brother or sister could have easily sneaked up to your uncle's room without being seen. Ellery, what are you sitting there like a dummy for?"

"I'm thinking," said Ellery, looking thoughtful.

"And have you thought out," asked his father acidly, "which one of the Halls their uncle meant when he said 'Hall' killed him? Do you see a glimmer?"

"Oh, more than a glimmer, dad," Ellery said. "I see it all."

CHALLENGE TO THE READER
Who killed Uncle Herbert from
Australia? And how did
Ellery know?

"Old 'erbert was right, dad," Ellery said. "Millie, drooling over the prospect of all those Australian goodies, couldn't wait for her uncle to die naturally. But she hadn't the nerve to murder him by herself—did you, Miss Hall? So you held out the bait of a three-way split to your brothers, and they willingly joined you in the plot. Safety in numbers, and all that. Right?"

The three Halls had grown very still indeed.

"It's always disastrous," Ellery said sadly, "trying to be clever in a murder. The plan was to confuse the issue and baffle the police—one of you being tied to motive, another to the weapon, the third to opportunity. It was all calculated to water down suspicion—spread it around."

"We don't know what you're talking about," said the drinking Hall, quite soberly, and his brother and sister nodded at once.

The Inspector was troubled. "But how do you know, Ellery?"

"Because Herbert Hall was a Cockney. He dropped his aitches; in certain key words beginning with a vowel, he also added the cockney aitch. Well, what did he say when I asked him which one of the three had stabbed him? He said 'Hall.' I didn't realize till just now that he wasn't saying 'Hall'—*he was adding an aitch.* What he really said was 'all' —all three of them murdered him!"

THE THREE STUDENTS

The membership of The Puzzle Club numbered six (one of whom, Arkavy the Nobel biochemist, was almost never free to attend a meeting), making it—as far as Ellery knew—the world's most exclusive society.

Its only agenda was to solve mysteries made up by the members and then, regardless of outcome, to slaver, sample, and gorge at the feast prepared by the master chef of their host and the Founder of the Club, Syres, the oil multimillionaire. Members took turns playing problem solver, and this evening the rotation had come round to Ellery again.

Having been duly installed to the "problem chair" in Syres's wide-open-spaces-style penthouse salon, Ellery tilted the bottle at his elbow and then settled back with his glass to face the music and its composers.

Little Emmy Wandermere, the Pulitzer Prize poet, had been designated to conduct the overture. "The scene is the office of the president of a small college," she began, "the office being situated on the ground floor of the Administration Building. President Xavier—"

"X," Ellery said instantly. "Significant?"

"You're a quick starter," the poet said. "In this discipline, Mr. Queen, significance lies in the ear of the listener. I should like to go on. President Xavier has one child, a grown son—"

"Who is, of course, a student at the college."

"Who happens to benothing of the sort. The son is a high-school dropout immersed in the study of Yoga and Zen."

"His name?"

"Ah, his name. All right, Mr. Queen, having consulted my instant muse, she tells me that the son was christened Xenophon, President Xavier having taken his doctorate in Greek history. Now Xenophon Xavier has just become engaged to be married—"

"*To* a student?"

"You seem to have students on the brain. Not to a student, no. She's a topless exotic dancer Xenophon met through his guru. May I suggest that you listen, Mr. Queen? The boy's father—and if you want to know President Xavier's Christian name, too, by the way, it's St.

Francis—has undertaken to provide the engagement ring. He's just come from visiting his safe-deposit box, in fact. The first thing President Xavier does on entering his office is to place the ring on his desk. It's a very valuable ring, of course, a family heirloom."

"Is there any other kind?" Ellery asked mercilessly. "Whereupon," and he paused to sip his Scotch, "enter Suspects."

Syres nodded. "A delegation of three students who represent three dissident groups at the college."

"One," said Darnell, the lawyer, "a law student named Adams."

"Two," said Vreeland, the psychiatrist, "a medical student named Barnes."

"And three," said Poet Wandermere, "a literature major named Carver."

"Adams, Barnes, Carver," Ellery said. "A, B, C. We're certainly relying on basics tonight. But proceed."

"Adams, the law student, demands that the football team's star pass receiver, who's been expelled from the school after a secret hearing," said Lawyer Darnell, "be reinstated on the grounds that he was the victim of a star-chamber proceeding and had been denied due process."

"The college expelled its star receiver?" Ellery shook his head. "This is obviously a fantasy."

"Derision, Queen, will get you nowhere," Dr. Vreeland said severely. "As for Barnes, like many med students he's sex mad, and he's there to demand that the curfew restrictions for coeds visiting the boys' dorms be lifted entirely."

"And young Carver is there," Miss Wandermere said, "to demand a separate and autonomous Black Culture Department, staffed entirely by blacks."

"There's a lively discussion, President Xavier promises to take the three demands under advisement, and the students exit." Syres held up his saddlelike hand. "Not yet, Queen! Xavier then goes to lunch, locking the only door of his office. He's away, oh, twenty minutes—"

"A fast eater," Ellery murmured.

"When he unlocks the door on his return, he notices two things. The first—"

"Is that the ring, which with convenient forgetfulness he'd left on his desk," Ellery said promptly, "is gone."

"Yes," Darnell said, "and the second is a folded slip of paper lying on the floor near the desk."

"Which says—?"

"Which says," and Dr. Vreeland showed his formidable teeth like a playful wolf, "in unidentifiable block lettering, naturally—are you paying attention, Queen?"

"Which says," Emmy Wandermere said, "as follows: 'On old Olympus' towering top / A Finn and German viewed a hop.' Terrible verse. I can thankfully say, Mr. Queen, I'm not responsible for it."

Ellery mumbled, "Would you mind repeating that?"

The challengers exchanged congratulatory smirks. Miss Wandermere cheerfully repeated the doggerel.

"Nonsense verse." Ellery was still mumbling. "Or . . ." He stopped and shook his head like a fighter shaking off a stiff jab. "Let's hack away the underbrush first. Was the door tampered with?"

"I'll make it simple for you," Syres said in a kind voice. "Entry was by the window, which had been forced. No fingerprints. No clues."

"I take it that during their visit to Xavier's office, Adams, Barnes, and Carver had the ring in plain view?"

"Right there on the desk," Dr. Vreeland said. "They all saw it."

"Who else knew the ring was in the office?"

"No one."

"Not even his son Xenophon?"

"Not even his son Xenophon."

"Or his prospective daughter-in-law?"

"That's right."

"Was the ring visible from the window?"

"It was not," said Miss Wandermere. "It was lying behind a bust of—"

"Xanthippe, I know. Was there an open transom above the door?"

"No transom at all."

"A fireplace?"

"No fireplace."

"And you wouldn't insult me by a secret passage. Well, then, the thief has to have been one of the three students. Which is the conclusion I assume you wanted me to reach."

"True," Darnell said.

"And Xavier is positive the paper with the verse wasn't on the floor when he left for lunch?"

Glances were exchanged once more. "We hadn't thought of that possibility," the oil man confessed. "No, Queen, the paper wasn't there when Xavier left the office."

"So it must have been dropped by the thief."

"Accidentally, Queen," the lawyer said. "It was later learned that the thief took a handkerchief out of his pocket to wrap around his hand—he didn't want to leave fingerprints—and as he did so, the paper fell out of his pocket."

"He made off with the ring," the poet said, "without noticing that he'd left the verse behind."

"So you don't have to ask any further questions," the psychiatrist said. "Tough one, Queen, isn't it? We were absolutely determined to stump you tonight. And by the superegos of Freud, Jung, and Adler, friends, I believe we've done it!"

"Give a fellow a chance, will you?" Ellery growled. " 'On old Olympus' towering top / A Finn and German viewed a hop.' "

"We've got him on the run, all right," the oil king chortled. "Usual one-hour time limit, Queen. Mustn't keep old Charlot's dinner waiting. What is it?"

Emmy Wandermere: "Oh, no!"

Dr. Vreeland: "Impossible!"

Darnell, incredulously: "You've got it?"

"Well, I'll tell you," Ellery said with unruffling brow, a vision of peace. "Yes."

CHALLENGE TO THE READER
Who stole the ring?
And how did Ellery know?

" 'On old Olympus' towering top / A Finn and German viewed a hop,' " Ellery said. "As verse, it's gibberish. That made me dig into my gibberish pile, which is eighty feet higher than Mount Everest. My curse is that I never forget anything, no matter how useless.

"Having recognized the nature of the verse, I knew the thief couldn't have been Adams, the law student, or the lit major—much as you tried to make Carver your red (or should I say black?) herring.

" 'On old Olympus' towering top' et cetera is a traditional mnemonic aid for remember the names of the twelve cranial nerves. The 'o' of 'On,' for instance, stands for 'olfactory'—the olfactory nerve; the 'o' of 'old' stands for the optic nerve; and so on. The verse is used in medical schools by students. The paper therefore dropped from the pocket of

Barnes, the med student, making him the thief of the ring."

"I could have sworn on my plaque of Hippocrates that you'd fall flat on your face when I suggested this one," Dr. Vreeland said glumly.

"Queen erat demonstrandum," Emmy Wandermere murmured. "And now, gentlemen, shall we render unto Charlot?"

THE ODD MAN

One of the unique encounters in the short and happy history of The Puzzle Club began, as so many interesting things do, in the most ordinary way.

That is to say, 7:30 of that Wednesday evening found Ellery in the foyer of Syres's Park Avenue penthouse aerie pressing the bell button, having the door opened for him by a butler who had obviously been inspired by Jeeves, and being conducted into the grand-scale wood-leather-and-brass-stud living room that had just as obviously been inspired by the king-sized ranchos of the Southwest where Syres had made his millions.

As usual Ellery found the membership assembled—with the exception, also as usual, of Arkavy, the biochemist whose Nobel achievement took him to so many international symposiums that Ellery had not yet laid eyes on him; indeed, he had come to think of the great scientist as yet another fiction his fellow members had dreamed up for mischievous reasons of their own. There was Syres himself, their hulking and profoundly respected host—respected not for being a multimillionaire but for having founded the club; tall sardonic Darnell of the John L. Lewis eyebrows, the criminal lawyer who was known to the American Bar, not altogether affectionately, as "the rich man's Clarence Darrow"; the psychiatrist, Dr. Vreeland, trim and peach-cheeked, whose professional reputation was as long as his stature was short; and wickedly blue-eyed little Emmy Wandermere, who had recently won the Pulitzer Prize for poetry to—for once—unanimous approval.

It was one of the strictest rules of The Puzzle Club that no extraneous matters, not of politics or art or economics or world affairs, or even of juicy gossip, be allowed to intrude on the business at hand, which was simply (in a manner of speaking only, since that adverb was not to be found in the club's motto) to challenge each member to solve a puzzle invented by the others, and then to repair to Charlot's dinner table, Charlot being Syres's chef, with a reputation as exalted in his field as that of the puzzlers in theirs. The puzzles were always in story form, told by the challengers seriatim, and they were as painstakingly planned for the battle of wits as if an empire depended on the outcome.

Tonight it was Ellery's turn again, and after the briefest of amenities he took his place in the arena, which at The Puzzle Club meant sitting down in a hugely comfortable leather chair near the superfireplace, with a bottle, a glass, and a little buffet of Charlot's masterly canapés at hand and no further preliminaries whatever.

Darnell began (by prearrangement—the sequence of narrators was as carefully choreographed as a ballet).

"The puzzle this evening, Queen, is right down your alley—"

"Kindly omit the courtroom-type psychology, Counselor," Ellery drawled, for he was feeling in extra-fine fettle this evening, "and get on with it."

"—because it's a cops-and-robbers story," the lawyer went on, unperturbed, "except that in this case the cop is an undercover agent whose assignment it is to track down a dope supplier. The supplier is running a big wholesale illicit-drug operation; hundreds of pushers are getting their stuff from him, so it's important to nail him."

"The trouble is," Dr. Vreeland said, feeling the knot of his tie (I wonder, Ellery thought, what his analyst made of that—it was one of the psychiatrist's most irritating habits), "his identity is not known precisely."

"By which I take it that it's known imprecisely," Ellery said. "The unknown of a known group."

"Yes, a group of three."

"The classic number."

"It's convenient, Queen."

"That's the chief reason it's classic."

"The three suspects," oilman Syres broke in, unable to conceal a frown, for Ellery did not always comport himself with the decorum the founder thought their labors deserved, "all live in the same building. It's a three-story house . . ."

"Someday," Ellery said, peering into the future, "instead of a three-story house I shall make up a three-house story."

"Mr. Queen!" and Emmy Wandermere let a giggle escape. "Please be serious, or you won't be allowed to eat Charlot's chef d'oeuvre, which I understand is positively wild tonight."

"I've lost track," Syres grumped. "Where were we?"

"I beg everyone's pardon," Ellery said. "We have an undercover police officer who's turned up three suspects, one of whom is the dope wholesaler, and all three live in a three-story house, I presume one to a floor. And these habitants are?"

"The man who occupies the ground floor," the little poet replied, "and whose name is John A. Chandler—known in the neighborhood as Jac, from his initials—runs a modest one-man business, a radio-and-TV repair shop, from his apartment."

"The question is, of course," Lawyer Darnell said, "whether the repair shop is just a front for the dope-supply operation."

Ellery nodded. "And the occupant of the middle floor?"

"An insurance agent," Dr. Vreeland said. "Character named Cutcliffe Kerry—"

"Named what?"

"Cutcliffe Kerry is what we decided on," the psychiatrist said firmly, "and if you don't care for it that's your problem, Queen, because Cutcliffe Kerry he remains."

"Very well," Ellery said, "but I think I detect the aroma of fresh herring. Or am I being double-whammied? In any event, Cutcliffe Kerry sells insurance, or tries to, which means he gets to see a great many people. So the insurance thing could be a cover. And the top floor?"

"Is rented by a fellow named Fletcher, Benjamin Fletcher," Syres said. "Fletcher is a salesman, too, but of an entirely different sort. He sells vacuum cleaners."

"Door to door," Ellery said. "Possible cover too. All right, Jac Chandler, radio-TV repairman; Cutcliffe Kerry, insurance agent; Ben Fletcher, vacuum-cleaner salesman; and one of them is the bad guy. What happens, Mr. Syres?"

"The undercover man has been watching the building and—isn't the word tailing?—the three men, according to his reports to his superior at police headquarters."

"And just after he finds out who the drug supplier is," Darnell said mournfully, "but before he can come up with the hard evidence, he's murdered."

"As I suspected," Ellery said, shaking his head. "Earning the poor fellow a departmental citation and the traditional six feet of sod. He was murdered by the dope boy, of course."

"Of course."

"To shut him up."

"What else?"

"Which means he hadn't yet reported the name of the dope supplier."

"Well, not exactly, Mr. Queen." Emmy Wandermere leaned forward to accept the flame of Dr. Vreeland's gold lighter, then leaned back puffing like The Little Engine That Could on a steep grade. She was trying to curb her nicotine-and-tar intake, so she was currently smoking cigarettes made of processed lettuce. "The undercover man hadn't reported the drug supplier's name, true, but in the very last report before his murder he did mention a clue."

"What kind of clue?"

"He referred to the supplier—his subsequent killer—as, and this is an exact quote, Mr. Queen, 'the odd man of the three.' "

Ellery blinked.

"Your mission, Mr. Queen, if you accept it—and you'd better, or be kicked out of the club," said Darnell in his most doom-ridden courtroom tones, "is to detect the guilty man among Chandler, Kerry, and Fletcher —the one of them who's been selling the stuff in wholesale lots and who murdered our brave lad of the law."

"The odd man of the three, hm?"

Ellery sat arranging his thoughts. As at all such critical stages of the game, by protocol, the strictest silence was maintained.

Finally Ellery said, "Where and how did the murder of the under-cover agent take place?"

Darnell waved his manicured hand. "Frankly, Queen, we debated whether to make up a complicated background for the crime. In the end we decided it wouldn't be fair, because the murder itself has nothing to do with the puzzle except that it took place. The details are irrelevant and immaterial."

"Except, of course, to the victim, but that's usually left out." Having discharged himself of this philosophical gripe, Ellery resumed his seat, as it were, on his train of thought. "I suppose the premises were searched from roof to cellar, inside and out, by the police after the murder of their buddy?"

"You know it," Syres said.

"I suppose, too, that no narcotics, amphetamines, barbituates, et cetera *ad nauseam*, no cutting equipment, no dope paraphernalia of any kind, were found anywhere in the building?"

"Not a trace," Dr. Vreeland said. "The guilty man disposed of it all before the police got there."

"Did one of the men have a record?"

Miss Wandermere smiled. *"Nyet."*

"Was one of them a married man and were the other two bachelors?"

"No."

"Was it the other way round? One of them a bachelor and two married?"

"I admire the way you wriggle, Mr. Queen. The answer is still no."

"The odd man of the three." Ellery mused again. "Well, I see we'll have to be lexical. By the commonest definition, odd means strange, unusual, peculiar. Was there anything strange, unusual, or peculiar in, say, the appearance of Chandler or Kerry or Fletcher?"

Dr. Vreeland, with relish: "Not a thing."

"In a mannerism? Behavior? Speech? Gait? That sort of thing?"

Syres: "All ordinary as hell, Queen."

"In background?"

Darnell, through a grin: "Ditto."

"There was nothing a bizarre or freakish about one of them?"

"Nothing, friend," Emmy Wandermere murmured.

Ellery grasped his nose more like an enemy.

"Was one of them touched in the head?" he asked suddenly. "Odd in the mental sense?"

"There," the psychiatrist said, "you tread on muddy ground, Queen. Any antisocial behavior, as in the case of habitual criminals, might of course be so characterized. However, for purposes of our story the answer is no. All three men were normal—whatever that means."

Ellery nodded fretfully. "I could go on and on naming categories of peculiarity, but let me save us all from endangering Charlot's peace of mind. *Did* the undercover man use the word odd to connote peculiar?"

The little poet looked around and received assents invisible to the Queen eye. "He did not."

"Then that's that. Oh, one thing. Was the report in which he fingered the supplier as being the odd man written or oral?"

"Now what kind of question is that?" the oil king demanded. "What could that have to do with anything?"

"Possibly a great deal, Mr. Syres. If it had been an oral report, there would be no way of knowing whether his word odd began with a capital O or a small o. Assume that he'd meant it to be capital O-d-d. Then Odd man might have referred to a member of the I.O.O.F., the fraternal order—the Odd Fellows. That might certainly distinguish your man from the other two."

"It was a written report," Darnell said hastily, "and the o of odd was a small letter."

Everyone looked relieved. It was evident that the makers of this particular puzzle had failed to consider the Independent Order of Odd Fellows in their scheming.

"There are other odd possibilities—if you'll forgive the pun—such as odd in the golf meaning, which is one stroke more than your opponent has played. But I won't waste any more time on esoterica. Your undercover man meant odd in the sense of not matching, didn't he? Of being left over?"

"Explain that, please," Dr. Vreeland said.

"In the sense that two of the three suspects had something in common, something the third man didn't share with them—thus making the third man 'the odd man' and consequently the dope supplier and murderer. Isn't that the kind of thing your undercover agent meant by odd man?"

The psychiatrist looked cautious. "I think we may fairly say yes to that."

"Thank you very much," Ellery said. "Which brings me to a fascinating question: How clever are you people being? Run-of-the-game clever or clever-clever?"

"I don't think" Miss Wandermere said, "we quite follow. What do you mean exactly, Mr. Queen?"

"Did you intend to give me a choice of solutions? The reason I ask is that I see not one possible answer, but three."

"Three!" Syres shook his massive head. "We had enough trouble deciding on one."

"I for one," Counselor Darnell stated stiffishly, "should like to hear a for-instance."

"All right, I'll give you one solution I doubt you had in mind, since it's so obvious."

"You know, Queen, you have a sadistic streak in you?" barked Dr. Vreeland. "Obvious! Which solution is obvious?"

"Why, Doctor. Take the names of two of your suspects, John A.—Jac—Chandler and Benjamin Fletcher. Oddly enough—there I go again!—those surnames have two points of similarity. 'Chandler' and 'Fletcher' both end in 'er' and both contain eight letters. Cutcliffe Kerry's surname differs in both respects—no 'er' ending and only five letters—so Kerry becomes the odd surname of the trio. In this solution, then, Kerry the insurance man is the supplier-killer."

"I'll be damned," Syres exclaimed. "How did we miss that?"

"Very simply," Miss Wandermere said. "We didn't see it."

"Never mind that," Darnell snapped. "The fact is it happened. Queen, you said you have three solutions. What's another?"

"Give me a clue to the solution you people had in mind, since there are more than one. Some key word that indicates the drift but doesn't give the game away. One word can do it."

Syres, Darnell, and Dr. Vreeland jumped up and surrounded Emmy Wandermere. From the looped figures, the cocked heads, and the murderous whispers they might have been the losing team in an offensive huddle with six seconds left to play. Finally, the men resumed their seats, nudging one another.

Said little Miss Wandermere: "You asked for a clue, Mr. Queen. The clue is: clue."

Ellery threw is head back and roared. "Right! Very clever, considering who I am and that I'm the solver of the evening.

"You hurled my specialized knowledge in my teeth, calculating that I'd be so close to it I wouldn't see it. Sorry! Two of the surnames you invented," Ellery said with satisfaction, "are of famous detective-story writers. Chandler—in this case Raymond Chandler—was the widely acclaimed creator of Philip Marlowe. Joseph Smith Fletcher—J. S. Fletcher—produced more detective fiction than any other writer except Edgar Wallace, or so it's said; Fletcher's *The Middle Temple Murder* was publicly praised by no lesser mystery fan than the President of the United States, Woodrow Wilson. On the other hand, if there's ever been a famous detective-story writer named Cutcliffe Kerry, his fame has failed to reach me. So your Mr. Kerry again becomes the odd man of the trio and the answer to the problem. Wasn't that your solution, Miss Wandermere and gentlemen?"

They said yes in varying tones of chagrin.

Ordinarily, at this point in the evening's proceedings, the company would have risen from their chairs and made for Syres's magnificently gussied-up cookhouse of a dining room. But tonight no one stirred a toe, not even at the promise of the manna simmering on Charlot's hob. Instead, Dr. Vreeland uttered a small, inquiring cough.

"You, ah, mentioned a third solution, Queen. Although I must confess—"

smile, "may I? I've given you people your solution. I've even thrown in another for good measure. Turnabout? I now challenge you. What's the third solution?" . . .

CHALLENGE TO THE READER
What is the third solution?

Ten minutes later Ellery showed them mercy—really, he said sorrowfully, more in the interest of preserving Charlot's chancy good will that out of natural goodness of heart.

"John A. Chandler, Cutcliffe Kerry, Benjamin Fletcher. Chandler, Kerry, and Fletcher. What do two of these have in common besides what's already been discussed? Why, they derive from trades or occupations."

"Chandler." The lawyer, Darnell, looked around at the others, startled. "You know, that's true!"

"Yes, a ship chandler deals in specified goods or equipment. If you go farther back in time you find that a chandler was someone who made or sold candles or, as in very early England, supervised the candle requirements of a household. So that's one trade.

"Is there another in the remaining two surnames?

"Yes, the name Fletcher. A fletcher was—and technically still is—a maker of arrows, or a dealer in same; in the Middle Ages, by extension, although this was a rare meaning, the word was sometimes used to denote an archer. In either event, another trade or occupation.

"But the only etymological origin I've ever heard ascribed to the name Kerry is County Kerry, from which the Kerry blue terrier derives. And that's not a trade, it's a place. So with the names Chandler and Fletcher going back to occupations, and Kerry to Irish geography, your Mr. Kerry becomes once again the unpaired meaning, the odd man—a third answer to your problem."

And Ellery rose and offered his arm gallantly to Miss Wandermere.

The poetess took it with a little shake. And as they led the way to the feast she whispered, "You know what you are, Ellery Queen? You're an intellectual *pack rat!*"

THE HONEST SWINDLER

"Who leads off this evening?" asked Ellery. It was his turn to crack the mystery.

"My gambit." Syres was the Founder of the Puzzle Club. The regular meetings took place in his Park Avenue penthouse, and his chef's *cordon bleu* dinners were never served until the challenged member had either triumphed or failed. So a hungry Ellery took the inquisitional armchair facing four of his five co-members—the fifth, Arkavy the Nobel biochemist, was in Glasgow attending one of his interfering symposiums —and was fortifying himself from the steam tray of Charlot's canapé works of art.

"The villain of tonight's Puzzle," began the multimillionaire who had made his oily pile in the Southwest, "is an old scamp, one of those legendary prospectors the West used to brag could live for months on beans and jerky in temperatures that would frazzle an ordinary man's gizzard or turn his blood to mush-ice."

"Old Pete's life," Darnell, the criminal lawyer, took up the tale, "has been one uninterrupted washout. Although he's tracked a hundred El Dorado-type rumors thousands of miles in his time, he's never once made the big strike. Only an occasional miserable stake scratched out of hard-pan has kept Pete alive. Doctor?"

The psychiatrist, Vreeland, tapped the ash surgically off his two-dollar cigar. "Finally the mangy old fox becomes desperate. Frustration, loneliness, advancing years have whittled his wits to a fine edge; he plots a cunning—no, why plagiarize the shrinking violet? a brilliant!— scheme. To carry it off he sells just about everything in the world he owns. It brings him enough to pay for a display ad in *The Wall Street Journal*."

"*The Wall Street Journal?*" Ellery helped himself to the Scotch, looking delighted. "What imagination, what panache! Exactly how does your villain word his ad, by the way?"

Little Emmy Wandermere, who had just won the Pulitzer Prize for poetry, offered him a sheet of paper. On it she had penciled in her swashy hand:

Finance My Uranium Hunt!
Impossible to Lose!!
5-Year Money-Back Guarantee!
Complete Refund
Even If Uranium
Is Never Found!
Old Prospector, Box 1313

"Hardly a *Wall Street Journal*-type ad," Ellery said. "I'll put it down to poet's license, Miss Wandermere. And the response to Pete's pitch?"

"Heavy," the oil tycoon said. "You know what I always say—a sure thing gathers no moss. The dough comes rolling in."

"Can you give me a figure, Mr. Syres?"

"Well, let's say five hundred suckers invest $100 each to stake the old skunk for five years. That's $50,000. Agreeable, Miss Wandermere, gentlemen?"

The poet, the lawyer, and the psychiatrist nodded solemnly.

"In short, Mr. Queen," Dr. Vreeland said, "if Pete should strike uranium, the investors can realize many times their investments."

"Would you believe like five thousand percent on their money?" winked the oil man.

"But even if he should fail," Lawyer Darnell chipped in, "every last investor at least gets back his original investment. That was Pete's offer."

"Do you mean that if I'd staked Pete to $100 of my money and he didn't find uranium, he'd give me my hundred back?"

"Your money, and that of every other investor."

Ellery meditated. The company waited. Finally Ellery said, "Did the old fellow find uranium, or didn't he?"

"If I may embroider the obvious, gentlemen?" The lady-poet's wicked blue eyes took on a faraway look. "Prospector Pete, better provisioned and outfitted than he's ever been outside his most beautiful dreams, sets out on his uranium quest. With the euphoria of his breed he spends years—in the deserts, the plains, the mountains, the glaciers, from Baja, California, to the Rockies to Alaska and all stops between— patient years of foot-slogging, climbing, chipping, digging, panning, or whatever it is you do when you're looking for uranium. The sun fries him, the rain waterlogs him, snow and ice make a Father Frost out of him. Many times he nearly dies of thirst. He runs the risks of bear and cougar and, worst of all, of loneliness. It does seem as if he deserves a happy ending, Mr. Queen, but he doesn't get it. He finds absolutely nothing. Not a squawk or a wiggle in his Geiger counter. Until finally the time limit in his guarantee is up and he hasn't a cent left."

"Whereupon," Syres said, "old Pete makes good the promise in his ad."

To which Darnell added, with magnificent simplicity, "End of story."

There was a tranquil hush.

"Well," Ellery muttered. "I see. His money's gone, he's failed to find uranium, and still he manages to pay back every one of his backers. In full?"

"In full."

"Then and there? Not ten years later?"

"Within twenty-four hours," Dr. Vreeland said. "Question: How does Pete do it?"

"I suppose I had better rule out the obvious. He hadn't found something else of value? Gold, say? Diamonds? Platinum?"

Emmy Wandermere looked sad. "Alas, as they used to say, Mr. Queen. He found nothing."

"Or just before the five years were up, his long-lost uncle—on his mother's side, of course—died in Poona, Illinois, and left him ten billion lakhs?"

"Please," Lawyer Darnell said, pained. "Our man Pete is penniless when he runs the ad, his prospecting efforts produce an unrelieved zero, he doesn't have an uncle, and at the expiration of the five years he can't claim a single negotiable asset. His equipment is worn out and not worth the match to set it on fire, and even his burro has died of exhaustion."

"Yet every investor gets his money back *in toto*."

"Every investor, every dollar."

"Hm," Ellery said, reaching for the Scotch again.

"You have the usual one hour, Queen," Syres said briskly. "After that, as you know, Charlot's dinner—"

"Yes, won't be edible, and I'm declared Nitwit of the Month." Ellery took an elegant swallow. "To avert both disasters I'd better solve your puzzle right now."

CHALLENGE TO THE READER

*How did old Pete manage to repay
the entire $50,000 after five years in spite of his failure
to find anything of value and winding up dead-broke?*

"The answer has to be," Ellery said gently, "that *he never touched the $50,000 in the first place*. Didn't spend a dime of it. So when the time limit expired he was naturally able to give the whole sum back.

"But if he never touched the principal, how did he manage to finance five years of prospecting?

"Simplest way in the world," Ellery went on. "When he first collected the $50,000 from his backers, he deposited the entire amount in a savings bank. At, say, five percent interest the $50,000 would bring him an income of $2500 a year. $2500 a year was a sumptuous grubstake to a desert rat with one ancient burro to his name and a lifetime's practice in living on next to nothing.

"Old Pete was no swindler, and he certainly wasn't the scoundrel you deliberately painted him to set me off the track. He was simply a businessman following time-honored business practice. And now, fellow-puzzlers, shall we partake of Charlot's goodies?" Ellery flourished his empty glass. "I'm ready to eat Pete's burro."

THE REINDEER CLUE

Note by Edward D. Hoch:

In the Fall of 1975 Fred Dannay phoned me with a problem. His agent had a deal with the National Enquirer *for a Christmas short-short by Ellery Queen. There had been no new novels or short stories with the Ellery Queen character since Manny Lee's death in 1971, and Fred didn't feel that he wanted to write one now. He asked if I would do it for a flat fee, with him making some editorial changes before it was submitted. Of course I agreed.*

Although I'd written the final Ellery Queen paperback, The Blue Movie Murders *(details are in my essay, "A Tribute," in the final section of this book), I felt a special obligation in using the Ellery Queen character. I decided the story should contain a dying message, since many of the last EQ short-shorts were built around this type of clue. The Children's Zoo at Central Park seemed the perfect setting, with a reindeer display for the holidays. I sent the story to Fred and we discussed a few minor changes on the phone. The story ran in the* National Enquirer *just before Christmas and I felt that it turned out well. It was reprinted in two anthologies (one of which I edited myself).*

"Ellery!" Inspector Queen shouted over the heads of the waiting children. "Over here!"

Ellery managed to work his way through the crowd to the entrance of the Children's Zoo. The weather was unusually warm for two days before Christmas and the children didn't mind waiting.

If the presence of a half-dozen police cars stirred any curiosity, it was not enough for anyone to question Ellery as he edged his way forward.

"What is it, dad?" he asked, as the Inspector closed the wooden gate behind him.

"Murder, Ellery. And unless we can wind it up fast there are going to be a lot of disappointed kids out there."

"Are they waiting for Santa Claus?" Ellery asked with a grin.

"The next best thing—Santa's reindeer. It's a Christmas tradition here to deck the place with tinsel and toys and pass one of the reindeer off as Rudolph."

Ellery could see the police technicians working over the body of a man sprawled inside the fence of the reindeer pen. Off to one side a white-coated man kept a firm grip on the reindeer itself as the police flashbulbs popped. Another white-coated man and a woman were standing nearby.

"Who's the dead man?" Ellery asked. "Anyone I know?"

"Matter of fact, yes. It's Casey Sturgess, the ex-columnist."

"You've got to be kidding," Ellery exclaimed. "Sturgess murdered in a children's zoo?"

The old man shrugged. "Looks like he was up to his old tricks." Sturgess had been the gossip columnist on a now defunct New York tabloid.

When the paper folded he'd continued with his gossipy trade, selling information in a manner that often approached blackmail.

Ellery glanced toward the woman and two men. "Blackmailing one of these?"

"Why else would he come here at eight in the morning except to meet one of them? Come on—I'll introduce you."

The woman was Dr. Ella Manners, staff veterinarian. She wore straight blond hair and no makeup. "This is a terrible thing, simply terrible!" she cried out. "We've got a hundred children and their mothers out there waiting to see the reindeer. Can't you get this body out of here?"

"We're working as fast as we can," Inspector Queen assured her, motioning Ellery toward the two men.

One, who walked with a noticeable limp, was the zoo's director, Bernard White. The other man, younger that White and grossly overweight, as Mike Halley—"Captain Mike to the kids," he explained. "I'm the animal handler, except today it's more of a people handler. Our reindeer is tame, but it's still a big animal. We don't let the kids get too close to it."

The Inspector motioned toward the body. "Any of you know the dead man?"

"No, sir," Bernard White answered for the others. "We didn't know him and we have no idea how he got in here with the reindeer. We found him when we arrived just after eight o'clock."

"You all arrived at once?" Ellery asked him.

"I was just getting out of my car when Captain Mike drove up. Ella followed right behind him."

"Anyone else work here?"

"We have a night crew to clean up, but in the morning there's only the three of us."

Ellery nodded. "So one of you could have met Casey Sturgess here earlier, killed him, and then driven around the park till you saw the others coming."

"Why would one of us kill him?" Ella Manners asked. "We didn't even know him."

"Sturgess had sunk to some third-rate blackmailing lately. You all work for the city, in a job that puts you in contact with children. The least hint of drugs or a morals charge would have been enough to lose you your jobs. Right, dad?"

Inspector Queen nodded. "Damn right! Sturgess was shot in the chest with a .22 automatic. We found the weapon over in the straw. One of you met him here to pay blackmail, but shot him instead. It has to be one of you—he wouldn't possibly have come into the reindeer pen before the place opened to meet anybody else."

Ellery motioned his father aside. "Any fingerprints on the gun, dad?"

"It was wiped clean, Ellery. But the victim did manage to leave us something—a dying message of sorts."

Ellery's face lit up. "What, dad?"

"Come over here by the body."

Ellery passed a bucket that held red-and-green giveaway buttons inscribed, "I saw Santa's Reindeer!" He ducked his head under a hanging fringe of holly and joined his father by the body. For the first time he noticed that the rear fence of the reindeer pen was decorated with seven weathered wooden placards, each carrying eight lines of Clement Clarke Moore's famous poem, "A Visit from St. Nicholas."

Casey Sturgess had died under the third placard, his arm outstretched toward it.

"He could only have lived a minute or so with that wound," the old man said. "But look at the blood on his right forefinger. He used it to mark the sign."

Ellery leaned closer, examining two lines of the Moore poem. *Now, Dasher! now, Dancer! now, Prancer and Vixen! / On, Comet! on, Cupid! on,*

Donder and Blitzen!

"Dad—he smeared each of the eight reindeer's names with a dab of blood!"

"Right, Ellery. Now you tell me what it means."

Ellery remained stooped, studying the defaced poem for some minutes. All the smears were similar.

None seemed to have been given more emphasis than any other. Finally he straightened up and walked over to the reindeer that was drinking water from its trough, oblivious of the commotion.

"What's its name?" he asked the overweight Captain Mike.

"Sparky—but for Christmas we call him Rudolph. The kids like it."

Ellery put out a gentle hand and touched the ungainly animal's oversized antlers, wishing that it could speak and tell him what it had seen in the pen.

But it was as silent as the llama and donkey and cow that he could see standing in the adjoining pens.

"How much longer is this going on?" White was demanding from the Inspector.

"As long as it takes. We've got a murder on our hands, Mr. White."

He turned his back on the zoo director and looked at his son. "What do you make of it, Ellery?"

"Not much. Found anyone who heard the shot?"

"Not yet. The sound of a little .22 wouldn't carry very far."

Ellery went back for one more look at the bloody marks on the Moore poem.

Then he asked Ella Manners, "Would you by any chance be a particularly good dancer, Doctor?"

"Hardly! Veterinary medicine and dancing don't mix."

"I thought not," Ellery said, suddenly pleased.

"You got something?" his father asked.

"Yes, dad. I know who murdered Casey Sturgess."

CHALLENGE TO THE READER
Who killed Casey Sturgess
And how did Ellery know?

Sparky the reindeer looked up from its trough, as if listening to Ellery's words. "You see, dad, there's always a danger with dying messages—a danger that the killer will see his victim leave the message, or return and find it later. Premeditated murderers like to make certain they've finished the job without leaving a clue. You told me Sturgess could only have lived a minute or so with that wound."

"That's right, Ellery."

"Then the killer was probably still here to see him jab that sign with his bloody finger. And are we to believe that in a minute's time the dying Sturgess managed to smear all eight names with his blood, and each in the same way? No, dad—Sturgess only marked *one* name! The killer, unable to wipe the blood off without leaving a mark, smeared the other seven names himself in the same manner. He obliterated the dying man's message by adding to it!"

"But, Ellery—which reindeer's name did Sturgess mark?"

"Dad, it had to be one that would connect instantly with his killer. Now look at those eight names. Could it have been Donder or Blitzen? Hardly—they tell us nothing. Likewise Dasher and Prancer have no connection with any of the suspects. Dr. Manners might be a Vixen and White could be a Cupid, but Sturgess couldn't expect the police to spot such a nebulous thing. No, dad, the reindeer clue had to be something so obvious the killer was forced to alter it."

"That's why you asked Dr. Manners if she was a dancer!"

"Exactly. It's doubtful that the limping Bernard White or the overweight Captain Mike are notable as dancers, and once I ruled Dr. Manners out as well, that left only one name on the list."

"Comet!"

"Yes, dad. The most famous reindeer of all might be Rudolph, but the most famous comet of all is surely Halley's Comet."

"Captain Mike Halley! Somebody grab him!"

Moments later, as the struggling Halley was being led away, Bernard White said, "But he was our only handler! We're ready to open the gates and who's going to look after the children?"

Ellery glanced at his father and smiled broadly. "Maybe I can help out. After all, it's Christmas," he said.

ESSAYS AND REMINISCENCES

ELLERY QUEEN

by Jon L. Breen

For more than four decades, Ellery Queen was the most famous and influential figure in American detective fiction. Queen the detective solved baffling crimes in books, magazines, motion pictures, radio, and television. Queen the author wrote novels, short stories, a stage play, film scenarios, radio scripts, and true crime essays. Queen the editor founded a magazine that is still the leader in its field 58 years later and guided and encouraged some of the best writers in the form. Queen the public personality appeared as platform lecturer and radio panelist. Queen the literary figure exchanged correspondence with some of the most significant people of the twentieth century. The celebrated critic Anthony Boucher once wrote, "Ellery Queen *is* the American detective story."

Frederic Dannay and Manfred B. Lee, the two cousins who wrote about detective Ellery Queen under the pseudonym Ellery Queen, formed the most successful and longest-lasting literary partnership in history. They had much in common. Both were born in 1905 in a Brooklyn tenement district, the offspring of Jewish immigrant families. Both attended Boys' High School in Brooklyn. Both changed their names to assimilate into the Great American Melting Pot, Daniel Nathan becoming Frederic Dannay, Manford Lepofsky becoming Manfred B. Lee. Both discovered a refuge in books early in life and developed literary ambitions, Dannay to write poetry, Lee to become nothing less than the Twentieth-Century Shakespeare. Both had an enthusiasm for detective stories. Both were devoted family men and successful parents, though their family lives were often troubled or tragic.

Their differences were also striking. While Lee spent all of his boyhood on the tough streets of the city, Dannay spent a big part of his growing-up years in Elmira, a small town in upstate New York. After high school, Lee went to New York University, leading a jazz band to help finance his education, while Dannay never attended. Dannay was quiet, somewhat introverted and professorial in manner. Lee was an extravert, more inclined to shoot from the hip in his dealings with others. Dannay, a workaholic, spent most of his time on indoor pursuits; outdoorsman Lee had a greater appreciation for nature. Their differences in personality and outlook—they once told an interviewer that they not only had different attitudes about detective fiction but different attitudes about everything—made their ability to collaborate successfully for so many years a miracle.

In 1928, Lee was a motion picture publicist, Dannay an advertising agency art director. Close since boyhood, they frequently met for lunch in Manhattan. When *McClure's* magazine offered a $7500 prize for the best new detective novel, the cousins collaborated on *The Roman Hat Mystery*. After verbally declaring them the winners, *McClure's* went out of business and the successor magazine gave the prize to another book. Still, their novel was published and became a major success; more followed, making Ellery Queen a household word for fair-play detective novels, somewhat in the pattern of the phenomenally successful bestseller S.S. Van Dine (Willard Huntington Wright) but far superior.

As their fame grew, they became founders and editors of the pulp magazine *Mystery League*, which lasted only four issues but foreshadowed editorial projects to come. The Dannay half of the team became a collector of books of detective short stories, his efforts resulting in the experimental anthology *Challenge to the Reader*. Early in the thirties, the team developed a second pseudonym, writing as Barnaby Ross *The Tragedy of X*, *The Tragedy of Y*, *The Tragedy of Z*, and *Drury Lane's Last Case*. While the identity of the two bylines remained a secret, the cousins went on the lecture circuit as masked combatants, Lee as EQ, Dannay as his bitter rival Ross. They had a stint as Hollywood scenarists and were radio panelists on *Author! Author!*, where one was known as Mr. Ellery, the other as Mr. Queen. The lecture-platform and radio appearances were an outlet for their lifelong competitiveness. Their respective roles were clearly defined, though long kept secret. Dannay devised the complex plots, with their well-planted clues, alternate solutions, and dazzling surprise twists, raising the formal puzzle from craft to art. Lee, a gifted novelist whose elegance of style and mastery of pace and character had few equals in the genre, turned Dannay's outlines into novels, short stories, and scripts. What they might have accomplished individually as writers of detective fiction can never be known, since (with a few odd exceptions) they never worked alone. Together, they formed the greatest single byline in mystery fiction annals.

A browse through the Frederic Dannay papers at Columbia University provides some fascinating insights into the partnership and its achievements. Dannay and Lee admitted that theirs was often a stormy relationship (the Gilbert and Sullivan comparison is not far from the mark), but it would be hard to imagine just how acrimonious the partnership could be without reference to their letters. Both Dannay and Lee were haunted by self-doubt, depression, and ill health; and each felt denigrated, devalued, or patronized by the other. Their exchanges by mail on the working out of *Cat of Many Tails* and *Ten Days' Wonder*, both written when Lee was living a continent away from Dannay in California, not only illuminate their creative processes but also highlight the misunderstandings, mutual insults, and recriminations that constantly threatened the health of their partnership. A casual reader of their correspondence would marvel that they managed to work as a team for over forty years, and might even conclude the two cousins hated each other. Surely the truth is that they loved each other, indeed shared a kind of openness and intimacy rare among heterosexual males, whether friends, business partners, or relatives. The comparison of their collaboration to a marriage—a constantly stormy but ultimately solid marriage—is inevitable.

In the first decade of Ellery Queen, even after their true identities had been revealed in 1936, the cousins' partnership was presented to the world as an equal one. But in Howard Haycraft's *Murder for Pleasure* (1941), Dannay was identified as the book-collecting, editorial half of the team, and he began to take on an independent identity in the field. The development troubled Lee, who believed he had been relegated to a lesser position in the partnership. Even a seemingly innocuous act deeply wounded Lee, as when Dannay, using a charming account of his own boyhood encounter with the Sherlock Holmes stories as an introduction to the anthology *The Misadventures of Sherlock Holmes*, began with the words, "This is one of the Queens speaking . . ." To Dannay, it seemed quite a reasonable way to approach the matter; to Lee, it was a betrayal of the partnership. When Dannay's fictionalized boyhood memoir *The Golden Summer* (1954) was published under his birth name of Daniel Nathan, the author's true identity was a secret for a time, though a fairly transparent one to anyone in the field. It was Dannay's only solo book.

Through the forties, radio and its business details were primarily Lee's bailiwick. Lee never wrote a novel on his own, though he reportedly had a standing offer for one from Random House editor Lee Wright; two collections of magazine true crime articles published under the Queen name were his sole work, though based on research material provided by the magazine.

In 1941, the same year Dannay produced the landmark anthology *101 Years' Entertainment*, he launched *Ellery Queen's Mystery Magazine*, still the premier periodical in its field. The great first decade of the magazine was a difficult, sometimes tragic one for Dannay in his personal life: a serious traffic accident late in 1940 that had left him hospitalized for weeks was followed by recurring health problems, the death from cancer of his first wife, and (following his marriage to his second wife) the long illness and eventual death of his third son, Steven. While all this was going on, Dannay's playful, informative, and enthusiastic story notes in the magazine and anthologies celebrated the joys of book collecting, editorial discovery, and games playing.

Manfred Lee made occasional editorial contributions to *EQMM* and their contract with publisher Lawrence E. Spivak specified he would take over the editorship in the event Dannay died or (during World War II) was drafted. But in reality and in the eyes of the mystery field, the magazine was Dannay's. At one point, Lee groused about the fact that his money was being used to pay Joseph T. Shaw, legendary former editor of *Black Mask*, to find potential reprints for the magazine, work that Lee could have been doing (and indeed later did for a time) himself.

As early as 1950, the team contemplated recruiting and training a stable of ghost writers, and they had earlier used ghosts on some juvenile adaptations of Queen movies and radio shows (Anthony Boucher taking over the plotter's role from Dannay) and on the series of juvenile mysteries signed Ellery Queen, Jr.—the author of the latter aroused the ire of Lee by farming out the writing of some of the books to a sub-ghost. In the sixties, with Lee suffering from writer's block (among other psychological and physical ailments), science fiction writers Theodore Sturgeon and Avram Davidson were brought in as uncredited third collaborators to turn Dannay's outlines into new Queen novels. Meanwhile, totally non-Queenian paperback originals, written by various ghosts and edited by Lee, appeared on the market to confuse fans. The team's efforts to keep the ghosting secret tested the loyalty of the *New*

York Times critic, *EQMM* columnist and longtime Queen friend and admirer Anthony Boucher, who at one point wrote to Dannay to warn him that a coming *Times* column would have harsh words about the ghosted paperbacks. Apparently informed by Dannay of Lee's precarious health and the bad effect such an attack in print might have on him, Boucher wired reassurances that the column had been killed. However, soon came the shattered Boucher's news that the column had run after all without his knowledge, though with some of its bitterest passages editorially cut—in the interest of length, not content. Though Lee finally conquered his writer's block, returning to the traditional collaboration for the last few Queen novels, the authorship of the very atypical fortieth-anniversary novel *Cop Out* (1969), which Dannay swore was the work of the cousins alone, has spurred controversy among Queen devotees because of its marked difference in style and approach from other genuine Queen novels.

After Lee's death in 1971, Dannay carried on his editorial duties but produced no more fiction. A last paperback original and a single EQ short story for *National Enquirer* were the work of Edward D. Hoch. The year after Lee's death, Dannay for the second time lost a wife to cancer.

In his last decade, Dannay married for a third time and became more visible, lecturing publicly for the first time in thirty years at a San Diego mystery writers' conference and even being interviewed on television by Dick Cavett. Shortly before his death in 1982, he retired from the magazine he founded—ironically, for commercial reasons, *EQMM* included no obituary nor any recognition of his passing, apart from a brief tribute in the present writer's book review column.

Why is the Ellery Queen story so dramatic and significant? The two cousins lived through many of the great events of the twentieth century, being affected by and responding to them in ways that were sometimes typical of their generation, sometimes surprising. They were associated with many of the significant writers of their time, both in and out of the crime-fiction genre. Apart from writing some of the most ingeniously plotted detective novels of their time (and all time), they created one of the few Golden Age detective heroes who grew and developed from book to book. They demonstrated an ability to adjust to changes in the field, to experiment with theme and subject matter, without sacrificing the qualities that made their work unique. The influence of Queen (primarily the Dannay half) on the development of the detective story in the century through discovering and encouraging new writers cannot be over-estimated.

The story of Ellery Queen is both a landmark in American literary history and a fascinating human story of the sometimes troubled face behind the enthusiastic and playful mask. While other seminal figures in crime fiction (Arthur Conan Doyle, Dorothy L. Sayers, Agatha Christie, John Dickson Carr, Ngaio Marsh, Margery Allingham, Dashiell Hammett, Raymond Chandler, Jim Thompson, James M. Cain, Rex Stout, S.S. Van Dine, Ross Macdonald) have been the subject of major biographical works, Ellery Queen, as significant and biographically interesting as any of them, has not. Apart from Francis M. Nevins's two book-length studies, they have also been comparatively neglected critically. A combination of factors has worked against them. In literary criticism, there is a general bias in favor of individual creation and against collaboration. The multi-faceted Queen has been viewed as a brand name (or even, with the sixties use of ghostwriters, a house name) rather than an author. For whatever reason, the full story of these two remarkable men remains to be told.

LEGACY

by Douglas and Richard Dannay

Of course, there were the novels (*Ten Days' Wonder, Cat of Many Tails, . . .*), the short stories (*The Adventures of Ellery Queen, Calendar of Crime, . . .*), the anthologies (*101 Years' Entertainment, The Misadventures of Sherlock Holmes, . . .*), the scholarship (*Queen's Quorum, The Detective Short Story*), the radio show (CBS, NBC, . . .), the television show (Dumont, NBC, . . .), the magazines (*Mystery League, Ellery Queen's Mystery Magazine*), and the Grandmaster's award given by the Mystery Writers of America. The legacy to the detective story genre is undeniable, but there was more . . . *The Golden Summer*, an autobiographical fiction of a ten year old's summer in 1915, was written by one Daniel Nathan . . . It wouldn't take Ellery Queen very long to deduce where the name Dannay originated: the DAN from Daniel, the NA from Nathan, the Y for sound and good looks. The Frederic would require some investigation before an admiration for Chopin was uncovered. *The Golden Summer* ended with these lines of poetry:

> May there be
> Forever in your heart
> A country stream,
> Forever in your dreams
> A wind that lifts,
> A field that sings.

Thirty-one years later came *O Lost and Lonely Star*, a difficult collection of poems exploring the relationships among family, friends, acquaintances, and religion, unpublished. It contained the following poem:

> One hot day our gardener,
> a walnut-man in his seventies,

---

came in to fret about the chinch bugs.
He found me at my desk,
facing a typewriter,
an unweeded manuscript growing wild.
When he left he said,
"I don't see how you do it—
if my life depended on it, I couldn't
    think up a story."

One cold day in winter
I saw the gardener shoveling our walk
free of snow. That wrinkled, hard-shell man,
past his biblical time,
tossed snow effortlessly,
singing loud opera in the flurried air.
I said to myself,
"I don't see how he does it—
if my life depended on it, I couldn't
    clear away that snow."

Luckily, he didn't have to and could spend his time weeding and taming
EQ manuscripts.

But the personal legacy was books, the love of a book not only for its
content but as a physical object of beauty, a collector's love. We
absorbed his feeling for books, his attitude toward them, his reverence,
and, surrounded by their wonder, we too became collectors—not that we
could ever approach what our father had built.

First there was the detective short story on which he was probably
the world's leading expert. His collection provided raw material for
Ellery Queen's Mystery Magazine and for *Queen's Quorum*, a critical judgment
of the best of the detective short story, an indispensable tool for
collecting the detective short story, and still quoted in rare book
catalogues because being included in *Queen's Quorum* enhanced a book's
collectibility. His collection contained the marvels of the field: Poe's
Tales in the original wrappers, *A Study in Scarlet* in the original wrappers
of *Beeton's Christmas Annual*, *The Adventures of Sherlock Holmes* inscribed,
The Memoirs of Sherlock Holmes in the dust jacket, the manuscript of "A
Scandal in Bohemia." But Dupin and Holmes were joined by Jacques

Futrelle's Thinking Machine (the book inscribed), Maurice Leblanc's Arsène Lupin, Freeman's John Thorndyke (the book signed), Chesterton's Father Brown (the book signed), Post's Uncle Abner, Philip Trent, Hercule Poirot, Lord Peter Wimsey, Charlie Chan, The Saint, Sam Spade, Perry Mason, Philip Marlowe, and, of course, Ellery himself, all represented in the mysterious first editions, a collector's Shangri-La.

The books were sold to The University of Texas. What else was there to add? And so our father then began putting together an incredible poetry collection, the greatest books by the greatest poets. These first editions would also be his, allowing him now to touch the greatness of a literary form he also loved.

His poetry collection was auctioned at Christie's in 1983: Beaudelaire, Browning, Byron, Chaucer, Coleridge, Crane, Dickinson, Eliot, Housman, Hughes, Keats, Kipling, Masefield, Masters, Omar Khayyam, Poe (an old friend!), Robinson, Rosetti, Sandburg, Shakespeare, Shelley, Tennyson, Thomas, Whitman. Masefield's *Reynard the Fox* was illustrated with 54 pen-and-ink and watercolor drawings in the margins, on blank pages, on endpapers. His copy, inscribed and with these wondrous illustrations, was one of only three such copies known: one had belonged to King George V, the other to Masefield's wife Constance. Even the poets might have difficulty appropriately describing such a book. This special book was auctioned again at Christie's and now once again belongs to our family.

In a sense, *our* serious collecting began with four books of poetry from that spectacular collection: to one of us, Housman and Robinson; to the other, Sandburg and Masters. It was *Spoon River Anthology* that inspired the creation of Wrightsville, which first appeared in *Calamity Town*. But why the books of Housman, Robinson, and Sandburg? Mystery is not unique to the detective story. It also lies at the heart of great poetry and at the heart of one's response to it.

Although our father's archive of manuscripts and correspondence is housed now in the rare book library at Columbia University, the Ellery Queen/Barnaby Ross books themselves, the physical books, were going to remain in the family. Still, they had to be divided between us. Much choosing followed, coin flipping over the piles of books we had brought to the dining room table in the Larchmont house, a Danny-Nathan-like golden summer activity. Negotiations went on easily as the books found new shelves in different homes. Perhaps, the most difficult moment arose over the nine digest-sized paperback collections he edited of the Dashiell Hammett short stories. They made an important contribution to a revival of interest in Hammett after the political quagmire he had fallen into, but the books were not all that valuable and wouldn't be all that hard to obtain in the rare book market—except that seven of the nine were inscribed by Hammett to our father. Inscribed! And one of the inscriptions said: "For Fred—and, Jesus, was I glad to see him again" So, which of us would get four? Not exactly a problem equivalent in difficulty to the one offered by Frank Stockton in "The Lady, or the Tiger?" (a *Queen's Quorum* title, by the way). But a seventh inscribed Hammett! What balanced that? Well, Stockton never did open that door.

So, now we're both into the hunt that was such an important part of our father's life, trying to fill in the gaps in his own Ellery Queen/ Barnaby Ross collection—inexplicable gaps for a great collector to endure, like *The French Powder Mystery* in dust jacket which he did not have. Maybe we'll succeed, but every book collector knows that even if you get every title you want, there's always a copy out there in better condition, a signed copy, an inscribed— Well, we're sure that there never were inscribed copies of those other two Hammett collections. We're absolutely sure, absolutely . . .

And why wasn't there a copy of *The French Powder* in dust jacket? Who knows? All any good mystery needs is a good detective. Ellery would be perfect, stepping into the heart of the mystery from a distant golden summer when it all began . . .

THE TEMPLE OF HIS WORD:
GROWING UP WITH ELLERY QUEEN

by Rand B. Lee

My father, Manfred B. Lee, died of a heart attack around 8 p.m., Eastern Standard Time on April 3, 1971. He died in the upstairs dressing room of our big white house on South Street in Roxbury, Connecticut, lying on the floor's bare oak planking. When he and my mother had moved into the house in 1951, the oak had been shamed by a coat of grey deck paint; they had stripped it together, inch by inch, marveling at the blockheadedness of anyone who could not comprehend the glory of old oak. I was not a year old. When my father lay dying, I was just twenty.

I was not present at his passing. I was in college, far away in Maryland, thrashing through thickets of sexuality and philosophy and self-doubt. My brother, Manfred B. Lee, Jr., had returned from serving with the Marine Corps in Viet Nam not long before. My sisters, Jacquelin, Patricia, Anya, and Christopher Rebecca, were scattered around the East Coast, with husbands or children or Greenwich Village cats. Not even my mother was present when my father died. Anthony Joseph and Jeffrey Robert, my eldest and youngest brothers respectively, were in the house that day, and they sent her downstairs to the kitchen so that she would not have to witness my father's death throes. Jeff said that Dad died quickly, without a word uttered; as my brothers knelt beside him, they witnessed the light of his sharp, wary intelligence fading from his eyes by perceptible degrees. "It was at that moment," Jeff told me, "that I knew human beings have a soul."

It was many years before I heard this version of my father's death. At the time of the actual event, the story Jeff and Tony told us was that our father had died in an ambulance rushing him to the hospital in nearby New Milford, nine miles away from little Roxbury. From the first, my mother insisted this was untrue. *Her* version of the story was that Dad had died in her arms in their bedroom, whispering, "Help me." It must have comforted her to think so.

The truth is probably an amalgam of all three tales: that Dad had his heart attack in the bedroom he shared with Mother; that after my brothers sent Mother downstairs, Dad became unconscious on the floor of the dressing room, Jeff kneeling beside him; and that he achieved brain death on the ambulance ride. But the mystery doesn't stop there. Now, twenty-eight years later, seventy years after my father and his cousin published their first book under the pseudonym of "Ellery Queen," everyone who was in the house that day is dead: Tony of a heart attack while jogging in 1987; Jeff, of AIDS in the spring of 1990 while—in an eerie replay of the events that claimed our father—an ambulance sped him toward a hospital in Cork City, Ireland; Mother in 1991 at that same hospital, while my sister Christopher and a cousin were taking a short break from their days-long vigil in the ward. One would, by this juncture, be deeply suspicious if these events had taken place in an Ellery Queen novel.

I must have been ten or eleven when I first found out my father was famous. We lived on 63 ½ acres in rural Roxbury, Connecticut, which in those days was virtually undiscovered. Our house, the house Dad died in, had been built in 1792. About a hundred yards from the kitchen door stood a second dwelling, a remodeled colonial school building that we called the Little House. My sister Christopher, whom we always called "Kit," lived in one half, and Dad had his study in the other.

Dad's study was normally off-limits. You were only officially permitted to go there when he was present, and his presence did not ensure your entry; you had to knock, timidly, first, and gauge by the tone with which he replied whether or not it was safe to cross the threshold. If my mother was Juno, passionately nurturing and vengefully possessive by turns, my father was Jove: autocratic, a good provider, brooding, sensual, and pleasure-loving. He thundered from on high when he was angry, brooking no back talk. That day he was gentle, and invited me inside. I passed into dimness.

I had been there before, of course, this *sanctum sanctorum* of dark wood and the scent of pipe tobacco, but the walk up the old carpet to my father's big, paper-littered, glass-topped oak desk seemed longer than usual. My father sat behind his desk looking like a benign pope. He was short and heavyset, with a full grey-and-black beard and a rich bass voice, and the whole place was full of his hierophantic presence. A lot of people thought he resembled Ernest Hemingway, and in fact, several days after the news wires were flooded with reports of that writer's death, Dad was walking through Grand Central Station in New York when a passing businessman raised a hat to him and remarked, "Good morning, Mister Hemingway." Dad nodded graciously and continued on his way, but he came home chortling to Mother, "'I'll bet that guy got a shock when he told his wife whom he had met!"

Shyly I looked around me at the paneled walls, lined floor to ceiling with full bookshelves, and noticed really for the first time that many of them were printed in languages other than English. When I asked my father what they were, he told me that they were books he had written with our Cousin Dan under the pen name of "Ellery Queen," and that people from all over the world read them. Something fell into place in my mind. I had known that Dad was a writer, and I had heard the name "Ellery Queen" used around the house; I also had memories of Dad sitting in front of the television set in the late Fifties, watching a TV show and making irascible notes on a pad while he did so. "What," I asked, "are they about?"

"They're mystery novels. The detective is named Ellery Queen, too. We decided to give our detective the same name as our pen name so readers wouldn't have to remember two names when they went looking for our books."

I was astonished. There was a world of books here, a lifetime of them. I asked if I could read them, and my father looked at me as though he, too, were seeing something he had never really noticed before. He said, "Well, which one would you like to start with?"

"With the first one." It seemed the obvious place to begin.

He grimaced. "Oh, son, that awful thing! Are you sure you don't want to start with one of the later ones?"

I was adamant. Smiling to himself, he got up from his desk, moving slowly. He pulled out a volume from the topmost shelf of the very first bookcase and held it out to me. I read the title: *The Roman Hat Mystery*. It was a thick book; I opened it carefully. There was a map of a theater inside it—the Roman Theater—a long list of characters, and an introduction by someone named "J. J. McC." It was a book, a real book, and my father had *written* it.

"Who's 'J. J. McC.' ?" I asked.

Dad looked embarrassed. "A silly idea Cousin Dan and I had. Here. Let me dedicate it for you." He took the book back to his desk, wrote an inscription in the front, and handed it back to me. "It really isn't very good, son."

I didn't care. My father was a famous writer. And he was pleased by my interest, I could tell, this huge, distant, omnipotent man, whom I had always feared and yearned for touch, look, praise from. I departed, carrying my treasure in excited hands.

It was indeed a dreadful book, and the next one, *The French Powder Mystery,* which featured a corpse discovered in a department store window, wasn't much better. I found the vast casts of characters impossible to keep track of, the convoluted plots impossible to follow, the mannered writing peculiar, and smart-alecky Ellery with his Twenties *pince-nez* peculiarly unattractive. But I liked the Challenges To The Reader, and loyally I kept on: through *The Chinese Orange Mystery* (which I thought pretty good: imagine, a corpse with all its clothes on backwards!) and then *The Dutch Shoe Mystery.* By *The Egyptian Cross Mystery*, I sensed a new note coming into the books: *Cross* was far darker and more violent than the previous books had been. *Halfway House* I thought dismal and frightening, but Dad assured me it marked the transition from his and Dan's youthful excesses to their first hint of writing maturity. From then on, the writing became more spare. "J. J. McC." vanished, as did the *dramatis personae* and Ellery's *pince-nez*, so did the literary quotes heading the chapters (which I adored, but which Dad confessed to me that he and Dan had made up, authors and all). I sailed out into a wide bay of Queen delights which I fished in ravenously for the next few years. I loved the Hollywood series, the Wrightsville novels, and the short story anthologies; I was not as crazy about the horrifying *Cat of Many Tails,* a serial killer novel, which Dad, Mom, and my sister Kit always thought of as the best Queen book.

I also discovered the Ellery Queen, Jr. juveniles, which I later learned were ghostwritten, albeit tinkered with extensively by Dad and Dan before publication. The only Queen books I refused to read were the Drury Lane novels (*Tragedy of X, Tragedy of Y, Tragedy of Z,* and *Drury Lane's Last Case)* because they didn't have Ellery in them. I read *The Tragedy of X* for the first time only last year.

Of course, I decided to be a writer, too. And possibly an actor—my mother's profession—but definitely a writer. I wrote plays with mythological themes, and bullied my younger brother Jeffrey and my poor nieces Sarah and Anne to act in them. My first novel, written on ruled notepaper, was a fantasy about a boy who is transported back in time to

Robin Hood's day and joins the band of merry men in Sherwood Forest (I was madly in love with Alan à Dale). My second novel was an Ellery Queen, Jr. takeoff about a bunch of spies who lived in a cave under the youthful detective's home town. I do not think I showed Dad these pieces; easily crushed, I was too fearful of what he might say about them. I know I showed them to Mother, who had written for radio, and (as she always did anything I essayed) she praised them to the skies.

Encouraged, I wrote a bloody piece set in the Trojan War; then, deciding the novel form was a trifle ambitious, moved on to write a series of science fiction short stories characterized by their extreme brevity, adolescent moodiness, imitative style, and paucity of plot. Dad had introduced me to science fiction. He had told me how he and Cousin Dan had been involved with starting up *The Magazine of Fantasy and Science Fiction* around the time I was born, and this had thrilled me no end. (Anthony Boucher, the first editor of *F & SF*, was my older brother Tony's namesake and godfather.) It is because of my love of science fiction that, for many years, my favorite Queen novel was *And On The Eighth Day*. (The runner-up was *The Finishing Stroke*, which still to my mind is the greatest country house murder mystery ever written.)

By the time I was 14 I had my own typewriter, and Dad and I had had our big Talk About Writing. In this talk, my father outlined his rules for budding authors. They were:

(1) *Read everything you can lay your hands on.*
(2) *Write what you know.*
(3) *Edit ruthlessly.*
(4) *Don't bother with writing courses. You learn to write by writing.*

Reading was easy; I already read everything: Superman comic books; Edgar Rice Burroughs; A. A. Milne (*Once On A Time*, his now-forgotten first book for children, I came to love even more than the Pooh stories); the Oz books; E. Nesbit's wonderful fantasies (*Five Children and It, The Phoenix and the Carpet*); Isaac Asimov's *Words From The Myths*; Robert Heinlein's *Have Spacesuit, Will Travel*. (Heinlein's Mother Thing was to resurface, decades afterward and quite unconsciously, as the model for the alien Damanakippith/fy in "Tales From The Net: A Family Matter," one of my early published short stories.) Writing what I knew was more problematical. I didn't want to write about real life; I wanted to *escape* real life.

It was years before it dawned on me that, in pursing a career as a mystery novelist, my father had seldom taken his own advice. The Queen books in which he did stand out from the crowd. Many of the femme fatales in the Queen books from the early Forties onward are modeled after my mother, Kaye Brinker. *The Glass Village* borrows setting and characters from the little town in Connecticut where I grew up. To research *Cop Out*, a late non-Ellery novel about a small-town policeman whose daughter is kidnaped, Dad rode around all night on patrol with some New Milford, Connecticut officers; the authenticity shows in a way it does not in his last books, written when he had virtually withdrawn from public life. But it is *Inspector Queen's Own Case* (originally titled *November Song*) that stands as the most sensitive and emotionally mature works in the Queen canon; it is in large measure an exploration of Dad's feelings about growing older. My father told me that in this book he built up the character of Richard Queen, Ellery's father, from memories of his father, Benjamin Lepofsky, and my maternal grandfather, Robert Hugh Brinker, of whom Dad was fond.

The editing advice Dad gave me was explicit, and I still try to follow it, however imperfectly: When you finish your first draft of a story, go back and cross out every adjective and adverb. Then put in only those adjectives and adverbs you feel you really need.

Despite my new appreciation for my father's fame, like all children of famous fathers I found it difficult to reconcile the image of him as a world-renowned author with my daily experience of him. At home, I knew him as a pot-bellied, tee-shirted, smoke-enveloped, irritable hater of parties, whose idea of Hell was having to make the journey into New York to meet with his publisher, or Dan, or attend some MWA dinner. He worked four hours a day in his study and spent much of the rest of the time doing crossword puzzles, driving to New Milford, or watching TV sports and news broadcasts, upon which he commented loudly with the transplanted New Yorker's love-hate for the Mets and the liberal's contempt for the stupidity and racism of Man. He ate voraciously, jealously guarding his stashes of refrigerated citrus salad and lox. Though he left the running of house, children, dogs, cats, birds, and gardens to my mother, he occasionally cooked for pleasure, and to this day I have never eaten beef and vegetable soup to compare with his: I used to marvel at the textures of the vegetables floating in the dark broth, and the thin golden sheen of the fat that haloed each morsel. With the cruelty of adolescence, I was deeply contemptuous of his bulk and nonathleticism, both of which I inherited (he had been a slender and rather beautiful young man).

But I was proud of Ellery Queen, and the rare glimpses I got into his working life thrilled me. Once I got to audit a workshop, held on a northeastern university campus, at which the Queen partners were featured lecturers. I sat in the back of the room, basking in reflected glory, impressed with the look of awe on the faces of the adult students as Dan (politely) and Dad (sourly; he was wearing a suit and he *loathed* formal dress) fielded questions about fiction-writing. Dan was short and bald like Dad, but much slimmer, and courtly. I liked him, though I knew him very slightly. My older sister Kit remembers him with fondness as always having been very kind to her, and after Dad's death, when I sold my first science fiction story to *Isaac Asimov's Science Fiction Magazine,* Dan paid me the high compliment of expressing the wish that he, not Asimov, had been the one to publish the piece.

Dad and Dan always had a contentious relationship. By the time I was a teenager, they had fallen into the routine of working long-distance between Connecticut and Larchmont, New York, and frequently I would pick up the extension phone to hear them arguing with one another. Dan was my father's first cousin, from a somewhat better-off side of the family, born Daniel Nathan (hence "Cousin Dan"); he had, by his account, an idyllic rural boyhood in upstate New York. Dad came from Brownsville, New York and was raised Brooklyn-poor. Everybody knows how, fresh out of college and working as admen in New York, they had originally collaborated on *The Roman Hat Mystery* in an attempt to win a mystery-writing contest sponsored by the now defunct *McClure's* magazine. The first prize was awarded to them; then *McClure's* was bought by a new publisher, who turned it into a women's magazine and awarded the prize to someone else. Frederick A. Stokes picked up the manuscript, which received fair reviews. Emboldened, they wrote another, then a third, and by the fifth, Dad told me, they had quit their jobs and were collaborating full-time.

They tried a number of ways of working together. Eventually, Dan ended up doing the primary editing on the *Ellery Queen's Mystery Magazine* and writing detailed plot outlines for the Queen books; Dad fleshed out the plot outlines and did the bulk of the actual writing of narrative, characterization, and dialogue. Or so my father told me; when I revealed this after his death in an article in *TV Guide* (it was an official secret for many years), Dan would not confirm it to reporters. But by his own admission, my father could not plot to save his life, and in my opinion Dan's great gifts were as an editor, anthologist, scholar, and puzzle-crafter.

In Kabbalah, God creates with Word. Words were worlds to my father, and so were names. My father fled himself into names. He was the eldest of three children and the only boy. His mother, Rebecca Lepofsky *née* Wallerstein, had wanted to call him "Manford" when he was born in January of 1905 ("She must have gotten it from some damn romance novel," he told me); the Jewish doctor who attended Dad's birth did not think the name appropriate for a Jewish baby, so he put down Dad's name on the birth certificate as "Emanuel." Oddly, there is a family story, which may be apocryphal, that not even "Lepofsky" was the family's real name: that it had been changed (from something like "Ashov" or "Arshov") when my paternal great-grandfather had been en route from Russia to the United States. According to the tale, great-grandfather had been informed by a fellow-immigrant that he needed an American name to get into America, and either the boat-savant had suggested "Lepofsky" as a good old American name or great-grandfather had known of a family named "'Lepofsky" who had emigrated and kept their name. In any case, he gave "Lepofsky" as his last name when he hit U.S. customs.

If this is true, then my patrimony is thrice-shrouded. In the Twenties, just before young Emanuel Lepofsky graduated *summa cum laude* in English from New York University's Washington Square College branch (where Jews, the Irish, and other undesirable minority students were shunted), he told his beloved faculty advisor and mentor, Dr. Munn, that his big dream was to become a professor of English at the college level. Dr. Munn looked at him and said, "Manny, no Jew will ever get tenure in the New York University system." It was Munn's attempt to protect my father from humiliation, but for my father it was the expulsion from Eden. Dad went into advertising, a profession he despised, and not long afterwards he changed his name to the most Gentile name he could think of and still maintain his nickname: Manfred Bennington Lee. Dad was not the only one to flee into names: Dad's sisters, Helen and Rena, and now widowed father, Ben, adopted "Lee" as their last names, too; and Cousin Dan changed his name from Daniel Nathan to Frederic Dannay.

Though I cannot think of one explicitly Jewish character in the Queen canon, Dad and Dan never denied that they were Jews: it was one of the first things Dad told somebody when he met them for the first time. A staunch voting liberal, he stood up, as Dan did, against the racism and antisemitism of the Forties and the McCarthyism of the Fifties (read *The King Is Dead*). Yet as occasionally happened over the years, when Dad was personally confronted with an antisemitic remark, he would withdraw into a shell, leaving it to my mother to defend him. The year Dad and Mom lived in Hollywood, the kosher butcher down the street thought *she* was the Jew and Dad was the Gentile.

Ellery Queen became my father's third escape route from disappointment. I am quite certain that there were times he enjoyed his and Dan's success. They bought one another Dunhill pipes when *The Roman Hat Mystery* won its award; he agreed to the drama of wearing a full-face mask in early Queen public appearances, when as a PR ploy the true identities of the Queen authors were kept secret. He knew, and I think (by and large) enjoyed knowing, other famous writers: William Styron, Agatha Christie, Taylor Caldwell (with whom he corresponded for many years), Rex Stout; in a brief stint as Roxbury's Justice of the Peace at the start of the 1950's, he very nearly performed the ceremony in which Arthur Miller and Marilyn Monroe were wed. However, Dan was the more outgoing of the partners, and because as an active editor Dan always maintained close ties with New York, it is Dan who had the more enduring circle of literary acquaintances.

One story my mother told me typifies my father's ambivalence towards his fame. Once, when he and Mother were attending a dinner party in William Styron's home, Dad—seated in a corner, as was his wont—was trapped by a gushing fan. It was rather late in the evening, and as Mother watched from across the room, the woman began talking with particular force and animation. Curious, Mother looked more closely, and realized (to her chagrin and delight) that my father was fast asleep in his chair, oblivious to his fan's increasingly desperate plaudits.

Despite his later reluctance for the limelight, my father was, by all accounts, a superb public speaker. When family funds were low in the Sixties, Dad went on a lecture tour, and when he returned (after having groused for weeks about the inconvenience and the exhaustion of the experience) he related with relish how he and the college boys had shared bull sessions till the wee hours. "The worst audience I ever had was a convention of morticians," he told me once. "I did all my best material, and they just sat there, completely without expression. When I was done, they applauded enthusiastically, and many of them told me afterwards how much they had enjoyed my talk. It was unnerving."

But in time his will to continue Queen dried up. Mysteries were not the respectable mainstream fiction he had always dreamed of writing. I believe this because of the defensiveness with which he told me frequently that his great goal was to "elevate the mystery genre to the ranks of serious literature," and from the close, impassioned watch he kept over his children's English as we were growing up; I have had my suspicion confirmed by my sister Kit, who told me recently that, depressed, Dad had once explicitly referred to himself as a "literary prostitute." In the Sixties, he suffered from severe writer's block, during which, desperate, he essayed a humorous work about our family's legion of pets tentatively entitled *Welcome To Bugsville* (a remark by my baby brother Jeff had inspired the title). It was to be published under his own name, Manfred B. Lee, not Ellery Queen. He abandoned the manuscript after only a few pages and never returned to it.

It was not his first attempt to write under his own name. I have in my possession a school copybook containing a novelette entitled "Testing His Mettle, Or, How A Boy Proved His Worth." Woodrow Wilson was President and World War I was not yet over when my father wrote this manuscript. It is a Horatio Alger swipe, mannered and stilted, a world of wealthy Gentiles, from its opening prologue ("A gentleman to see you, sir") to its final chapter ("The Reconciliation"). Written in pen and ink in a careful longhand, it is signed "By Emanuel Lepofsky, Thirteen Years Old." The "Thirteen Years Old" is crossed out in pencil, and below it stands the emendation, "Twelve and One Half Years Old." At the back is a schoolboy's word list: hard words, nowadays. "Acquiesced" lacks the final "c". It is the only word misspelled.

The other manuscript is bound in a heavy metal notebook. It dates from the mid-Twenties, about the time Dad changed his name from Lepofsky to Lee. The inside cover bears the legend, "Please Return This Folder and Its Contents to: Manfred Bennington Lee, 1346 Bergen Street, Brooklyn, New York." It gives his telephone number, too: "Decatur 7499." The notebook is divided into sections of short stories, some of them not bad. The stories are the work of a raw young writer attempting sophistication, and it is perhaps not fair to quote from them; still, one passage stands out in my mind. It is from "Post-Amor," the first story in Section One, "A Man's Notes On Women." The note of worldliness amuses me, because my father told me he had had his first sexual experience only a few years before, with an older woman, when he was playing violin with his college band at a resort in the Catskills.

The story begins: "Too many bubbles have passed in the water flowing under the bridge. Too many bubbles, too much water. The bridge might have been an enormous structure of cobweb and rose-leaf in the first place. Perhaps it never had a material existence. Fantasy and desire were always indeterminable airy things. In any case the bridge of cobweb and rose-leaf has wavered and trembled, crumbled and blown away like any dream. And whether it was a real bridge or not, too much water and too many bubbles passed under it. Of that I am convinced."

My father spent his life attempting to reinvent himself, and in the end, his compromises failed him. But they did not fail us. As Manfred B. Lee, co-author of the Ellery Queen novels and short stories—not Emanuel Lepofsky, university English professor—my father gave pleasure to millions, and it is as Ellery Queen that he will be remembered. I wish he had known how much we all wanted to love him.

Three days after my father's death, I received what must have been one of the last letters he ever wrote. It is not much: it expresses concern over his sense that I was not enthusiastic about the college I was attending, and closes with his love for me. I keep it hidden away in my scrapbook. I had feared and adored him for so long, patterning my intellectual and artistic development after his, that his sudden absence left me centerless. I sought a center to replace him for many years. Along the way I became many things that would have baffled and embarrassed him had he lived to see them: a Fundamentalist Christian; then openly gay; then a spiritualist.

Still, I never stopped writing, never completely. Overshadowed though I have felt by my father, troubled though I have been by being neither Jew nor Christian yet somehow both, and as much as I have tried to build my life into something not his but distinctly mine, his Word is within me, joining us, as deeply as blood and bones. And I am grateful.

THE AUTHORSHIP OF
THREE LATE ELLERY QUEEN NOVELS

by Douglas and Richard Dannay

There is increasing confusion concerning the authorship of three of the Ellery Queen novels: *The Player on the Other Side, And on the Eighth Day* . . . , and *The Fourth Side of the Triangle*. Before misinformation becomes fact, we would like to clarify the matter.

The Player on the Other Side was *not* completely ghost-written by Theodore Sturgeon. Frederic Dannay prepared/created a 42-page outline of the book, and Mr. Sturgeon wrote the novel based on the outline. Manfred B. Lee then extensively revised the Sturgeon manuscript. There were also other revisions by Mr. Dannay.

And on the Eighth Day . . . was also written from an outline prepared/created by Frederic Dannay, an outline of 66 pages. Avram Davidson wrote the novel based on this outline and the novel was then extensively revised by Mr. Dannay and Mr. Lee.

The Fourth Side of the Triangle was again written from a Frederic Dannay outline, this time of 71 pages. Again it was Mr. Davidson who finished the novel and he based his work on the outline. The book was revised by Mr. Lee and Mr. Dannay.

In H. R. F. Keating's *The Bedside Companion to Crime* (The Mysterious Press, 1989), Mr. Keating cites an article sent to him by Geoff Bradley, editor of the British magazine *CADS: Crime and Detective Stories*, to the effect that *The Player on the Other Side* was entirely written by Mr. Sturgeon. This simply is not true. The concept of *The Player on the Other Side* is pure Queen—as are the concepts of *And on the Eighth Day* . . . and *The Fourth Side of the Triangle*. All three books were extensively revised by Mr. Lee and/or Mr. Dannay. Working, from a detailed outline was standard Queen procedure, and we don't think it would be unfair to consider them as Ellery Queen novels.

Published statements about authorship become part of the factual literature of mystery fiction and are likely to be cited by others who do research in the genre. We both fear that some of the misinformation about the authorship of these three books may already have become information. We are not so much trying to set the record straight as to publicize the facts and let people draw their own conclusions based on them. Some scholars may still feel that *The Player on the Other Side* should not be placed "squarely in the Queen canon." If that decision is based on the facts, then so be it. It won't be the first time people have looked squarely at the facts and come to different conclusions.

REMEMBERING MY HANAI FATHER

by Richard A. Smith, M.D.

Rarely does a child have the opportunity to pick his father. However, I did. And I picked one whose profession was murder.

It happened in the mid-forties shortly after I met Anya Lee's mother Kaye. The occasion was the annual mother-daughter dinner at Center Junior High School in Norwalk, Connecticut. I had arranged to be their student-waiter because I had a crush on Anya. Kaye sensed a special relationship brewing and invited me to their home a few days later. A fateful invitation.

Meeting Kay's husband Manny was a memorable event. There was warmth and gentleness in the bear hug with which he first greeted me the Saturday morning Anya introduced us. During that first encounter I was unexplainably attracted to this man who was to become the most important male in my life. I initially bristled as his half-inch beard scratched across my face in an embrace to which I was to become accustomed. He was genuinely pleased to meet his daughter's classmate about whom he and Kaye had obviously talked.

My father died when I was three months old. My mother, who worked as a house cleaner, remarried into an abusive relationship with an unpleasant alcoholic. Life became increasingly difficult for her, me and my older brother Julius. At 17 Julius joined the Navy, leaving me to contend with a contentious step-father. My mother was a wonderful, thoughtful and caring woman who, in her uncanny and loving parenting, sensed and encouraged my relationship with Manny Lee as it blossomed into a "father-son" relationship she knew I needed.

Happy enough to be with Anya and Kaye, it seemed I couldn't get enough of being in Manny's presence. Initially I spent many of my weekends at their home in Norwalk and then a few miles away in Westport where they moved the following year. Weekends began to stretch into weekdays. Soon I became a part-time member of the

Manfred Bennington Lee family. As I learned many years later in Hawai'i, I had found my *hanai* father. ("*Hanai* father" is a Hawaiian term used to describe a man who becomes an unofficial "adoptive father" to a child in need of a caring male presence or father figure at some stage of growing up.)

Over the next few years I spent considerable time living with the Lee family, celebrating with them new arrivals and the raising of seven more of their children. During this time my relationship with "Pop" deepened and formed a secure framework for enduring my teen years and beyond. My relationships with each of the other kids was, and continues to be today, one filled with the dynamics of a passionately loving and caring family.

I spent many evenings in his study, sleeping on the sofa behind him as he worked through the night. Although he occasionally wrote during the day, his occupation with murder was mostly at night.

Rackety-tac-tac-rickety-tac-thump was the repetitive rhythm and sound which ushered me to sleep many of those nights. Using only his two index fingers, he pecked fast and in long bursts on a bulky, old, manual typewriter. He would type continuously and furiously, non-stop for 10-15 minutes. Then he'd stop and stare out the large plate glass window in front of him. It was as if he saw the action in his stories on the screen of darkness before him. Then he would suddenly drop his eyes and attack the typewriter again, recording what his mind had just experienced.

He would occasionally stop and sit quietly between scenes, lighting up and puffing away on alternate pipes he kept in a pipestand on his desk. (He left me those pipes in his will.) Turning around he often scanned the library covering the room's walls as if inspiration came from between the covers of one of hundreds of books sitting quietly on the shelves.

There were prolonged periods of silence during which he enveloped himself in pipesmoke. He would emerge to again attack that writing machine with which he turned out the most magnificent of his genre.

I had no idea how famous Manny Lee was when I first visited Anya. In retrospect, it took me years to appreciate what the five or six "Edgars" kept over the living room fireplace signified in the business I later learned was personified earlier by Edgar Allan Poe. What I did know, however, was that when I walked into his life, the world changed for me.

It was no longer an amorphous ocean in which I felt I could easily get lost. I had no idea how important Manny was to the rest of the world. However, I sensed early on how important he was to me. I needed him and he knew it. I lucked out when I fell into his world as an adolescent.

Pop was constantly talking to me about my life as a Black American male—creating real life scenarios which he knew I would encounter. As a Jew he was well acquainted with the kind of discrimination I might (and did) encounter in the years to follow. He wanted me prepared to deal with the America rushing headstrong into the latter half of the twentieth century.

Perhaps it was the nature of his profession that he was always playing "what if" games with me. It was not until many years later that I realized I had been taught contingency planning by a master of alternative scenario development.

As a good father should, he insisted (sometimes overly so I thought at the time) that I examine—before, during and after—the consequences of decisions and actions before I took them. He wanted me to learn early to predict the good and bad realities my decisions could produce.

Manny Lee pushed me to dream . . . to think big pictures . . . about what my interests were and could be as I approached adulthood. Perhaps it was the openness of his inquiring mind which introduced me to the importance of "connections" in life.

Whether as fruitful or frivolous exercises of the intellect, purposeful or non-directed journeys of the imagination, he often pushed me to examine how people, events and phenomena in my life might be connected. I see now that obvious and not-so-obvious connections in our lives collectively describe who and what we are and the environment in which we live. I give much attention to connections in my life today because Manny Lee shared with me his thriving on making them in his personal and professional lives.

As in most families there were some rough spots in our relationship.

I angered him when I told him in 1951 I wanted to go on a summer workcamp for college students to work with Methodist missionaries in pre-Castro Cuba. He was opposed to religious prosetelyzing and figured that was the purpose of the workcamp. He wanted me to broadly determine my spiritual and vocational directions. His opposition centered on not having my life narrowly defined by one specific religion. However, I received a church scholarship to underwrite the experience. That tipped the balance and I went. As it turned out, it was one of the most important decisions of my life.

The experience, working alongside a nurse among the poorest of the world's poor in Cuba's Oriente Province, was an epiphany for me. It was there I received my calling into medicine. Not merely as a doctor, but as a trainer of health care providers somewhere between a nurse and a doctor. To make a difference in the world, I wanted to multiply my hands a thousandfold for delivering essential services to populations most distant physically and economically from basic health care services.

Pop was elated and amazingly apologetic when I returned from the experience firmly determined to become a physician to the disadvantaged of the world. I remember him listening attentively to the story of one of his kids and a wondrous summer working among people in desperate need. On numerous occasions he had lamented a human condition that needed the attention of us all. I had brought that attention home.

On another occasion, when I wrote my first short story, I sent it to him for a critique. In a letter fully half as long as my story, he was brutal. I remember thinking he was actually cruel. However, what he was was principled. He criticized me mercilessly, reminding me that he was an experienced editor and that I had asked him for his honest thoughts. He responded as a professional, not as a father. He pointedly pointed me away from journalism.

When I sold a television series to CBS in 1968 he was my loudest cheerleader.

As the co-creator of Ellery Queen, Pop made an indelible mark in the world of literature. In the personal lives of numerous individuals—mine being one of them—he was an especially powerful force. He prepared me well as he defined the *hanai* father. There is need for more like him.

Thanks Pop . . .

AT WORK AND PLAY WITH FRED DANNAY

by Francis M. Nevins

On the night of Friday, September 3, 1982, six and a half weeks short of his seventy-seventh birthday, the life of Frederic Dannay ended. Even so many years later, each time I realize he's gone I feel an emptiness.

For the millions of readers who loved the adventures of Ellery Queen which he wrote in collaboration with his cousin Manfred B. Lee, Fred's death meant the end of a noble tradition in mystery fiction: the tradition of the detective as towering intellect, the tradition whose last surviving giants were Rex Stout and Fred himself. I was one of those readers. I discovered Ellery Queen in my early teens, the formative years where the heroes a person adopts can last a lifetime. I can still see myself sitting in a creaky old rocking chair in front of my grandmother's house during the heat of the 1957 summer, lost in ecstasy as I wandered with Ellery through the labyrinths of *The Greek Coffin Mystery*. Through my high school and college years I found and devoured in haphazard order all the other Queen classics: *The Egyptian Cross Mystery, The Tragedy of X, The Tragedy of Y, Calamity Town* and the unforgettable *Cat of Many Tails*. Fred wrote no fiction after Manny Lee's death in 1971, but while he lived there was always the hope that he would. When Fred died, Ellery Queen died irrevocably with him.

For the writers who appeared regularly in *Ellery Queen's Mystery Magazine*, which Fred founded in the fall of 1941 and actively edited for almost forty years, his death meant the end of the most exciting and fruitful of professional relationships. He wasn't easy on his contributors. He made them work and rework stories until every detail had taken its place in a harmonious mosaic, and thereby taught them more about the storyteller's art than any course or textbook could possibly teach. I was one of those writers. Our first meeting was in 1969, soon after I'd begun work on my book *Royal Bloodline: Ellery Queen, Author and Detective* (1974). I can still see myself stepping off the New Haven Railroad commuter train at Larchmont station and shaking hands for the first time with Fred and his wife Hilda and riding in their car to the Dannay home on Byron Lane. Fred was not just co-operative but flattered that somebody was actually writing a book about Queen, and over the next few years he helped me in countless ways. It was only after we'd come to know each other well that he began to hint that perhaps I'd enjoy writing a mystery myself. I slaved over a story for two months and finally mailed it to him. Its inspiration was a line from one of my favorite Queen novels, *Ten Days' Wonder* (1948), and I was sure that he'd like it.

A few weeks later he invited me to Larchmont again. We had dinner at a lovely old seafood restaurant and returned to Byron Lane and sipped brandy in his living room as he ripped that story of mine apart with a surgical precision that I now realize was more than justified by the sheer unadulterated silliness of what I had written. Then we began to build the story up again. He taught me what I should have done not by telling me in so many words but indirectly, by emphasizing the wrong steps I'd taken and leaving it to me to make them right. I spent the next couple of months rethinking and rewriting that story from first word to last. Finally in fear and trembling I mailed him the revised version. And this time he sent me a contract. "Open Letter to Survivors" was published in *EQMM* for May 1972. During the month that issue was on the nation's newsstands, every time I entered a store and saw my name on that blue-and-white cover along with the names of all the other contributors it was all I could do to restrain myself from shouting "HEY!! THAT'S ME!" to everyone within earshot.

Over the next ten years Fred bought many more stories from me: some about law professor Loren Mensing who went on to appear in three of my novels (*Publish and Perish* [1975], which was dedicated to Fred, *Corrupt and Ensnare* [1978]. and *Into the Same River Twice* [1996]); some about Milo Turner, the confidence man with an identity for every occasion, perpetually fated to solve one crime in the process of committing another, and featured after Fred's death in my novels *The 120-Hour Clock* (1986) and *The Ninety Million Dollar Mouse* (1987); some with no series character at all. Even though *EQMM* still survives today, the special thrill of working with Fred and being buoyed by his praise and instructed by his line-for-line criticism is something I shall never know again.

When Fred wanted something changed in a manuscript, the reason most of the time was that he sensed how readers would react and saw that a change was needed to forestall that reaction. I learned a vast lesson in the workings of his editorial mind from an incident in the second story I sold him and the first tale about Loren Mensing, "After the Twelfth Chapter" (*EQMM*, September 1972). In the last paragraph of the story as I wrote it, Mensing warns a black militant who has been involved in the case that the police will be keeping him under close surveillance for a while. "The black man said nothing, as though it were raining and Mensing had told him it was raining. Then he nodded, without changing expression, and walked away. Mensing felt unclean and directionless and afraid, like a man trying to fight a forest fire he knows is out of control." When the story was published I discovered that Fred had deleted the word "unclean" from the last quoted sentence. I wondered why, and after a moment's thought I saw it: the word conveyed the subtle suggestion to the reader that the black character was not on the friendliest terms with soap and water. Fred had seen this instinctively, known it wasn't what I'd intended, and cut. When I asked him later if that was indeed the reason he'd dropped the word, he replied that he'd already forgotten but it might have been something like that.

Early the following year I sent him a story in which I used the basic device of Conan Doyle's classic "The Six Napoleons" in an up-to-the-minute Loren Mensing adventure with an airplane hijacking, Arab terrorism, a conveyor belt in a dog food factory, and a band of former Green Berets turned armed robbers. My title for that story was "Six Thousand Little Corsicans." Fred thought readers wouldn't remember that the island of Corsica had been Napoleon's birthplace and so would miss the allusion to Conan Doyle—which is why the story's published title was "Six Thousand Little Bonapartes" (*EQMM*, December 1973).

I suspect that every contributor to the magazine could tell similar anecdotes about benefitting from Fred's editorial expertise. He himself once told me about an author whose most recent story was set in Victorian London and required the *fin-de-siecle* touch of a Robert Louis Stevenson but somehow failed to convey the period mood. Fred simply took down his copy of *Dr. Jekyll and Mr. Hyde* and, every time the manuscript described some action or object that was also in Stevenson's story, he replaced the author's description with the precise words Stevenson had used, thereby improving the tale immensely and getting the proper flavor by the most direct, economical and accurate means. For anyone wondering whether this was a violation of copyright law, it wasn't:

Stevenson has long been in the public domain.

Fred did all his work at home. He never went to New York on business and never met most of the people who worked on the magazine. Every afternoon the associate editor in Manhattan would make up a package containing the day's submissions (except those that were hopeless), attach comments to each story, and mail the parcel to Byron Lane. Fred would read each story but would not read the comments until he'd formulated his own opinion. When a story needed changes, he would discuss them with the author over the phone or in letters, usually handwritten. I have dozens of those letters, as does everyone who ever sold a few stories to *EQMM*, but Fred's correspondence with me went way beyond the professional. Reflections about himself, remembrances of times past, health problems, gentle hints that my latest submission to him was too long, thoughts on writers and writing and editors and critics and the current scene—a cornucopia of insight into his life and times that I will always treasure.

In one letter, dated December 6, 1971, Fred mentioned that he and Hilda were "planning to take a trip—probably a cruise to the Caribbean. We are waiting for a confirmation of a Feb 5 sailing on the Michelangelo." Hilda became seriously ill on that cruise and died of cancer soon afterwards. For the next several years I watched Fred dying by inches. Photographs of him taken in 1973 show the empty, devastated face of a man waiting for the dark to claim him.

Then good luck came his way when he found (to cite the title of one of the final Queen novels) the last woman in his life. In 1975 Fred met and married the former Rose Koppel, whose love and care saved him and gave him the reason at age 70 to be glad once again that he was alive.

For the next few years after his third marriage Fred and I served together on the board of Mystery Library, a publishing project of the University of California. Each year, very late in August or early in September, we and the other board members would be flown out to San Diego for our annual meeting. Fred was diabetic, and one of my jobs after we breakfasted each morning at the University cafeteria was to take his Prohibition-style flask and go back through the serving line and fill it with the orange juice he needed to sip during the day to maintain his blood sugar level. I often wondered (and so did he) how many UCSD students and faculty saw that flask and, like Sergeant Velie in an EQ novel, drew the obvious but wrong conclusion. In the evenings after business and dinner were over, Fred would often hold court. We would gather around him, some of us literally sitting at his feet, and he would reminisce about his near half-century in the genre. As he talked one could almost see them coming back to life: people like Conan Doyle who was still walking the earth when Ellery Queen first appeared, and Dashiell Hammett who had been one of Fred's closest friends in the time between his return from World War II and Fred's second marriage, and so many others.

We talked on the phone every few weeks and he would always invite me to spend an evening with him in Larchmont whenever I was on the east coast. Usually I would stay for three or four hours but by my subjective clock each visit lasted just a few seconds. Our conversations ranged over the length and breadth of the genre we both loved. It was in his living room that he shared with me some of the hidden history of the Forties and Fifties. He told of how he had planned a series of Hammett story collections during World War II but was stymied by the veto of Lillian Hellman, who hated those early stories and had Hammett's power of attorney while he was serving in the Aleutians. (The collections were okayed, Fred said, only after publisher Lawrence Spivak met privately with Hellman and put some pressure on her which neither of them later discussed.) He described the poisonous atmosphere of the early Fifties, the days of Joe McCarthy and HUAC and the witch hunts, when Hammett was facing a jail sentence for refusing to reveal the contributors to a left-wing bail fund, and one of the women in Hammett's life threatened to report Fred as a Communist sympathizer unless he made a large contribution, supposedly to the Hammett legal defense fund. (Fred told her to go to hell and nothing happened.) He told me of John Dickson Carr's battle with cancer and asked if I had any suggestions against the day when Carr's monthly review column for *EQMM* would have to be given to someone else. (I suggested Jon Breen, who did in fact take over from Carr and is still the magazine's reviewer today.) Agatha Christie, Rex Stout, Anthony Boucher, the outrageous Michael Avallone, even literary giants like Hemingway and Faulkner who occasionally had dealings with Fred, they all came alive for me in his living room during those wondrous evenings. If only I were blessed with a photographic memory, what a book I could write just from our conversations! I do remember vividly the time, perhaps a year or two after I had received an Edgar award for *Royal Bloodline*, when I stepped into the Dannay living room and saw a copy of the book prominently displayed on an end table. "How thoughtful!" I said. "Whenever you invite a writer for a visit you put out something they wrote." Fred shook his head. "No, Mike," he said. "You don't understand. That book is *always* there." There was no mirror in the room but I would bet money I blushed.

I made a special trip to New York when Fred was guest of honor at a Lotos Club banquet celebrating the fiftieth anniversary of the publication of *The Roman Hat Mystery*, and another excursion to Waukesha, Wisconsin when Carroll College awarded Fred an honorary doctorate— one of the proudest moments of his life. The last time I saw him was in New York in the spring of 1982, the night of the annual MWA Dinner. He wasn't feeling well and had arranged for a limousine to take himself and Rose back to Larchmont right after the banquet. We shook hands and said goodbye on Sixth Avenue in front of the Sheraton Central, neither of us knowing how little time he had left. On the first Friday of that September he died.

For those who were privileged to know Fred on a personal basis, his death meant the end of an infinitely precious friendship. We had many divergent interests and opinions but our feeling for mystery fiction brought us together and gave birth to our feeling for each other. We shared tragedies and triumphs, happy moments and sad. But for me the best times were when we would get together and talk for hours on end about the writers who had come before Fred and those who were his contemporaries and those who were coming after him and, as I grew older, those who were coming after me. I never felt so much a part of a living tradition as I did on those occasions. Since Fred's death that vital link has snapped and the excitement of his presence lives only in memories.

He was the closest to a grandfather I've known. Without him I would never have written a word of fiction worth reading. Every writer and reader and lover of mystery fiction owes him debts none of us can pay. What he gave us—as writer, editor and friend—will live as long as any of us live who remember.

FRED DANNAY AND MANNY LEE

by Hillary Waugh

Fred Dannay, one-half of the writing team of "Ellery Queen," I knew well because we were both involved in the activities of Mystery Writers of America (known as MWA). His cousin, Manfred B. Lee, the other half of the Queen team, however, I only met once.

The occasion was the idea I had that MWA should tape interviews with our illustrious members while they were still with us, and record them for posterity. And, certainly, no mystery writer was more famous than "Ellery Queen."

Thus it was arranged that I would interview Fred and Manny for the archives with Chris Steinbrunner, another dedicated MWAer, doing the taping.

The pseudonym "Ellery Queen" came into being when Manny and Fred decided to enter a mystery writing contest in the late nineteen twenties, "We were so naive," Fred said, "we had no idea that the word 'queen' had homosexual implications." Thus they wrote their first mystery novel, entitled *The Roman Hat Mystery*. The contest was ultimately aborted, but their novel, nevertheless, won the prize and it was published in 1929.

Though Fred and Manny thought they were writing only a single novel, detective Ellery Queen proved so popular that more stories were demanded and they found themselves with a career as mystery writers. In fact, the Ellery Queen stories were so good that mystery critic Anthony Boucher once said, "Ellery Queen *is* the American mystery story." The writing and plotting were so clever that the question arose, "Who wrote the Ellery Queen Stories? Who *is* Ellery Queen?" Speculation included a number of prominent and esteemed authors.

Fred and Manny were more than willing to feed the mystery and, on the lecture circuit, one of them would wear a mask and pose as the mysterious author.

The taping lasted an hour but the three of us were having such a good time we talked for another hour while Chris shut down the taping. I only wish we'd taped that second hour for that was the most fun.

Fred and Manny reported that, when they came to Hollywood, William Powell and Myrna Loy had one film left to go on their contracts. A screen-writing couple had one script to do before they retired to Italy. The studio decided to wrap it all up in one film, and gave them Dashiell Hammett's book *The Thin Man* which had been collecting dust on their shelves.

The movie was shot on a back lot and since nobody bothered to look at the rushes, the writing couple decided to do a script the way they wanted to instead of the way they were supposed to.

As a result, the studio heads didn't see the picture until it was completed. They were horrified at what had been done, but it was too late to make changes. Audiences, on the other hand, loved it and it became a smash hit. As a result, Powell and Loy were signed to long-term contracts and ultimately made 17 pictures together, including several *Thin Man* sequels, and the method of making mystery movies was upgraded.

I can't close without mentioning Rose Dannay, the wife Fred married late in life. She was a delight and got Fred up and around and doing things. I once said something to Fred about being the most esteemed mystery writer and he said, "I'd rather be the oldest mystery writer." To that goal Rose certainly contributed.

They both attended the Third International Congress of Crime Writers in Stockholm in June 1980 when he must have been around eighty himself, and they even took a trip up to the Arctic Circle where, in June, the sun never sets.

That was the last time I saw him. It's twenty years ago now, but it doesn't seem that long.

He and Manny are both long gone now, but my memory of them is fresh and, fortunately, we do have them on tape in our archives.

TRIBUTE TO FRED DANNAY

by James Yaffe

In 1943, when I met Fred Dannay, he was half of the most successful collaboration in literary history and the best known detective story writer in the world (though Agatha Christie fans might argue this point). He was thirty-eight years old, and I was sixteen, and the relationship between us could hardly have been more improbable. He was an editor and a grown man, I was a writer and a teen-age kid, and he was about to publish my first short story.

Fred was the half of "Ellery Queen" who edited *Ellery Queen's Mystery Magazine*, a comparatively new publication in those days. I was told that the other half of the team—Manfred B. Lee, Fred's cousin and collaborator—had no interest in editing. He lived way out in the country—the real country, not the Westchester commuting suburb in which Fred lived—and he had many children and little time for any professional activity beyond his share of writing the more or less annual Ellery Queen novel. I met him only a few times, and he was always cordial and polite, but clearly the public world of the Detective Story and of other detective story writers had little appeal to him; his commitment seemed to be to his private life and to the fictional world that he and Fred had created together.

Fred had a private life too. He was married three times—his first and second wives both died—and he had three sons, one severely brain-damaged, the tragedy of his life, I often thought. He spent a lot of time with his family. In addition, since boyhood he had suffered from diabetes, a disease that requires constant attention. It is easy to imagine how much care, effort, and anxiety this caused him every day of his life.

But he also had twice as much energy as almost any other human being I have ever met, and along with his work on the novels, he found time to turn out every month a mini-anthology of the best new detective short fiction being written in America, to attend meetings and serve on the boards of God knows how many professional organizations, to write articles, prefaces, and reviews on the state of the detective story, to collect first editions, and to read, I would guess, every new example of his chosen genre that was published every year.

And to talk about detective stories too. He could do this for hours on end. He never pontificated, never laid down the law, though his experience and achievement certainly entitled him to; but he argued— oh, did he argue!—passionately about his likes and dislikes, with his eyes shining, his arms waving, and his vocabulary growing riper and riper. On his favorite subject—his vocation, his hobby, his calling—I never heard him express an opinion that wasn't backed up by feeling, and his feelings were never lukewarm.

I was fifteen years old, beginning my junior year of high school, when I sent a story to *EQMM*. I had been reading detective stories almost as long as I could remember, including everything ever published by Ellery Queen, and somewhere in the back of my mind was the vague fantasy of some day Being a Writer. I had written bits and pieces, off and on, for several years, but nothing that I ever had the nerve to submit for publication—until now. When Fred read my manuscript—I think that, unlike many editors, he actually must have read, or at least glanced at, every manuscript that came to the magazine's office—he spotted it immediately, of course, as the work of a child. A despicably precocious one. He bought the story, sending me the first money I ever earned as a writer, a check for one hundred dollars. My father gave me the hundred out of his wallet, had the check laminated and framed, and kept it on the wall of his office for many years afterwards; I have no idea what finally became of it.

A few months later, when the story was about to appear—by this time I was sixteen—Fred summoned me to the *EQMM* headquarters where he and I were to give a joint interview to a feature writer from the *New York World-Telegram*. Where *EQMM* was concerned, Fred always had a good instinct for public relations.

My first impression of him was almost completely obscured and distorted by the emotional turmoil that boiled within me—part nervousness, part bewilderment, and a good part, I'm afraid, adolescent arrogance: wait till my friends at school heard about this! Still, that confused first impression remains in my memory. I remember a short man, with a little mustache and not much hair on top of his head, shaking my hand vigorously, with no flabbiness or halfheartedness, unlike the way grown-ups mostly shook hands.

The story appeared, and a few others after it. I got out of high school, went to college, served in the Navy for a year and a half at the end of the war, went back to college, set out to earn what living I could as a writer, and somehow, as time passed, and without my fully realizing it, my relationship with Fred stopped being a professional one and turned into a friendship.

It has taken me many years to understand the nature of that friendship. While it was going on, I never valued it as much as I should have. Fred and his first wife, and later his second wife, had me for dinner four or five times a year. They were long evenings during which we talked and talked, yet he gently refrained from asking me any questions about my personal life. (A big change from my weekly dinners with my parents.) We talked about current events, politics, new books and plays and movies, what was happening in the world of publishing. Many things outraged Fred, and he was an enthusiastic and accomplished griper. I started writing for television, which interested Fred very much; he was involved in several different TV versions of Ellery Queen, and was full of fascinating horror stories, gripes of a high order, about his dealings with television executives.

I poured out my own gripes on him too, mostly about the ups and downs of my writing career. He gave me advice, all of it sound and sensible, never overbearing, never showing any impatience with my self-opinionated naivete. But never pulling his punches either; in his gentle way he often told me things I didn't want to hear, things I wish I had listened to more carefully.

I never thought of myself as learning from him. I never thought of him as a teacher or a mentor, and very likely he never thought of himself that way either. But a friendship between two people who are twenty-two years apart in age has to have something of the teacher/mentor element in it. And that's exactly what Fred was to me. Through his enthusiasm, his energy, and his passion, through a certain consistency in his attitudes and his values regardless of what subject he was talking about, he taught me the most important lesson that a young writer can learn. I will sum it up now, though I can't possibly do it as effectively as Fred did, by virtue of not really trying to do it at all.

The lesson was that good work matters, and shoddy work is a disgrace. By good work, he meant the best that you could do along the lines that suited you. By shoddy work he meant cutting corners, falling into lazy habits and fuzzy thinking, letting yourself be satisfied with less than the best you could do.

Fred was a detective story writer, and a certain kind of detective story writer, an advocate of the traditional "puzzle" story, in which the writer plays a game of wits with the reader, in which we experience the most exquisite pleasure when the writer baffles us, leads us by the nose, stretches our curiosity to the snapping point, and ultimately dazzles us with the ingenuity of the final surprise. A great detective story writer is like a great baseball pitcher dueling with a great batter, like a great ballet dancer hurling his body into a leap that defies gravity, yet with the utmost grace. But to bring off these heart-stopping effects requires self-discipline, logic, absolute fairness in adhering to the rules of the game. In other words, that perfect mixture of imagination and hard work which is what all artists mean by "craftsmanship."

The first time I ever heard Fred raise his voice and saw him wave his arms furiously was just after he had finished reading a new book by a detective story writer almost as prominent as Ellery Queen. Nobody was more generous about his rivals than Fred—he published them all in *EQMM*, with prefaces that were full of the joy he got from their work— but he had to light into this particular author's new book because it deeply offended his sense of craftsmanship. In it the author had committed dozens of serious detectival sins—mysterious events were planted early on that the author never bothered to explain; characters behaved in ways that made no sense psychologically; worst of all at the end the detective announced his solution to the crime by saying, in effect, "I felt in my bones that the murderer had to be So-and-so"; no relevant clues were brought out, no structure of logic was erected, to support the solution for those who didn't happen to share the detective's bones with him. Fred ended by throwing up his hands with a deep despairing groan: "How could he let such shoddy work be published? Doesn't he have any self-respect? For God's sake, doesn't he take any *pride* in his craft?"

I listened to this tirade with a kind of awe. Fred was, after all, the first dedicated professional writer I had ever met. I couldn't imagine, in those days, how anyone could get so excited over a few feeble clues and some stale plot twists in a mere detective story. After all, nobody expected any of these writers to be Shakespeare or Joyce. But in the following years I heard many similar outbursts from Fred, and more than once they were directed at me, for something I had had the poor judgment and bad faith to submit to *EQMM*. Slowly the lesson was hammered into my mind. The quality of a writer's work—of anybody's work, in any field—has nothing to do with pretentiousness or profundity. It is better to produce a good detective story than a shoddy epic.

A long time has passed. I can hardly claim that I have never done shoddy work since those days, or that I have never been able to deceive myself about its shoddiness. But sooner or later the self-deception catches up with me, and I can hear Fred Dannay's voice exploding in my head:

"For God's sake, don't you take any *pride* in your craft?"

This has been his most precious—and sometimes most uncomfortable—legacy.

FREDERIC DANNAY, BSI

by Bill Vande Water

The Baker Street Irregulars, those ardent students of the life and work of Sherlock Holmes, observe many traditions at their meetings: they toast *The* Woman, read Elmer Davis's Buy Laws, sing the risqué ballad of "Aunt Clara." Among the oldest traditions, begun by Frederic Dannay in 1943, is a complimentary copy of the current issue of *Ellery Queen's Mystery Magazine* for each member and guest.

Dannay had very much enjoyed his first dinner the year before. In gratitude he planned a surprise issue of *EQMM*. He bought a puzzle Christopher Morley had created for a Sherlockian nephew, commissioned a Sherlockian cover design, and arranged to have advance copies of the magazine ready for the dinner.

When Morley questioned whether the general reader would be interested in the puzzle, Dannay replied: "Any new light thrown on the Sacred Writings . . . is of vital interest to all Devotees of Doyle and Sycophants of Sherlock. If you are still fearful, good Chris, you may henceforth consider the Editor and all readers of this magazine new members of your family-circle—'nephews,' equally afflicted with that incurable malady, 'sherlockophily.' "

Dannay had contracted that "incurable malady" at the age of twelve. He was ill with an ear infection when an aunt brought him the library book that would change his life: *The Adventures of Sherlock Holmes*:

> I opened the book with no realization that I stood—rather, I sat —on the brink of my fate. I had no inkling, no premonition, that in another minute my life's work, such as it is, would be born . . . A strange rushing thrill challenged the pain in my ear. *The Red Headed League*! What a combination of simple words to skewer themselves into the brain of a hungry boy! I glanced down quickly—*The Man with the Twisted Lip*—*The Adventure of the Speckled Band*—and I was lost! Ecstatically, everlastingly lost!

... and all the Queen's horses and all the Queen's men couldn't put Ellery together again ... my doom had been signed, sealed, and delivered in the *Adventures*.

He finished the book convinced he "had read one of the greatest books ever written." In the same essay he adds that in "the mature smugness of my present literary judgement, I still consider *The Adventures of Sherlock Holmes* one of the world's masterworks."

Dannay has become so well known as a scholar and collector that it is easy to assume he viewed the Holmes stories solely in those terms. It is true that one of his primary interests was the stories themselves, their place and influence in the history of the genre. But as readers of Queen soon learn, the first solution may not be the only one. Dannay was also an avid Sherlockian and, at times, very much the Irregular. Scholar and Sherlockian combined to produce Queen's classic 1944 anthology of pastiche and parody: *The Misadventures of Sherlock Holmes*. (The Irregular stepped in to preface his own piece in the book—a radio play on the unsolved case of James Phillimore—with a letter to Holmes himself, apologizing for bringing up one of his failures.)

To celebrate the simultaneous publication of the *Misadventures*, Edgar Smith's *Profile by Gaslight*, and Christopher Morley's *Holmes and Watson: A Textbook of Friendship,* a special "trilogy" BSI dinner was held in April 1944. A *Life* magazine photograph taken at the dinner shows Dannay about to inject himself with an enormous hypodermic. He was soon to need a seven percent solution of something; not everyone was as pleased with the book as Dannay was.

If calling the stories "Sacred Writings," was an in-joke to Irregulars, it was literal truth to Adrian and Denis Conan Doyle. Sir Arthur's sons considered parodies sacrilege, and objected to pastiches as diluting the estate's (meaning their own) income. A complex legal situation enabled them to force the withdrawal of the book in 1945.

The 1946 BSI Dinner started a classic Sherlockian year for Dannay. Manfred B. Lee attended the dinner with him, for the first and only time. The first issue of the *Baker Street Journal* appeared, with Ellery Queen listed among the associate editors. (The second issue would reprint the story of his first meeting with Holmes, and the fourth a letter on Sherlockian elements in *The Tragedy of Y*.) Finally, the first of the *Queen's Awards* anthologies was published, including Irregular Bliss Austin's story in which contest judges Haycraft and Morley use Holmes's methods to solve the murder of their fellow judge, Ellery Queen.

In 1950 the Irregulars proudly proclaimed Dannay a full member. Presenting him with the Investiture of "The Dying Detective" (a play on his frequent use of the 'dying clue'), Morley quoted Dr. Mortimer's comment to Holmes in *The Hound of the Baskervilles*: "It is not my intention to be fulsome, but I confess that I covet your skull."

Dannay was equally proud to belong. Listing his Sherlockian first editions, he included two copies of *The Dying Detective*, then added to the catalog his certificate of investiture and the attached Irregular Shilling "representing the Conanical proof of Ellery Queen's membership in The Baker Street Irregulars." Photographs taken at the '50 dinner show him, a twinkle in his eye, playing Col. Moran to Morley's Moriarty, as Sherlock Holmes (Clayton Rawson) escapes from the ropes in which they have bound him.

Dannay's editorial decisions also reveal the many sides of his Sherlockian character. (It is an altogether fitting tribute that the cover of Irregular John Nieminski's *EQMM* index shows a deerstalkered Holmes reading the first issue of the magazine.) The scholar printed Michael Harrison's analysis of Doyle's sources for the names of Holmes, Watson and Baker Street. The Sherlockian "nephew" published an essay by Tom Stix, Sr. pointing out seven mistakes in "The Red Headed League." But it was Dannay the Irregular who couldn't resist pointing out an eighth mistake. Over the years he wrote introductions to nearly 100 Sherlockian parodies, essays, poems and pastiches published in the magazine.

References to Holmes turn up in the introductions to other stories as well. In the midst of urging readers to search the used bookstores for the short stories of Karl Detzer, he relates his own discovery of the rare first American edition of the *Memoirs of Sherlock Holmes* which, unlike the British edition, contained "The Cardboard Box."

Dannay always remained alert for Sherlockiana, old and new. He reprinted, with appropriate commentary, Rex Stout's scandalous proof that "Watson Was a Woman." He raided the *Baker Street Journal* for physicist Banesh Hoffman's pastiche, which has Holmes using Irregular scholarship to prove Shakespeare had knowledge of the hydrogen bomb, and printed former agent Thomas McDade's comparison of Holmes's methods with those of the FBI.

When, in 1974, Irregular historian Jon Lellenberg found an unknown parody by A. A. Milne, Dannay immediately bought it for *EQMM*. In introducing it he not only gives him finder's credit, but goes on to plug Lellenberg's collection of parodies by John Kendrick Bangs.

A complete list of Dannay's Sherlockian writings would fill a small book, and even then the irregular possibilities in Dannay's career would not be exhausted. In *A Study in Terror* (how grateful the Sherlockian world was to learn that Queen had written only the Queen portion and *not* the pastiche part of that book!), Grant Ames claims Sherlockian expertise and is immediately put to the question. In true Irregular fashion Ellery fires quotation after Canonical quotation at him, all of which he correctly identifies. But the final quote, which Ames also identifies, is not from Doyle, but one of Queen's own books.

This byplay hints at an area of the Queen/Holmes connection not yet adequately explored. What, for example, was the name of Ellery's Aunt? Clara? Or perhaps even Irene? And exactly why, in Francis M. Nevins' *Royal Bloodline*, does the true story of the *Misadventures* come exactly in the middle of page 221? These and other questions beg for the sort of irregular investigation Dannay always enjoyed.

THE IMPOSSIBLE MR. QUEEN

by Robert Adey

There is no dispute that Ellery Queen was one of the finest practitioners of the well written, well plotted, rationally resolved fair play detective novel. These points of excellence, elegantly combined, were his trademark for over forty years, and, if asked to say whether Queen had a fondness for one particular plot gimmick, I would unhesitatingly have nominated the dying message clue, a constituent, sometimes minor, often major, that he employed with skill and ingenuity time and time again, never better than in his late novel, *Face To Face*.

However there is another plot device, generally regarded as the preserve of his friends and contemporaries, John Dickson Carr and Clayton Rawson, which Queen by no means neglected, the impossible crime. Over a period spanning almost thirty years the inventive cousins produced a steady, if not exactly prolific, stream of miracle problems. In their earlier writings they appeared only at novel or novelette length, but later when their novels began to reflect the post war shift from golden age predominance of formula and plot to greater emphasis on characterisation and psychology, such deft mechanics were reserved for short stories.

We must look first at their sixth novel, *The American Gun Mystery* (1933), the first to feature impossible crime. The setting is the Colosseum, a gigantic sports arena which is to stage Wild Bill Grant's rodeo, "the largest aggregation of cowboys and cowgirls in the world." Ellery, his old man, and Djuna, their young major domo, attend the opening night and are stunned when, during the first event, a rip roaring ride round the arena by 40+ horsemen, the lead rider, star and former cinema idol Buck Horne, falls dead, shot through (with almost unbelievable accuracy) by a .25 bullet.

The Queens take charge, bring in a full squad of detectives and, in a quest for the murder weapon, search the arena, all surrounding areas and buildings, each and every one of the performers and the backroom staff and more than 2000 members of the audience. But to no avail—which in a nutshell is the impossible problem. Just how could the gun have been spirited away or so well hidden that it could not be found in what had in effect become a sealed area?

Later, just to emphasise the point, and after numerous other subplots have been played out, a second murder occurs in precisely the same circumstances as the first. Once again an exhaustive search proves fruitless. Ellery doggedly continues to piece it all together and in the finale reveals the true identity of the murderer, the name under which he has been masquerading and the whereabouts and hiding place of the missing pistol.

As an impossible crime conundrum this has the advantage of neatness both in the posing of the problem and its solution, even though this aspect of the plot might just as easily have fitted into a piece of short story length. It is only one of a number of linked plot elements which include blackmail, missing money and a slew of complex human relationships, all of which go to make up a very diverting detective novel.

Ellery himself is, at this early stage of his career, still very much a pince nez polisher and exotic phrase dropper, much given to musing and mulling and clearly the literary descendant of Van Dine's still flourishing Philo Vance.

The following year (1934) saw the publication of *The Chinese Orange Mystery* set in the Hotel Chancellor (the venue also for the later short, "The Adventure of the Dead Cat") at which a tubby little man, muffled up to the eye-brows, arrives on the 22nd floor and is directed to the private office of Donald Kirk, publisher and postage stamp and precious stone expert. He is asked to wait for Kirk in the adjoining room but when Kirk and his companion, Ellery Queen, arrive later its communicating door is found to be bolted from the other side. When access is gained via a second door, the unfortunate visitor is discovered to have been bludgeoned to death.

But rather more puzzling, every single item in the murder room, including the dead man's clothing, has been turned back to front— topsy turvy as the chapter heading has it. The only other occupant of the office, Kirk's assistant, swears that he did not leave his position throughout, yet heard nothing untoward that might throw light on this bizarre situation. Mysteries pile on. No one knows who the victim is nor the reason for his visit, and even when the mighty machinery of the New York Police Department grinds into action, his identity remains an impenetrable mystery. Again who is the enigmatic Irene Llewes and why do a set of books belonging to the irascible old man Kirk suddenly disappear? Blackmail is in the air but who is the victim and who the perpetrator?

Ellery of course explains all and the solution to the topsy turvy puzzle, enthralling in its pursuit, is both delightful and logical even if a trifle far-fetched. As for the solution of the locked room (which wasn't really locked) that stands as a somewhat flawed monument to complexity. Flawed because, try as one might, it is virtually impossible to follow the minutely detailed explanation of the technique employed as furnished by Queen, a technique equally impossible to believe that the murderer could have dreamt up and executed at such short notice.

So if not strictly an excellent locked room novel (though it was the one that got this particular reader hooked on Queen) it is nonetheless an excellent detective novel which also features a locked room style murder.

Ellery? Well, he rather drawls and sprawls his way through this relatively early opus, still very much the dilettante gentleman detective, even at one precious moment exclaiming " 'Nothing, my aunt's foot' as dear Reggie [Fortune] would say."

Just a year later came "The Lamp of God" (or "House of Haunts" as it first appeared in the *Detective Story Magazine* for November 1935), with its rather spooky remote Long Island backdrop. The action centres on the dilapidated "White House," next to "Black House" in which supposedly wealthy recluse, Sylvester Mayhew, has recently died, after reputedly hiding a fortune in gold. Ever since Mayhew's death his lawyer, Thorne, a good friend of Ellery, has sat guard to prevent the deceased's odious brother-in-law, Dr. Reinach, from locating and removing the loot, but now they all await the arrival by boat of Mayhew's long lost daughter, brought up in England, and Mayhew's rightful heir.

On repairing to the Long Island retreat with daughter Alice in tow Ellery meets Reinach's downtrodden wife, his burly and probably disreputable factotum and, later, Mayhew's unbalanced sister, who is still looking for her own daughter dead these three years.

After a less than convivial evening they retire to their cold and cheerless White House bedrooms and next morning Ellery rises to discover that the house next door, the Black House where the money is, has vanished from the face of the earth. How this seeming miracle has been accomplished is the core of the problem Ellery faces and, to make things worse, snow cuts off the party from the outside world.

This dramatic and atmospheric story, beautifully and logically resolved, owes as much as any of Queen's work to the influence of John Dickson Carr. It would have come as no surprise had Sir Henry Merrivale suddenly come booming into view, but he doesn't and Queen doesn't need him and settles all accounts neatly and ingeniously.

Vanishing house stories are few and far between and this is, with Will Scott's short story from *Giglamps*, easily the best of them. In fact I'll go further. At novelette length, which this is and no easy form to master, it vies for first place in my affections with Carr's magnificent tale, "The House In Goblin Wood," and only loses out by one word.*

Which brings us to *The Door Between* (1937) in which attractive engaged person, Eva MacClure, while visiting the home of her father's fiancée, prize winning writer Karen Leith, sits waiting outside Karen's bedroom door, thereby effectively if not literally sealing the author in. Concerned at the passage of time Eva enters the room and to her horror finds the author near death with her throat cut, all other exits from the room barred and no sign of the killer.

Panic stations for prime suspect Eva, who inadvisedly touches items in the room and generally plays the archetypal witless heroine. Enter unlikely hero, private eye Terry Ring, who in a trice sizes up the situation, falls head over heels for Eva and unlocks one of the other doors to provide her with a loophole—of sorts.

Inspector Queen, a logical man, naturally thinks otherwise, but his son and heir provides support, moral and practical, to the beleaguered couple. Much is made of the Japanese connections in this case—Karen had spent a lot of time there, as had her deceased sister and Dr. MacClure (Eva's cancer specialist father), her house has a Japanese garden, she dresses and takes tea in the Japanese manner, has a Japanese maid—even a Japanese bird in a cage. But it is only much later in the

---

* That word is "fall" uttered early in the piece by the recently arrived Alice Mayhew. However in England, where we are told she was raised, that word is never used to denote a season. "Autumn" is invariably used. A rare slip from the normally word perfect Mr. Queen, particularly when later the false Alice Mayhew, raised in the US, is clever enough to say petrol, when an American would have said gas(olene). Pernickety perhaps but worth drawing attention to in a plot where subterfuge and substitution go hand in hand.

narrative, by which time Eva has (rather unconvincingly) changed suitors and admitted what happened in the murder room, and the truth has emerged about Karen's sister and the authorship of the best selling books, that Ellery provides a stunningly simple answer to the locked room problem.

Unlike the earlier books Queen meets here for the first time a fully fledged locked room murder, and it is this problem which is the book's central theme.

Ellery himself is more mature than in his earlier outings and there are fewer of the mannerisms and affectations which marked, if not marred, previous investigations. Perhaps the least satisfactory feature is the liaison between, and behaviour of, Eva and her unlikely swain, gumshoe Ring. Given that Ring's manoeuvre of unlocking one of the murder room's other doors was perhaps necessary to widen the scope of the plot, it seems nonetheless a somewhat damnfool thing to do, particularly at barely a moment's notice.

But that's love, I suppose.

Queen's final novel of the impossible is *The King Is Dead* (1952). As the book opens the Queens, *père et fils*, are virtually kidnapped from their own home and whisked away by plane to Bendigo Island, situated Heaven knows where—but certainly not in America—and the home of "King" Bendigo, munitions magnate and one of the most powerful and ruthless men in the world. There he resides with his wife Karla, his two brothers, Judah and Abel and an entourage of guards, servants, scientists and military men, the most sinister of whom is Colonel Spring, "head of Public Relations."

King Bendigo (or to give him his correct name, Kane) has been receiving death threat letters, each successive one of which is more precise in its terms. The Queens' job, sanctioned by the US authorities, is to find out who is sending them and end the threat.

They set to work, receiving occasional help from Abel Bendigo, the island's prime minister, and Spring and his staff, but often, when they need it, none at all. Nonetheless they quickly trace the source of the letters and confront the culprit. However they prove absolutely powerless to stop the threatened attack, even after they have insisted that Kane continue his daily business inside the heavily fortified, well guarded Confidential Room with its single entrance. For as the death threat writer in the Queens' presence points an empty gun at the outside wall of the Confidential Room and pulls the trigger, Ellery on a hunch insists that the room be entered and there discovers Bendigo shot down and his wife, the only other occupant, unconscious. The guards confirm that nobody has gone into or come out of the room and a rigorous search fails to turn up any weapon which might be responsible for the shot. The forensic evidence shows that the bullet that hit Bendigo had been fired from the weapon which the Queens had seen pointed at the wall from outside.

The attack was not fatal and, while Bendigo is on the road to recovery, the Queens begin the slow process of investigation, again mostly on their own and with precious little help from their hosts. They are struggling to make any sense of it so Ellery flies back to the US to visit the town where the Bendigo boys grew up—that little slice of middle America with which he happens to be already so familiar, Wrightsville. Something of a stretch maybe to accept that out of all the myriad towns in the US this happens to be the one, but that's poetic licence for you, and this part of the book is not only thoroughly entertaining but also supplies the vital clues to help to solve the mystery and provide a very clever, fair solution to the problem of the gun that could fire through solid walls. As the Queens fly home the book achieves an explosive finale.

This is a very down to earth performance by Ellery, a much stronger and more determined person than in days of yore. If the book loses something by being set, largely, outside the US, it more than makes up for it by the pace and flair of the plotting. As for the impossible puzzle it is a very clever variant on the straightforward locked room theme and has only been matched in this particular form of ingenuity by the likes of Joseph Commings' "The X Street Murders."

For Queen's short fiction we backtrack a number of years to the October 1946 issue of *Ellery Queen's Mystery Magazine* and the first appearance of "The Adventure of the Dead Cat." Nikki Porter and Ellery attend a costume party (where everyone is dressed as a cat) and a game of murder is played. When the lights go up it is found that a real murder has been committed in a nearby room and the question is how did the murderer manage to cross a totally cluttered room in the pitch black without making a sound or falling flat on his, or her, face. The solution is a little pedestrian by Queen's standards but perfectly fair, and as a piece the story works very well.

Queen's next short is "The Dauphin's Doll" (*EQMM*, December 1948), a considerable improvement over its predecessor. Indeed this tale of impossible theft displays such skill and inventiveness that I would rate it as Queen's most accomplished miracle story at this length.   An eighteenth century doll with a fabulously valuable diamond is displayed for one day only in a well known department store. Inspector Queen is responsible for security and a major headache emerges in the form of master jewel thief, Comus, who calmly announces that he will steal the diamond right from under everyone's nose. Appropriate measures are taken to prevent him, including, most crucially, locking the doll and diamond inside a glass cell which is under public and official scrutiny from the moment the exhibition starts. But when it finishes, lo and behold, it is discovered that somehow a switch has been made and the real diamond has disappeared. The solution provided is a model of logical deduction and one of Queen's most inspired.

And following it, "The Three Widows" (*This Week*, January 29th, 1950), a very short, very clever poisoning case in which Queen has to work out how poison could have been administered when the victim's regime of eating and drinking has been extremely closely monitored. The solution is another little gem and reveals Queen at his most innovative.

"Double Your Money" (originally and far more imaginatively "The Vanishing Wizard" from *This Week*, September 30th, 1951) makes it three bull's eyes in a row and features a guarded room from which a crooked financier manages to make himself disappear, despite the presence of Ellery and others outside his office suite. On entering they find no financier and the only other exit locked on the inside. The answer is one that might be worked out by the more experienced reader, but so well handled that the enjoyment is unspoilt.

In his next impossible outing, "The Black Ledger" (*This Week*, January 26th, 1952), Ellery is charged with transporting a highly incriminating document by train to Washington but is waylaid en route by the monstrous Moriarty figure whom the document would incriminate. He is rigorously questioned and mercilessly searched (to the skin) but the documents remain hidden.   How Queen accomplishes this provides the impossible twist, and a very good one it is, though perhaps best not to dwell too long on whether the criminal Croesus would really have allowed him to finish his journey unharmed.

In "Object Lesson" (*Saturday Evening Post*, September 11th, 1955) Ellery gives an impromptu master class on detection at a local school and at the 59th minute of the 11th hour demonstrates where a small sum in stolen notes can be so cleverly hidden by one of the pupils that it almost remains undetectable. This very satisfying and moral tale could easily be the manual on how to write a good detective short story.

Queen's next miracle short (and well worthy of that description) is "Snowball In July" (*This Week*, August 31st, 1952) in which a crucial witness has to be brought from Canada to ensure the conviction of desperate criminal, Diamond Jim Grady. The only snag is that the train on which the witness is travelling disappears into thin air between stations. One of the classic problems of the impossible crime canon, which has formerly attracted the attention of no lesser personages than Arthur Conan Doyle and Melville Davisson Post (to name but two). Queen deals with the matter extremely neatly and, in so doing, provides a story which is a favourite among aficionados.

So to the final short, "E = Murder" (*This Week*, August 14th, 1960), and two for the price of one with both a locked building murder and a dying message clue. Eminent government scientist Dr. Agon dies horribly in his office at the top of a security Tower Block to which access is strictly limited, but manages to leave an enigmatic one letter clue to the killer. Queen provides the double solution but neither element shows him at his brilliant best. Probably the weakest of the Queen impossibles, bowing out with his least convincing tale of the miraculous.

Ellery Queen wrote some of the finest examples of the art of the impossible (and we will leave his radio plays for another time) throughout the golden age of detective fiction and beyond. His own special niche, within this already highly specialised field, was not however the dastardly deed in the locked and bolted room (though he managed it with considerable aplomb in both *The Door Between* and *The King Is Dead*) but that equally troublesome business of arranging incredible disappearances, and, as we have seen, he could accomplish it with perfect ease, whether it was a train or a .25 automatic pistol.

A most versatile man, our Mr. Queen.

(*I would like to acknowledge my debt to Francis M. Nevins's* Royal Bloodline.)

ELLERY QUEEN—MAN OF GOD

by Steven Steinbock

In the beginning it was without form, a darkness that kept shifting like dancers.

Rather an auspicious beginning for any book, be it the *Book of Genesis* or the *Gospel According to John*. But in this case, it is neither. The above is the opening line of Ellery Queen's *Ten Days' Wonder* (1948), the tale of Howard van Horn's journey into the abyss of insanity, wrestling with himself and with the God of the Ten Commandments.

Throughout the novels and stories of Ellery Queen, the rational mind is supreme over seemingly supernatural events. When it appears that an "impossible" crime could only be committed by something otherworldly, the scion of the 87th Street brownstone discovers a logical explanation. As much as Ellery dismisses any "higher power," theology trickles in, as it does in the final passages of *Cat of Many Tails* (1949)—a story like our present one about a world gone mad—in which the Viennese psychotherapist Bela Seligman tells Queen, "There is one God; and there is none other but he."

Emanuel Lepofsky was brought up in a non-religious family going back as far as anyone can remember. Russian Jewish immigrants, Benjamin and Rose Lepofsky were more likely to participate in intellectual and socialist salons than in anything religious, God forbid. They instilled in their children a disdain for organized religion. According to family legend, one of Manny's uncles made a point each year on Yom Kippur of eating a ham sandwich on the synagogue steps.

As Manny neared his graduation from NYU, he shared with his faculty advisor his dream of becoming a university English professor. "Manny," the advisor told him, "no Jew is ever going to get tenure in the New York university system!" Shaken and embittered, Lepofsky had his name legally changed to the most "gentile-sounding" name he could come up with: "Manfred Bennington Lee." His cousin Daniel ("Danny")

Nathan followed suit, changing his own name to "Frederic Dannay."

The two cousins kept their ethnicity hidden beneath levels of identity, compounding their name change by writing under the pseudonyms of Ellery Queen and Barnaby Ross. Dannay maintained his Judaism, taking his family to Passover Seders at the homes of relatives, celebrating the Bar Mitzvahs of his two sons, and sitting shiva upon the death of his wife, Hilda.

By contrast, Manny Lee raised his children in the Episcopal Church, explaining that they needed "something to reject." Despite his silence on matters Jewish, Manny's non-Jewish second wife, Catherine ("Kaye") Fox Brinker, was a vigorous defender of Jews and the State of Israel, and a vociferous opponent to antisemitism. If a Yiddish word or a Jewish comment were uttered in the Lee home, it was more likely to come from Kaye's mouth than Manny's.

Like his creators, the fictional Ellery Queen was a rationalist, skeptical of religion and theological notions. "Rationality, that was it," we are told in "The Lamp of God." "No esoteric mumbo jumbo could fool that fellow. Lord, no! His two feet were planted solidly on God's good earth." (Note how Queen cleverly evokes God even as he's denying Him). The power of the human intellect reigns in Queen's world. God appears only as a silent partner, an uncredited collaborator in Ellery's detections.

Religious elements—biblical motifs, names, and images—are used throughout the canon of Ellery Queen. "The Adventure of the Mark of Cain," an early Queen radio play, brings biblical allusions into a case of murder at the estate of late-millionaire John Cain. Again, in *The King Is Dead* (1952), Queen confronts totalitarian arms dealer "King" *Kane* Bendigo, a despot surrounded by his brothers *Abel* and *Judah*. In *And On the Eighth Day* . . . (1964) Queen's own name is interpreted as Elroï (Hebrew: "God Sees") Quenan (=Canaan?).

Nowhere do we find more religious props packed into the early (period one) Queen novels than in *The Egyptian Cross Mystery* (1932). Ellery and his father, Inspector Queen, travel to West Virginia where, on Christmas morning, the headless body of the town's schoolmaster was found nailed to a T-shaped signpost at a T-intersection, while a blood-swabbed "T" was found marking the dead man's door. In the course of the novel, there are more crucifixions, as well as totems, nudist cults, carpets decorated with "Trees of Life," a doctor named "Temple," a man who claims to be an

Egyptian Sun God, a generations-old Balkan blood feud, a discussion of the similarities of the St. Anthony Cross and the Egyptian "ankh," and a dead man who—like Lazarus—keeps coming back.

When events in the Queen stories appear to be the work of God's hand, it is often an evil god, a malicious meddler in human destiny. In "The Lamp of God" (1935), Queen tells us that "miracles don't happen any more, unless they are miracles of stupidity or miracles of natural avarice." Then, when an entire mansion disappears overnight, his reaction is "this is either a bad dream or the end of the world." Before the denouement, Queen's response to the impossible disappearance softens: "I never claimed . . . to be a magician. Or even a theologian. What's happened here is either the blackest of magic or palpable proof that miracles can happen." (In the end, of course, Ellery discovers a clever and diabolical—if unlikely—explanation for the building's disappearance).

During WWII and in the years that followed, the Queen novels took a major shift in tone and style. Gone were the walking stick, the pince nez, and the multisyllabic affectations. Classical plotlines with intricate puzzles evolved to a more somber search for moral truth. The *new* Ellery is a brooding young writer trying to work in peace but always pulled into the cause of justice. Just as he struggles with writer's block, he struggles to maintain a rational outlook in a world gone mad. He believes himself to be an Agnostic and an Empiricist. The only gods he will reluctantly allow are Pure Intellect, and Chaos.

Calamity Town (1942) might not at first appear to be a "religious" novel, but it marks a spiritual departure from previous EQ novels. As the first of the "Wrightsville" novels, it is more a character study than pure puzzle. The "challenge to the reader" is a moral one. Under an assumed name, Ellery comes to the New England town of Wrightsville seeking a quiet place to finish his novel. What he finds is Spoon River crossed with Peyton Place, a town tainted with bad blood, infidelity, and poisoning. *Calamity Town* has the pastoral quality of *Ruth*, the moral ambiguity of *Job*, and the existential naturalism and a sense of futility of *Ecclesiastes*. Ellery stands "looking at the old elms before the new Courthouse" when he observes:

> The old was being reborn in multitudes of little green teeth on
> brown gums of branches; and the new already showed weather

streaks in its granite, like varicose veins. There is sadness, too, in spring, thought Mr. Ellery Queen. He stepped into the cool shadows of the Courthouse lobby and was borne aloft.

Without taking the theological notions too far, EQ has planted a deeper meaning and biblical overtones into the novel with chapter headings like "Burnt Offering," "The Last Supper," "The Aramean," and "Easter Sunday." One should also note character names such as "Wright" and "Haight" (Right and Hate), a pastor named "Doolittle" and the self-righteous Miss DuPré ("do pray"?).

Ten Days' Wonder (1948), third of the "Wrightsville" novels, is reminiscent of Poe's "The Fall of the House of Usher," being the tale of the collapse of a man and his family as seen by an old friend. Queen returns to Wrightsville to aid his old friend Howard van Horn, a young sculptor in the midst of a psychological breakdown. Howard has been suffering long blackouts during which he believes he may be committing frightful crimes. As events unfold and a blackmail plot comes to light, it becomes apparent to Queen that his friend has been systematically—but unwittingly—violating each of the Ten Commandments. On the tenth day, in a tragic denouement, Queen discovers a horrific truth—one that cannot be explained here without revealing too much. Suffice it to say that here and in later novels, evil is committed by a malevolent godlike figure.

The farther we get from the Golden Age of classical detection, the more Ellery becomes disinclined to solve crimes. Like Jonah at Nineveh, Ellery is a reluctant prophet. He is dragged into criminal situations out of necessity or by accident.

It is such an accident that brings Ellery to solve a murder at a religious community in the 1964 novel *And On the Eighth Day* . . . . Lost somewhere on the California-Nevada border, he comes upon a mysterious utopia where crime is unknown. Theft and murder force Ellery to employ his deductive talents. "There had been a murder most foul in Eden, and the task of arraignment, indictment, and pressure for judgement was now his." While superficially *And On the Eighth Day* . . . has obvious religious content, and has been called Queen's "religious allegory," this book is rather short on ideas and cumbersome in style.

The Player on the Other Side (1963) is perhaps the most theologically revealing book in the entire Queen canon. On the surface, the themes seem to be stamp collecting and chess. But upon close analysis, we find a convergence of all the religious motifs previously used by Queen—the reluctant prophet, the world gone mad, trouble in Paradise, and the acts of a malevolent god—woven into a brilliant novel.

Ellery, the reluctant prophet, is summoned to solve a series of murders that have been orchestrated by an invisible, omniscient being. The chess-game is one of Good versus Evil, Truth versus Chaos, Revenge, and Death. While Ellery plays the hand of Truth, the invisible "player on the other side" uses his own prophet, his "chosen one," as a pawn in murder. The invisible killer, who fashions himself as none other than God, instructs his pawn: "you cannot speak my name" and reminds him that "I possess all powers . . . and I am everywhere." The first letter of prophecy to the simple handyman is signed "I am (but you know who I am!), Y"—recalling God's message at the burning bush: "I am that I am."

At the conclusion of *The Player on the Other Side*, as Ellery and Inspector Queen are contemplating the meaning of the case, we are given a glimpse into the authors' theology. Ellery quotes from Thomas H. Huxley, the great British who coined the term "agnostic" and managed to remain friendly toward the Church while championing Darwinism. In his essay "A Liberal Education," Huxley used the metaphor of a chess-game to describe reality:

> The chess-board is the world, the pieces are the phenomena of the universe, the rules of the game are what we call the laws of Nature. The player on the other side is hidden from us. We know that his play is always fair, just, and patient. But also we know, to our cost, that he never overlooks a mistake, or makes the smallest allowance for ignorance.

For Ellery Queen—the fictional detective as well as his creators and Theodore Sturgeon who collaborated on this novel—God is that Player who, as in chess, is our companion as well as our opponent. Like Jacob at the shore of the Jabbok, Queen wrestles with God until the break of dawn.

It is instructive that Queen evoked Huxley, who, while often at odds with organized religion, admits to something higher than himself. Although not quoted by Queen, the subsequent paragraph of Huxley's essay challenges the image of Satan playing chess with man for his soul.

"Substitute for the mocking fiend in that picture a calm, strong angel who is playing for love, as we say, and would rather lose than win—and I should accept it as an image of human life." Such a God is the ultimate practitioner of "fair-play."

If there remains for reader any doubt about the theological nature of the detective story, or of the religious insights of Ellery Queen, consider these words, which serve as the final leaf from *In the Queen's Parlor* (1957):

And Poe said: Let there be a detective story. And it was so. And when Poe created the detective story in his own image, and saw everything that he had made, behold, it was very good. And he cast the detective story originally in the classic form. And that form, as it was in the beginning, is now and shall be, world without end, the true form. Amen.

WE MAY AS WELL CONTINUE BEING CARROLLISH: A BOW BEFORE THE QUEEN

By Bill Ruehlmann

I've held up one of our books to the glass, and then they hold up one in the other room.

— Alice

Somebody's either playing a monstrous prank; or there's a devilishly clever and warped mentality behind all this.

— E.Q.

When I was in seventh grade, I arrived at McDonogh School, a boys' military academy in McDonogh, Maryland, with considerable apprehension and a copy of *101 Years' Entertainment: The Great Detective Stories 1841-1941*, edited by Ellery Queen.

The 995-page Modern Library Giant edition, massive to me then, now long out of print, contained 50 ingenious tales celebrating the titular centennial-plus-one elapsed since the publication of Edgar Allan Poe's "The Murders in the Rue Morgue," generally credited as the first short story officially employing a freelance flatfoot, in this case the nocturnal know-it-all named C. Auguste Dupin.

My apprehension quickly transformed itself into a permanent impatience with authority, but my admiration for the book remains undiminished to this day. Herein, besides the incomparable Ellery, were Hercule Poirot and The Thinking Machine, Lord Peter Wimsey, Arsène Lupin and Sam Spade, among others. The absolute fascination—and surcease—these birds provided certainly must have been part of the reason that I became the only boy in McDonogh experience to be placed on report for reading *Mike Shayne Mystery Magazine* during study hall instead of the less interesting textbook wrapped around that diverting periodical.

In detective stories there was always some solid, revelatory reason behind what seemed to be patently absurd behavior; it was my experience that this did not routinely seem to be the case in martial matters.

Now we are celebrating the seventieth anniversary of the first appearance of seminal editor/author Queen, a.k.a. Frederic Dannay and Manfred B. Lee, with the posthumous printing by Crippen & Landru of previously unpublished material, an occasion that leads me to pull down once again that marvelously astute and breezy anthology that helped get me through two years of full-dress formations, inspections and parades.

Dannay and Lee began with *The Roman Hat Mystery* (1929), Ellery's first official fictive exploit. So I suspect it was a far from arbitrary choice on their part to include, dead-center in *101 Years' Entertainment*, another criminous encounter with a chapeau, "The Mad Tea Party," the final tale of Dannay and Lee's first volume of short stories, *The Adventures of Ellery Queen: Problems in Deduction* (1934).

"At this point," the *101 Years'* compilers noted archly, "according to purple tradition, you should be reading a whimsical statement by the Publisher to the effect that under threat of corporeal-violence he got the Editors to include one of their own stories. We scorn this feeble subterfuge. Including 'The Mad Tea Party' was strictly our own idea."

It's a good yarn—but then so are they all good yarns in *The Adventures*, and *The New Adventures* (1940), too, for that matter.

Were the collaborators having a little further fun for the benefit of their discerning readers?

Hat trick:

Fans will recall that "The Mad Tea Party" concerns Ellery's summons to the Long Island estate of Arliss-like actor Richard Owen, who has arranged for friends to perform the no-room *Alice in Wonderland* encounter *à la* Lewis Carroll, with himself as Mad Hatter, for birthday-boy Jonathan, his son.

Ellery is escorted down the metaphoric rabbit-hole by Owen's chauffeur, the blond, squinty-eyed, bunnyesque Mallin ("You're a little late, aren't you, sir?"). It's only a hop to the porch of the fairy-taleish house, "a large rambling affair of gables and ells and colored stones and bright shutters, set at the terminal of a winding driveway flanked by soldierly trees," and the front door stands invitingly ajar. Inside the detective comes upon a rehearsal for the birthday tea party, at which

Ellery is smitten by Alice-like Miss Willowes, "whimsically girlish in a pinafore."

Of course the only certifiable child of the piece, Master Jonathan, is a thoroughly objectionable creature who talks like an adult while the cigarette-puffing Alice by the end seems to be engaged in making a serious pass at our hero, who had himself made careful note throughout of her "slim" legs, as well as the maid's "trim" ones. The Rev. Charles Lutwidge Dodgson would undoubtedly have sat up straight. But the authors are bent on making the curious curiouser, and variations on that word boil about the story like black pepper in the Duchess's kitchen.

The plot turns on a clock and a mirror, reminiscent of the ones in *Through the Looking-glass*, and Ellery's manipulation of a crucial verse in "The Walrus and the Carpenter." But one will also note the Queen's insistence on being arbiter of justice himself. "I assume I possess—er—ex officio qualifications." Ellery's off-with-his-head predilection allies him, of course, with many similarly vengeful ministers of vengeance, from Philo Vance to (beginning in 1947) Mike Hammer.

Prefigured, of course, by Lewis Carroll's famous mouse, whose "long and sad tale" ends thus:

" 'I'll be judge, I'll be jury,' said cunning old Fury; 'I'll try the whole cause, and condemn you to death.' "

Even Ellery confesses to a certain amount of inquisitorial glee in cornering the culprit: "Had to torture him, I suppose. It's a weakness of mine."

EQS&M.

The reader has been warned: "You're about to witness a slightly cock-eyed exercise in criminal ingenuity." But more is afoot than Ellery's clever explanation, which we won't spoil here. For example, everyone is drugged, but unlike Alice, who drinks with impunity, the Owen assemblage is not absolved of hangovers.

A case could be made that Ellery dreams all or that the text is a figment of the willowy Miss Willowes's reading imagination (resolved, naturally, in a library), but, as the Queen said to Alice, let's go on with the game.

Why does Ellery, who "hesitated between two volumes" (the other was undoubtedly *Alice*), select *Huckleberry Finn* for bedtime perusal? Is it mere "blithe reading on a dour night" or another account of a surprise death, belatedly discovered (Pap's)? And written behind one more pseudonymous, but also evasively dual, mask (Samuel Clemens/Mark

Twain)?

Which reminds us, that dark architect Paul Gardner of "The Mad Tea Party" takes on at once the portmanteau image of webspinner Erle Stanley and Perry's detective Drake.

Meanwhile the "cold knob" to "the wrong room" seems not only emblematic of *Alice* but of the mystery form itself. Which returns us to *101 Years' Entertainment* and why Dannay and Lee chose "The Mad Tea Party" as exemplary of their work. In part, it harks back to the question the Mad Hatter asks Alice: "Why is a raven like a writing desk?"

She doesn't answer, but the anthology seems to.

A raven is like a writing desk because both connect with an inkwell: Poe's.

Further, in *Through the Looking-glass*, Alice observes that the squared-off countryside seem marked out for "a great huge game of chess that's being played—all over the world . . ." So very like the cerebral combat of detective fiction. And Alice says she aspires to be a Queen in that inventive endeavor.

So much more fun than being a pawn!

Later the Queen offers another insight: "I'm just," she confides, *"one hundred and one,* five months and a day."

Also—like Ellery, Father Brown and Dr. Fell—she announces herself quite capable of believing six impossible things before breakfast.

Thus the Queen, the game and the anthology are a single endeavor, which effectively, as the monarch accuses the Hatter, murders time.

At least it does for me. Military school, that world of green lawns and long marches, seem like a dream now, but "The Mad Tea Party" remains as real as when I first read it, more than 40 years ago—as is, still, the wonderful diversion of detective fiction. I find myself exactly like that other Bill, who shoots through the chimney in *Alice*.

Something comes at me like a Jack-in-the-box, and up I goes like a sky-rocket.

TWAYBLADE

by Catherine Aird

My rather strange title comes not from the world of crime-writing but from that of ancient botany. "Twayblade" was the word used in 1578 by the famous horticultural lexicographer, Henry Lyte, to describe the orchid *Listera ovata* and means "two-leaf." I think that "two-leaf" is also an apt description of the good anthologist: it is in addition, quite serendipitously, yet another way of describing the two parts of that splendid whole which comprised Ellery Queen—Frederic Dannay and Manfred B. Lee.

In my view the good anthologist is of "twayblade" construction because he has two quite separate functions: the selection of the contents of the anthology and the composition of the introductory essay which usually accompanies it. Probably these are tasks of equal importance— one without the other undoubtedly lacks a certain savour. The educated palate needs both salt and sugar to enjoy the full flavour of that of which it is partaking.

Taste—good taste—is very important in another sense, too. The duty of choosing exactly what goes into an anthology has got quite a lot in common with the role of the wine-merchant, not the least of which is the requirement that both have to meet the demands of very specialised cognoscenti! In addition, similar skills are called for in recognising what is true vintage material, and differentiating between what is best for consumption now, what will stand the test of time, what will continue to mature even further, and, on the other hand, but equally important, that which should be consciously set aside because it will neither bear consumption now nor last—let alone travel across the Atlantic.

It is probably safe to say that the crime-writing genre itself—unlike the world of the oenophile—is still sufficiently youthful for there to be no need to worry about the good old—the real vintage—detective story passing its peak in our lifetime . . .

The first of the *Queen's Awards*—that for 1946—demonstrates something else which the good editor must have: the courage of his convictions. Here a short story by William Faulkner, one of the greatest names in American literature then and now, takes second place to one by Manly Wade Wellman, at that time a comparative newcomer to detective fiction.

My hypothesis is that this particular volume—one of the earliest out of the half a hundred and more Ellery Queen collections which were to succeed it—can stand for a paradigm of them all.

You will know that the series began as a short story competition for which there were eight hundred and thirty-eight manuscripts submitted —so even the preliminary reading could have been no sinecure. Entries were solicited in June 1945 from an immediate post-war world of servicemen and women, amateur or professional writer, experienced or novice, and came from all parts of the globe and the United States of America—save, for some quite unfathomable reason, North Dakota.

The finalists of this massive entry were winnowed down to a shortlist for the ultimate arbiters—Christopher Morley and Howard Haycraft and, of course, Ellery Queen. From this list fifteen prize-winning short stories were chosen to which one extra-mural one was added. The anthology was declared a new beginning and the future of the detective-crime short story said to be bright indeed.

It was.

It is the composition of the sixteen tales in this book which in my opinion bears analysis after half a century—and in the light of both the passage of time and the changing mores of the real world—as well as the crime-writing one.

The anthology also included an introduction and a paragraph headed "Caveat Lector" (or Reader Beware) modestly suggesting that those who wanted to get straight to the stories themselves should ignore the editorial comments and start with the text. These notes are in the main about the authors, their literary history and so forth rather than more general judgements on the genre. Most unusually though, both ante and post scripts were appended to each tale.

There is no doubt that the stories make up an excellent conspectus of the sub-genre, running as they do the gamut of types of crime fiction from the classic deduction of the American Indian detective—this the winner of the first prize—to the clever murder within the theatrical milieu so beloved by Ngaio Marsh.

More than this, though, they demonstrate an unsung choice by the editors which is infinitely more subtle than it seems at first reading. It is by no means as random a selection—even of the best—as the reader might have thought. The compilation actually includes examples of almost all the then current types of crime-writing—which is surely no editorial accident.

There is the simple but beautifully logical who-dunit of "A Star For a Warrior" by Manly Wade Wellman and a pair of unusual how-dunits —Ngaio Marsh's "I Can Find My Way Out" (too, too simple—worryingly so—when you know how), and "Count Jalacki Goes Fishing" by T.S. Stribling (very clever, this). The last also contains this piece of received wisdom: "One single criminal clue is like a geometrical point; it establishes direction but doesn't locate a point. Two clues . . . should define the crime . . . fairly accurately."

The traditional tale with the deceptively surprise ending is "Malice Domestic" by Philip MacDonald, then already an old hand at crime-writing. Another old hand—or perhaps I should say "old China hand" —Helen McCloy penned "Chinoiserie" set in old Peking in the 1860's. This echoes real-life in one respect at least in that it is told from the point of view of a suspect who doesn't know what the police are doing, or why.

There are a brace of what could loosely be called secret service stories including "Handcuffs Don't Hold Ghosts" by Manning Coles. These seem a little dated now although this is by no means the fault of the author or the editors. Not even the most accomplished of crystal-ball gazers could possibly have foreseen the changes to come in the ensuing fifty years in the nature of spy and espionage fact, let alone fiction.

And the stories fairly described by the editors as hard-boiled half a century ago would not, I fear, make the running in that category today. Things aren't what they were . . .

On the other hand Michael Innes' "Lesson in Anatomy" shows the Oxford and Cambridge School of academic crime-writers to have changed less than most. Ellery Queen scored a notable first in publishing Detective Inspector John Appleby's debut appearance in short story form in this collection. And in this true blue university tradition one of Michael Innes' characters describes another thus: "He is a bit of a humbug, of course—all philosophers are. And he is not a good man, since it is impossible for a Vice-Chancellor to be that." Things are what they were, after all . . .

There is a mandatory psychological piece and one from a representative of that—in this case—rather less than charming group of precocious infants known as "manhunting minors."

One of the clues in Frances Crane's story "The Blue Hat," which is centred around a wedding, is that age-old bridal dress requirement of:

"Something old, something new
Something borrowed, something blue."

A parody of this couplet would provide the reader with good clues to the deliberately wide-ranging contents of this, the first Ellery Queen's awards anthology:

"Something bold, something new,
Nothing borrowed, nothing blue."

Actual parody may be found in the story outside the collection and which completes the volume. This is an ingenious work punningly called "The Final Problem." It involves the competition judges—well-known authors Christopher Morley and Howard Haycraft, and Ellery Queen—and Ellery Queen's father Inspector Richard Queen. It is based on the quite tenable premise that the characters—and readers—are all Sherlock Holmes aficionados. The action of the mystery includes the death—the murder—of Ellery Queen.

Don't worry: like the death of Sherlock Holmes himself, it is greatly exaggerated.

LEGACY OF AN EDITOR

by Janet Hutchings

The editorial legacy of Ellery Queen surrounds the staff of *Ellery Queen's Mystery Magazine* in the most tangible, physical way. One wall of the current editor's office is covered with the nearly six hundred issues of *EQMM* Queen himself edited, and next to them a floor-to-ceiling bookcase houses the dozens of anthologies that bear his name, in hardcover, paperback and special newsstand paperback editions. Shelved on another wall are the single-author short story collections "presented" by Queen. On most work days, letters from one or more of the distinguished authors Queen introduced to the magazine arrive in the office's in-box or computer e-mail. Or a visitor will appear in the reception: someone who knew editor Queen personally.

As every reader knows, Frederic Dannay was the man behind the signature "Queen" or "Ellery Queen" when it appeared in *EQMM* as the cognomen of the magazine's editor; Ellery Queen the writer, on the other hand, was the partnership of Dannay and his cousin, Manfred B. Lee. Seventeen years after the death of Frederic Dannay, there are still more objects one can point to in *EQMM*'s editorial office that were Queen's own work than there are magazines or books or papers by the magazine's subsequent editors.

Let's try to imagine this office seventeen years hence. By then the number of issues and anthologies created by editors other than Queen will almost equal those he edited himself, and the number of authors who can claim to have shaken hands with him will have dwindled to a very few. Queen will no longer have the sheer physical presence he has at the magazine today, but the person who sits behind the editor's desk in the year 2016 will still be surrounded by his legacy, for the legacy of a truly great editor—and Queen was one of the very best—goes beyond the authors he discovers and the individual books and magazines he edits. A great editor changes the way people think and establishes standards of taste that carry beyond his own time. No one in the mystery field has ever done this more completely or with more enduring effect than Frederic Dannay.

When Dannay launched his first mystery periodical, *Mystery League*, in 1933, a wealth of fine crime writing was being published in the better pulp magazines, but because of the pulps' lurid packaging, readership generally didn't extend to those who considered themselves connoisseurs of "literature." Dannay set out to change that; he wanted the American reading public to think of his beloved genre as "a genuine literary form," and with that end he determined that *Ellery Queen's Mystery Magazine*, the second periodical he put on the market, would take the respectable shape of a book, with book quality paper and printing.

EQMM's design was only the first step up the slope Queen scaled seemingly effortlessly in the years to follow. It wasn't very long before *EQMM* was being hailed as not only the finest periodical in the genre, but a favorite of literati such as Dorothy Parker. Dannay had succeeded in raising mystery fiction and particularly, as he put it, he "raised the sights of mystery writers generally"—in other words, he changed the way writers themselves thought about their craft.

Frederic Dannay accomplished his transformation of the mystery genre not from *EQMM*'s official offices, but from his home in Larchmont, New York. Long before telecommuting became fashionable, Queen employed the telephone lines to maintain thoroughgoing control of the magazine he founded and the story anthologies that bore his name. A lesser editor might have thought it enough to have set the publication's goals and tone, and have left the nitty-gritty to other members of the staff. Not Queen.

On hearing that Crippen & Landru were preparing a volume celebrating Queen's accomplishments, several *EQMM* authors offered to share with us their experiences with Fred Dannay in his capacity as editor. Dorothy Salisbury Davis, an MWA Grand Master whose work for *EQMM* dates from *EQMM*'s Seventh Annual Worldwide Short Story contest of 1952, had much to say about Queen's hands-on control of his magazine. She told us of Dannay's dictation by telephone of sometimes extensive letters to authors. A secretary at the New York office, she relates, would take down what Dannay had to say, type it, affix the Queen "signature" with a rubber stamp, and send his correspondence out to the many places across the globe in which he had discovered talented writers. Those letters might explain anything from a title change to extensive revision of a manuscript.

Said Bill Pronzini, an author whose work Queen admired:

He [Queen] was an editorial tinkerer—often changed story titles, and substituted words and phrases and rewrote sentences in the text—and I'm not really comfortable with that sort of thing without being consulted. But I never once disagreed with an editorial change Fred made in any of my manuscripts; and only once did I dispute a title change, and then mildly. His revisions were always carefully considered from the writer's point of view and invariably made a thought or plot point more clear, sharpened characterization, improve dialogue or narrative flow.

Many of Queen's editorial "tinkerings" survive today in the several long-running series of *EQMM*'s most prolific and cherished short story writer, Edward D. Hoch, who writes:

Fred suggested occasional ideas for stories, things for Nick Velvet to steal, new characters I might try. On at least two occasions, with Rand and Dr. Sam Hawthorne, he immediately recognized the potential for a lengthy series in just the first story. And in both cases he suggested important changes in my protagonist's name. Rand was shortened from my original "Randolph," perhaps to suggest James Bond. And my "Dr. Sam" acquired the New Englandish family name of Hawthorne.

Editor's changes are not always so kindly interpreted as "suggestions," as they are in Ed Hoch's letter. But we know that Queen's changes usually met with acceptance even when authors disagreed with him. Multiple *EQMM* Readers Award winner Clark Howard recalls that Dannay couldn't always explain why he wanted a certain revision, but says, "I respected him enough that he didn't have to."

The reverence writers felt for Frederic Dannay had its roots, in part, in the enormous status Ellery Queen enjoyed as a writer. With one hundred fifty million copies of his books in print worldwide, he was known to nearly everyone who ever picked up a work of popular fiction. Added to this was Dannay's extensive, scholarly knowledge of the literature of crime and detection. Whatever sort of mystery fiction they write—be it hardboiled, cozy, pure detection or suspense—writers knew they were in the hands of an editor who understood what they were trying to achieve.

For readers, Queen's vast knowledge of crime fiction and the use he made of it in his publications was revolutionary. Dannay believed that the intelligent reader of literate Golden Age whodunits would enjoy well-written private eye and espionage and pure suspense stories too, if the best writers of these tales were presented to them in a single book—alongside their favorite Golden Age authors. It was something that had never been tried before, and it worked like a charm. During *EQMM*'s first decade, as Dannay reprinted stories he'd gathered for his own personal library of crime fiction (the most complete collection in the world), slowly adding previously unpublished stories by both famous and unknown authors, *EQMM*'s circulation soared. To both writers and readers he had become *the* editor.

The esteem, and sometimes awe, in which writers, especially new-comers to the magazine, held Queen made it easy for him to inspire and draw from writers ever better work. By the sixties, *EQMM* was receiving stories from new writers who had grown up with the magazine and were among its most loyal readers. One of those readers-turned-writers, William Bankier, still thinks of Fred Dannay with affection. A simple complimentary remark from Dannay as he introduced one of Bankier's stories was enough to encourage the young writer to develop his unique talent. Clark Howard, who began selling stories to *EQMM* in 1980, describes his brief conversations with Dannay as "memorable moments. Talking to a living legend is always a fine experience."

By the sixties and early seventies, Queen *had* become a living legend as an editor, but fame never caused him to become unapproachable. Friends such as Dorothy Salisbury Davis recall that he loved nothing better than to put his feet up on a chair and talk about the craft of the mystery, both the short story and the novel. He was warmly welcoming, and for that reason, the writers remember him with fondness as well as respect.

As for the editors of *EQMM* (present and to come), we cannot but think appreciatively of Frederic Dannay, for we work within the structure he created. So sound were the principles and ideals on which Dannay founded his magazine that *EQMM* remains today essentially Queen's house. Entertainment combined with insight into the human condition, that is how Frederic Dannay once described the best mystery fiction—

and that is what he dedicated *EQMM* to providing. Over the years, *EQMM*'s subsequent editors have made a few minor renovations: an out-of-style paper removed from a wall; a room or two added to accommodate new developments in the field. But never an alteration to the fundamental design, which was meant to be encompassing and grand —including, as Queen said, the best the genre had to offer, both old and new—always of the highest literary quality.

A TRIBUTE

by Edward D. Hoch

The first adult novel I ever read, at age nine, was *The Chinese Orange Mystery* by Ellery Queen. I guess you could say it changed my life, and it explains why my early short story submissions always went first to *Ellery Queen's Mystery Magazine*. It was not until 1962 that I made my first sale there, but after that my stories appeared in *EQMM* with increasing regularity: one in '63, two in '64, four in '65, five in '66, etc. It was not unusual for me to receive a phone call from Fred Dannay discussing some aspect of my most recent submission, and he was disturbed when I won the MWA Edgar Award for a story in *The Saint Magazine* after his managing editor had rejected it for *EQMM*.

Over those early years I introduced a number of my series characters in *EQMM*, and Fred often advised me on which characters to keep and which to drop. We saw each other at MWA functions, and I visited him at his home in Larchmont. During that time I met Manny Lee only twice, at Edgar Awards dinners, but found him a friendly and likable man. By 1970 it was an open secret that the original paperbacks published under the Ellery Queen name were being written by others and edited by Manny, and I suggested to Fred that perhaps I could try one. Manny Lee contacted me and asked for an outline. After I submitted it he wrote me a detailed letter on March 29, 1971, suggesting a number of small changes and telling me to go ahead with the project. A few days later he died, and when I received the letter two days after his death it was like a voice from the grave. Although the paperbound originals had been strictly Manny Lee's project from the beginning, Fred Dannay said that with Manny dead he would edit my manuscript of this final novel, *The Blue Movie Murders*.

I sent it to him a few months later, and after he'd had an opportunity to read it he suggested I come again to his home in Larchmont to discuss his changes. I remember that I spent an entire summer's afternoon there, going over the manuscript page by page. For me, it was a lesson in editing from a master. He preferred fewer commas than I usually used, and fewer words. He found a phrase like, "He shrugged his shoulders," to be redundant. "You can't shrug anything but your shoulders," he told me, and of course he was right. To this day I remember that, every time I see the phrase in someone else's book. There were red editing marks on virtually every page of that manuscript, and when my wife Patricia retyped it for me she was as impressed as I was by Fred Dannay's editorial skills. *The Blue Movie Murders* was published in February 1972, the last of the Ellery Queen paperback originals, and the only one in which Fred Dannay and Manny Lee both played a part.

Fred often suggested projects to me, including story ideas for my Nick Velvet series and new characters that I tried from time to time. In 1971 he suggested a six-part serial, with each part complete in itself but with a cliffhanger leading to the next one. It became "The Will-o'-the-Wisp Mystery," originally published as by Mr. X. Fred had such trust in me by this time that he began running the series in *EQMM* before knowing how it would end. He asked me only one question: "Will I be surprised?" I told him I hoped he would be.

Also in 1971 I submitted a non-series story that Fred decided warranted another byline. Since the story was a variation on "Dr. Jekyll and Mr. Hyde," he suggested the pseudonym of "R.L. Stevens," after Robert Louis Stevenson. The "Stevens" tales continued to appear in *EQMM* until Fred's death, usually in the same issue as a Hoch story.

By 1973 I was appearing in every issue of *EQMM*, and would publish only one more novel before devoting my full efforts to the short story. When Allen J. Hubin relinquished the editorship of *Best Detective Stories of the Year* after the 1975 volume, Fred contacted the publisher and suggested that I take over the job. It was a series I continued to edit for the next twenty years, under two publishers.

Over the years I saw Fred Dannay at infrequent but memorable intervals. In 1979 my wife and I attended a dinner celebrating the fiftieth anniversary of the first Ellery Queen novel, *The Roman Hat Mystery*. Two years later we journeyed to Stockholm with Fred and Rose Dannay, and a large contingent of MWA members, for the Third International Crime Writers Congress. I remember attending a dinner party there with Fred, Julian Symons, Dorothy Salisbury Davis, Hillary Waugh, the Swedish writer Iwan Hedman, and the Japanese writer who hosted the party,

Shizuko Natsuki, among others. I still have an anthology of Japanese mysteries autographed by all thirteen of us who attended.

It was around this time, in 1980, that Fred asked me to take over a column previously written for *EQMM* by Otto Penzler. He suggested I use the pseudonym "R.E. Porter" (for Reporter) and I did so. The column ran for sixty issues of the magazine, until 1985.

After Fred's death in 1982 my close relations with his magazine continued through the two editors who succeeded him, Eleanor Sullivan and Janet Hutchings. Each of them has carried on the highest quality of the Ellery Queen tradition in *EQMM*, not as easy task during a time when the mystery story has changed so much since its Golden Age.

It was the Golden Age that launched Ellery Queen as one of its brightest stars. His work inspired me to become a writer, and as an editor he contributed much toward making me a successful one.

EQMM

By Michael Gilbert

I was considering recently the plight of the crime short story in Great Britain. It might not be going too far to include it in the obituary column for, in truth, it is practically dead. Dead for want of appropriate top-class outlets.

And after such a full and glorious early life!

I am thinking not only of the Sherlock Holmes stories. I am old enough to remember a time when no pater-familias would be welcomed home from his city office unless he brought with him the latest copy of the *Strand* magazine with splendid Holmes and Watson and villainous Dr. Moriarty in it. And on a very slightly lower scale I thought of H.C. Bailey, so delightful in his short Reggie Fortune stories and to me almost unreadable in his full length novels. And of the immortal Father Brown, whose story "The Oracle of the Dog" I would pick, if I was forced to choose, as one of the best short crime stories ever written.

With the killing of that excellent periodical, *Argosy*, the night finally fell. Along with the *Strand* and the *Grand* and *Pearson's* and the *Windsor*, they had been condemned, one after another, to death. But at this point there was a gleam of light from across the Atlantic. As Winston Churchill quoted in a similar situation—"But Westwards, lo, the land is bright." The steady flame of Ellery Queen was alive.

At this point I turned to the shelves in my cupboard where copies of *Ellery Queen's Mystery Magazine* were piled. I counted ninety of them.

The number of September 1964 pulls back the curtain on earlier history. It was headed "250th Issue." And as the preface puts it:

It just doesn't seem possible! 250 issues of *EQMM*! And we remember, as if it were last month, the very first issue of 23 years ago—the magic memory of Volume 1, Number 1—the planning, the enthusiasm and high hopes of *EQMM*'s first appearance in a field in which only the so-called 'Action' mystery printed on pulp paper, was known and accepted.

It contained what was identified as "Story no. 3000"—"The Perfect Stranger" by Rufus King. The story concluded with what might be regarded as a perfect coda for *EQMM*. "You cannot kill a man," observed the prelate, "who does not die." Long may its flame burn brightly enough to cross the Atlantic and warm the hearts of readers in this benighted and deprived land of ours.

My own connection with *EQMM* does not, of course, go back as far as No. 1. (I wonder if anyone retains a copy of it. It must be almost as valuable as the first printing of the first Sherlock Holmes story "A Study in Scarlet," reputed to be worth many thousands of dollars*). At the time when it appeared, in 1941 I was occupied with other activities than writing.

It was on the issue of December 1952 that I found I had scribbled, across the front cover, the proud words "First Michael Gilbert." The scribble obscured the face of a scientist, who appeared to have been murdered in a picture accredited to Salter. (More about these illustrations later.)

It is seven issues after, in July 1953, that I attain the honour of being mentioned on the front cover. When I add that I am at the bottom of a group that includes Cornell Woolrich, A.H.Z. Carr, John Galsworthy and Lawrence Blochman it will be seen that the standard was high.

If a complete listing of the contributors is made it would, I am sure, include all crime writers of any notability who were functioning between 1941 and the present day in England, America and many of the European countries as well. In addition to the well-known detective story masters and mistresses—Julian Symons, John D. Macdonald, Agatha Christie, Dorothy L. Sayers, Q. Patrick, Stanley Ellin—the list is too long to reproduce in full—it is both surprising and refreshing to note that it contains the honoured names of Franz Kafka and Anton Chekhov.

The planning of the cover must have presented problems to the editorial staff. On many occasions they contented themselves with the

---

*Publisher's note: The first issue of *EQMM* is very collectable, but it has not yet commanded the price of the first edition of "A Study in Scarlet." *EQMM* was a success from the start, and (as Dannay had hoped) many people retained their copies of Volume 1, Number 1.

setting out, in colourful array, the names of the contributors but there are also occasions, particularly in the more recent numbers, when there is an actual illustration. In some of them, I understand, fans of Ellery Queen allowed recognisable pictures of themselves to appear in a number of hazardous situations.

In one such the gentleman concerned is shown regarding, with understandable dismay, the descent of a heavy axe, suspended by a cord, which is in imminent danger of being burned through by a lighted candle; but my favourite is the evocative, but less immediately dramatic picture of the middle aged lady looking out of her window, whilst a trickle of blood comes down from the ledge of the window above.

Of the stories themselves it is sufficient to say that the majority of them are fine examples of their craft. If I was forced to chose the best—an almost impossible task—it would surely be "The Black Kitten" by A.H.Z. Carr, which was First Prize Winner in 1955. When it reappeared fourteen years later, in the October number of 1969, the editor commented, "With the passing of the years it has not lost one atom of its profoundly disturbing quality. When Mr. Carr asked some of his closest friends to read it, he was, he says 'startled at the intensity of their reactions.' "

Let it stand, therefore, as the epitome of this matchless collection of crime story fiction.

AVOIDING MR. QUEEN

by Peter Lovesey

If you can find them after half a century, the short story collections called *The Queen's Awards* are fascinating to read. In 1946, *Ellery Queen's Mystery Magazine* launched an annual short story competition that attracted most of the top names in crime writing. I have a copy of the second book, published in 1947, and the contributors include John Dickson Carr (as Carter Dickson), Leslie Charteris, Edmund Crispin, Michael Innes, Harry Kemelman, Philip MacDonald, Helen McCloy, Hugh Pentecost and Roy Vickers. Not a bad line-up. Yet the most original contribution comes from Ellery Queen himself. Each story is topped and tailed by the editors. The foreword is mainly about the authors; nothing startling in that. The afterword or tailpiece is the fascinating bit, for Ellery Queen analyses the stories and shows how they were constructed and why they work so effectively. It's a huge bonus, an invitation to look behind the scenes at the Magic Circle.

Here, for example, is Queen on Dickson Carr's "The House in Goblin Wood":

> The author's sense of timing is flawless. When Henry Merrivale's mystification reaches its most profound state, along comes Chief Inspector Masters with a simple, all-inclusive solution—the revelation that one of the rooms in the cottage was equipped with a trick window. So that's the answer to the impossible disappearance!—just another "gadget"! But the author is merely playing cat-and-mouse with his reader: instead of evoking the supernatural and then dispelling it (the usual procedure, and good enough for most practitioners), the author evokes the natural, only to dispel that and sink the story even deeper in the supernatural. The trick window, is a straw man, set up to be promptly demolished.

What a privilege it is to have one master giving an in-depth commentary on another's craft. Interestingly, Ellery Queen doesn't destroy the magic by explaining how the tricks are set up. He enhances it. And his choice of approach varies from story to story. In the afterword to Philip MacDonald's story, "The Wood-for-the-Trees," he demonstrates how the intricacies of plot are reconciled with the character and mood of the piece.

Queen's expert dissection of these and other stories provides a master-class for mystery writers. It encouraged me to try the form. In 1973 I had published four novels and was ready to dip my toe into short-story writing. Relying heavily on what I had learned from the tailpieces in *The Queen's Awards*, I put together a story called "The Bathroom" and optimistically sent it off to *Ellery Queen's Mystery Magazine*. Back came a rejection letter. Clearly I hadn't paid enough attention in the master-class.

It was not until six years later that I had a story accepted by the magazine. By that time I had seen Fred Dannay, the surviving partner of the writing team that was Ellery Queen, at the Crime Writers' International Congress in New York and heard him speak about editing the magazine. Seen and heard. I can't claim to have met him then; I was too awed to approach the great man.

More of my stories appeared in the magazine. In one issue they used my picture on the cover. Buoyed up by this star treatment, I did something totally stupid that makes me cringe when I recall it. I re-submitted "The Bathroom." Surely, I told myself, it wasn't such a bad story, and now, seven years on, nobody will remember it was rejected.

I heard nothing at all from New York. Mortified, I was forced to conclude that Ellery Queen did have a long memory; he'd rejected the story once, so why send a second letter? Had I ruined my chances of ever having another story published?

Then another international conference came along, this time in Stockholm. I'd enjoyed the first, so I turned up in Sweden, cheerful and confident—until I saw the list of delegates. Prominent among them was Fred Dannay. How embarrassing! I was tempted to take the next flight back to England.

I spent the first day and a half of the conference trying to keep at a safe distance from Mr. Dannay. You might think he was easy to spot in a crowd, because he wore thick dark-rimmed glasses and was bearded. However, he was a slight figure apt to disappear from view behind writers larger in size. I was constantly at risk from Christianna Brand or Julian Symons stepping aside to leave me eye-to-eye with my nemesis.

For all my watchfulness, it happened, of course. It was written in the stars. Towards the end of Saturday I stepped into an elevator and there were two other people inside. Fred Dannay, with Rose, his wife.

The doors closed behind me.

No escape—and I was wearing my name-tag. I smiled and nodded and tried not to appear as alarmed as I felt. He leaned forward for a closer look at the label. He said, "Peter Lovesey. I know your name."

Top of your blacklist, I thought.

"You've written some stories for the magazine."

I forget my stumbling reply. I waited for him to tell me it was unforgivable to submit a story after it had been rejected once.

The eyes twinkled behind the heavy specs, and he just said, "Keep them coming, won't you?" Then the doors opened and he and Rose stepped out.

I'm certain he knew.

Shortly after I got home from the conference a letter arrived from Ellery Queen accepting "The Bathroom." It was published with a different title.

And I've kept them coming since.

A LETTER FROM AN ARCHANGEL

by H.R.F. Keating

Some time early in the year 1966 *Red Herrings,* the journal of the Crime Writers Association, announced a short story competition run by *Ellery Queen's Mystery Magazine,* confined entirely to CWA members. I remember thinking at the time that it was a generous act indeed for an American magazine to offer money to British writers, although then I had no idea that such generosity was typical of Fred Dannay, *EQMM's* editor-in-chief, and, of course, one half of the legendary mystery author Ellery Queen.

I decided there and then that I would enter. I had never before written a crime short story, indeed only a handful of colourfully romantic schoolboy tales and deeply literary undergraduate ones. I had no idea how to go about a story of detection. All I could think of was to take an idea I had toyed with for a book and squeeze it till it fitted our rather generous—that telltale word again—given allowance of words. That idea was for a mystery set wholly among the twelve-year-old boys at a British boarding school. So I wrote it in that squeezing way, beginning work on it, as I remember, one long evening baby-sitting for a neighbour. I finished it. I sent it off.

Then in April 1966 there came a letter from—I almost said God— but at least from an archangel. It was signed Frederic Dannay "Ellery Queen." And it was long, two handwritten pages. It is too long to quote in full now. But—think of this for a young author, still quite unsure of himself—it began: "I thoroughly enjoyed reading 'Who Killed Cock Robin?' (and so, by the way, did my wife), and I want to compliment you on the honesty and integrity of your story."

I am tempted to ask what crime magazine editor, or what mystery publisher, today would put those two qualities at the top of their list, above sales possibilities or sexual spiciness? Not that Fred did not take into account that *EQMM* had to keep its readers happy. So he went on to say he had some doubts that the "prep school" setting would make difficulties for his readership, and inquiring, a little plaintively, "what exactly is a boot-hole?" (It was in my days a room, rather dark and smelly, lined with compartmented shelves where football boots were exchanged for elastic-sided "indoor shoes").

So he asked if he could withhold final judgment until the closing date for the contest. By that time, as it happened, Christianna Brand had put in her entry, and so "Who Killed Cock Robin?" got simply Second Prize (I am happy to say that when, in 1970, Fred ran another contest limited to British writers I did earn its first prize: Christianna had to be content with a "Special Award").

Fred's letter telling me when the story would appear, re-titled as "The Justice Boy," began "I don't think of you now as H.R.F. Keating. What do your friends and family call you? And surely you should think of me as Fred." Fred's penchant for changing titles became a sort of standing joke among the writers who admired him. But, it is worth noting, that most such changes were made for good editorial reasons. In that first long letter he wrote to me he explained " 'Who Killed Cock Robin?' has a humorous connotation over here, and your story is certainly not humorous in the ordinary sense."

I wrote a good many stories for Fred after that first one. More than one of them he characterised in his introductions as "odd." I don't think anyone other than Fred would have published them in a crime magazine. They were barely mysteries except, to quote, "in the sense that there is a mystery hidden in every human action and reaction." He used those words in presenting a story called "Memorial to Speke" (He added that "perhaps" the title should have been "The Adventure of the Glace-Fruits Coffin"). However, the story justified his decision to publish it, if ever a story did. Years later a kind American wrote to me to say he had had such fond memories of the little tale that, visiting London, he had made a special pilgrimage through Kensington Gardens in the footsteps of the boy carrying that coffin and its parrot corpse.

I recall, too, a different sort of change Fred asked for with another story, one which by today's recklessly liberal standards makes him look a bit of a fuddy-duddy, but which was made with good reason back in 1971. The story was set in the 1930s and for its plot I required the victim to be a man socially unacceptable. So, naturally, with my interest in all things Indian, I made him an Indian. But he had to be the lover of the wife of the finally revealed murderer. A white woman taking as her lover an Indian: potential readers' hands held wide in horror. So to and fro across the Atlantic bargaining went on. We settled at last on a Spaniard. And Fred, generously, led his June 1971 issue with the story.

Only once did I cross the wires-humming Atlantic and meet Fred face to face. And, as is the way of things, I find I can remember almost nothing of the occasion. Not where it was, nor when. One thing only has stayed in my mind. Fred's face looking at me and glowing—the only word—with enthusiasm and above all generosity.

A CHALLENGE TO THE LISTENER:
ELLERY QUEEN ON THE AIR

By David S. Siegel

Fans of Ellery Queen who first discovered the foppish detective in 1929 with the appearance of *The Roman Hat Mystery*, would have to wait at least ten years before they could listen to a far more sophisticated Ellery on the radio. Indeed, at least two film versions of Queen novels (*The Spanish Cape Mystery*, 1935, and *The Mandarin Mystery*, 1936, both released by Republic Pictures) were available to fans prior to Ellery's radio debut on June 18, 1939 with an episode entitled "The Adventure of The Gum-Chewing Millionaire."

Approached by CBS producer George Zachary who was interested in producing an hour long detective series that would invite listeners to match their wits against a master detective, Dannay and Lee served a brief apprenticeship learning the fundamentals of radio by writing scripts for two ongoing crime programs, *Alias Jimmy Valentine* and *The Shadow*, without credit and at minimal pay (their starting salary was $25.00 a week, $10.00 less than what their first short story had sold for six years earlier).

The cousins also wrote and starred in their own program, *Author! Author!"* a combination game/panel/melodrama show that was aired for a short time (4/7/39 to 2/12/40) on the Mutual network. The program featured both Dannay and Lee who introduce themselves as "Mr. Ellery" and "Mr. Queen," and a panel of rotating guests that included prominent figures such as poet Ogden Nash and writer Carl Van Doren. Listening to the single episode of the program that survives (the very first episode), one can admire the wit of the cousins and panelists but also understand why listener's did not find the show as entertaining as *Information Please*, a program it was supposed to rival.

When *Ellery Queen* finally debuted, it was heard on CBS on Sunday evenings from 8:00-9:00 p.m. Initially broadcast on a sustaining basis (i.e., without a sponsor) as a summer replacement for the *Screen Guild Theater*, the series was picked up by Gulf Oil in 1940.

On February 25, 1940 the show switched to a thirty minute format and continued on the air until 9/22/40. After a fifteen month hiatus, the program returned to radio, this time on NBC and sponsored by Bromo-Seltzer. With the exception of the performance of "The Adventure of a Bad Boy" on the hour long Ford Theater program (1/4/48), *Ellery Queen* remained a thirty minute program until its final performance on 5/27/48.

In 1945 the program returned to CBS with Anacin as its sponsor and in June, 1947 the program moved to Hollywood and back to NBC. The final 27 programs of the series were aired on ABC

While Dannay created the weekly plot skeleton, Lee's job was to flesh out the script. This pattern, for which they received $350 a week, was followed until the end of the 1944 season at which time Dannay left the series and Lee continued with Anthony Boucher as his co-author.

The one original radio character who did not appear in the Queen novels until 1943 (*There Was An Old Woman*) was Nikki Porter, Ellery's secretary. Like Margo Lane of *The Shadow* fame or Lorelie Kilbourne of *Big Town* and Lenore Casey of *The Green Hornet*, every radio hero had to have an adoring female to admire him (and, on occasion, to be saved by him). Marion Shockley, who would eventually become Mrs. George Zachary, was the program's first Nikki.

The program's original cast included Hugh Marlowe as Ellery and veteran radio actor Santos Ortega, who would later be heard as Nero Wolfe, as Ellery's father, Inspector Richard Queen. Robert Strauss (of *Stalag 17* fame) played Doc Prouty, the medical examiner and Howard Smith played the rough and sometimes gruff Sergeant Velie. Rounding out the company were Ken Roberts, the announcer and Bernard Herrmann (of Alfred Hitchock fame) as musical director.

Over the nine years the program was broadcast, there were several cast changes: Carlton Young succeeded Marlowe as Ellery to be followed by Sydney Smith, Lawrence Dobkin and finally by Howard Culver. Ortega continued to play Inspector Queen until the show moved to Hollywood when Bill Smith and later Herb Butterfield took that role. The role of Doc Prouty was later taken over by Arthur Allen, and Sergeant Velie was portrayed by radio actors Ted de Corsia, Ed Latimer and Alan Reed. Nikki Porter was played by Helen Lewis, Barbara Terrell, Gertrude Warner, Charlotte Keane, Virginia Gregg and finally by Kaye Brinker (no reflection on Ellery's ability to keep a secretary).

Succeeding announcers were Bert Parks, Ernest Chappell, Don Hancock and Paul Masterson. Succeeding musical directors were Leith Stevens, Lyn Murray, Charles Paul, Chet Kingsbury and Rex Koury. When the program moved to Hollywood, Tom Victor took over as director from George Zachary, to be followed by Bruce Kammon, Phil Cohen, Bill Rousseau, Dick Woolen and Dwight Hauser.

What really made the radio series unique, as well as so popular with listeners, was the Queen technique of halting each program just before Ellery was ready to reveal the name of the criminal in order to give both the audience at home and a guest sleuth (or two) in the studio an opportunity to "match wits" with the Master Detective. In fact, studio executives who were not initially impressed by the program, quickly changed their views when an electrical problem at a Chicago station carrying the program caused the program to go off the air just as the "solution" was about to be revealed. The number of listeners who jammed the station's switchboard was so great that the program not only remained on the air but also garnered its first sponsor.

When, at one point early in the program's run, director-producer Zachary tried to change the format by substituting people from the studio audience for celebrity guests, reaction from the radio audience was swift and clear and the celebrities were quickly brought back. A major factor for the program's success was the fun of hearing the likes of Gypsy Rose Lee, Bill Stern, Frank Buck, Dorothy McGuire, Guy Lombardo, Ed Sullivan, Jack Dempsey, Eva Gabor, Sally Rand, Celeste Holm, Milton Cross, Red Barber, Milton Berle, Gloria Swanson and a host of others (who were paid $25.00-$50.00 for their appearance) guessing and coming up with the same wrong answers as the audience at home did. Indeed, if one were to list all of the famous personalities of the entertainment, literary and sports world who appeared as guest armchair detectives during the run of this program you would see a Who's Who of Great Names.

Considering all the network changes and the time of day and day of the week changes, it is remarkable that the program remained on the air for more than 600 weekly broadcasts over a nine year period. What is truly sad is that (to the best of my knowledge) only 14 episodes of the series exist on audio recording (at this time) in addition to a single Australian version and the Ford Theater program. None of the 35 full hour episodes survive.

Also surviving are 76 of the hundreds of 60 second *Ellery Queen's Minute Mysteries* that were produced many years later. Although bearing the Queen name, the fillers were not written by Dannay and Lee, and the cousins' only involvement with the episodes was the royalty checks they received for the use of the name.

Over the years, some of the radio scripts were rewritten as short stories and appeared in various Queen collections such as *Calendar Of Crime*. Other stories were abridged and published in fan magazines of the day such as *Radio and Television Mirror* to help publicize the radio program. In a few cases, scripts appeared in *Ellery Queen's Mystery Magazine*.

Note: For additional information your attention is directed to:

John Dunning, *On The Air: The Encyclopedia of Old Time Radio* (Oxford U. Press, 1998)

Francis M. Nevins, Jr., *Royal Bloodline: Ellery Queen Author and Detective* (Bowling Green University Popular Press, 1974)

Francis M. Nevins, Jr. & Ray Stanich, *The Sound of Detection: Ellery Queen's Adventures in Radio* (Brownstone Books, 1983)

Chris Steinbrunner, various articles

CHALLENGE TO THE ARTIST:
THE COMIC BOOK STORIES OF ELLERY QUEEN

by Mike W. Barr

The third decade of this century saw the immense popularization of a genre of fiction: the intellectual detective story, the "whodunit," and the advent of arguably its finest practitioner, Ellery Queen, author and sleuth. The fourth decade saw the immense popularization of a medium, the comic book. Just as Manfred B. Lee and Frederic Dannay took their creation to the new medium of radio, so did they introduce their character to comic books, with mixed—but always intriguing—results.

At first glance, the subject and the medium would seem a perfect fit. While narrative fiction forces the detective story writer to describe every clue in prose, and thus risk either telegraphing the punch or not providing the reader with enough information, comic books are told through a mix of prose and pictures. Thus a clue the author wishes to reveal but not draw the reader's attention to can be included as a visual detail, leaving the reader—and his acuity—to fend for themselves. To fully exploit the visual medium of comic books requires the knack of combining words and pictures, realizing that both are necessary to fully serve the most important element—the story. For these reasons, an Ellery Queen comic strip would seem like a natural, but there has never been one.

While the number of comic book stories containing the character of Ellery Queen is fairly easy to determine—the existence of an Ellery Queen comic book series yet to be uncovered seems unlikely—who is responsible for them is not. The famous article on Ellery Queen in the November 22, 1943 issue of *Life*, "Ellery Queen: Crime Made Him Famous and His Authors Rich" by John Bainbridge, says Lee and Dannay have "provided the material for a series of Ellery Queen comic books." This could mean either that Lee and Dannay were simply overseeing the comic book version of their creation, or going so far as to commission artwork from many of the commercial studios existing in the 1940s, and supply scripts themselves, as they did with the *Adventures of Ellery Queen* radio show.

Ellery Queen made his comic book debut in 1940.   Perhaps appearing first was a ten-part adaptation of the E.Q. radio play, "The Adventure of the Secret Partner" (which had aired on August 27, 1939), in the *Gulf Funny Weekly* from #366 (April 26, 1940) to #375 (June 28, 1940), a comic book distributed free by Gulf gas stations to its customers.   In this serial, clues are obligingly pointed out to the reader by a star in the corner of the panel containing the clue.   According to Francis M. Nevins, Jr. and Ray Stanich in *The Sound of Detection: Ellery Queen's Adventures in Radio*. Gulf Oil assumed sponsorship of the radio show in late April of 1940, by which time the comic adaptation of "Secret Partner"—not one of Queen's best radio plays, to judge by the adaptation—was just appearing in print, but had to have begun being produced weeks earlier; perhaps some canny executive figured the most mileage for their advertising buck could be had by sponsoring the E.Q. radio show, as well, or perhaps Lee and Dannay, always the canny businessmen, pushed for E.Q.'s appearance in the *Weekly* to give them a foothold in the exciting new medium of comics.

At about the same time, or a little later, a series of E.Q. stories, running under the blanket name "The Adventures of Ellery Queen" (perhaps as a tie-in with the Queen radio show, though the comics made no mention of the show), began running in *Crackajack Funnies* published by the Whitman Publishing Company. *Crackajack* was a typical anthology comic of its time, each 64-page issue trying to be all things to all readers with original features and strip reprints of many different themes. Big-time syndicated strips like "Red Ryder" and "Wash Tubbs" slummed with originals like "The Crusoes," "Gabby Scoops" and "The Owl," a masked detective/adventurer who was the closest thing *Crackajack* had to a super-hero. An occasional "Tarzan" text feature, credited to Edgar Rice Burroughs, also appeared. The *Overstreet Comic Book Price Guide* credits the E.Q. feature with beginning in issue #23, the May 1940 issue, calling it the character's "first comic book appearance," which, depending on how far ahead of the cover date the issue was distributed, could be true, or it could either tie or come in a close second to Ellery's first appearance in the *Gulf Funny Weekly* of April 26,1940. Eleven of the twenty E.Q. *Crackajack* stories appear to be newly written for that comic (with widely-varying quality), and there were nine adaptations of Queen

Crackajack Funnies, July 1940, copyright 1940 by Ellery Queen

prose or radio work, or uses of clues extracted from stories in a method that today would be called "sampling." The very first episode, "The Adventure of the Coffin Clue," was taken from the Queen short story "The Adventure of the Invisible Lover." The second installment, in *Crackajack* #24, "The Adventure of the Blood Red Stamp," is a fairly faithful version of Queen's first short story, "The Adventure of the Penny Black," though through the alchemy of adaptation a story which contained no murders now has no less than three, as well as a rooftop climax in which Ellery shoots it out with the killer. (Intones Sergeant Velie, "No crook has a chance against Ellery Queen!") The entry in *Crackajack* #25 is a good adaptation of the short story "The Adventure of the Hanging Acrobat," while the E.Q. exploit in #26 is an adaptation of the short story "The Adventure of the Three Lame Men." The original versions of these stories can be found in *The Adventures of Ellery Queen* (1934), E.Q.'s first short story collection. #33, a story whose background is motorboat racing, utilizes the murder method from another sports story, "Man Bites Dog" from *The New Adventures of Ellery Queen* (1940). #34's investigation into the murder of an art collector transplants the titular clue from Queen's second novel, 1930's *The French Powder Mystery*. To my knowledge, #36's "Adventure of the Twin Eye-Glasses" has no prose or broadcast precedent, but contains the first comics use of a subgenre Queen virtually patented, the dying message. #37 uses one of the clues from "The Adventure of the Teakwood Case" from *Adventures*, while #42, the final installment of the series, saved the best for last: an adaptation, faithful to the structure of one of the better Queen radio plays, "The Adventure of the Dying Scarecrow" or "The Adventure of the Scarecrow Men,"broadcast 1/7/40 under the title "The Adventure of the Snowman Who Bled." (If this rings a bell, the script was rewritten into the half-hour format and broadcast on 1/20/44 as "The Adventure of the Scarecrow and the Snowman, which is available on tape. The script itself was printed in pamphlet form by Crippen & Landru as a tribute to Ellery Queen as Ghost of Honor at the 1998 Malice Domestic mystery convention.)

The *Crackajack* and *Gulf* stories are the only Ellery Queen comic book stories to draw plot material from the prose and radio canons. These stories are generally faithful to the structure of their prose roots, though there are occasional action sequences added which contribute little to the quality of the tales. Inspector Queen and Sergeant Velie are generally present in the *Crackajack* stories, with Ellery's "pert secretary," Nikki Porter, appearing in #s 36, 40 and 42. All three appear in the *Weekly* adaptation. Few clues exist as to who the writer(s) and artist(s) were for these two series, though certain similarities in the art indicate the same artist may have drawn both series for the *Weekly* and *Crackajack*, and both series present Queen's trademark "Challenge to the Reader" before the solution is revealed. Some of the stories fail to utilize the full potential of the comics medium; sometimes the art is too vague to enable the reader to fully perceive the visual clues, sometimes actions obviously occurring in a drawn panel are described in redundant prose ("Suddenly, a sandbag falls on Tex. Ellery yells . . ."), but this is an error comic book writers make to this day. One of the *Crackajack* artists, according to Ron Goulart ("The Comic Book Adventures of Ellery Queen" in *The Armchair Detective*, 12: 3, Summer 1979) was long-time comic book pro Will Ely, later a successful gallery painter. Ely told Goulart that his editor, Oscar Lebeck, may have scripted some of the stories. Frederic Dannay told Goulart that the deal had been set up by their literary agent, and that the scripts were by neither him nor Lee, though they did have the right to approve all scripts and art. *Crackajack Funnies* itself survived the series by only one more issue before the magazine folded with #43, the January 1942 issue. It was seven years before Ellery Queen returned to comics in an authorized capacity.

I say "authorized" because Queen, who was also popular with the comic book writers of the day, supplied—albeit without credit, let alone payment—plots to at least two of comicdom's most beloved crime-fighters, both in the year 1943.

Chronologically, *Batman* #18 (August-September 1943, reprinted in *Detective Comics* #443, October-November 1974) is dated later, but was probably published at about the same time, due to the by then prevalent custom of predating comic books, to give them as much shelf time as possible. The first story in that issue, "The Secret of Hunter's Inn!" (scripter unknown, art by Jerry Robinson), is the second encounter of Batman and Robin with the criminal team of "Tweedledurn and Tweedledee," twin brothers patterned after the characters of the same name from *Alice In Wonderland*. (Queen himself would also play variations on the motif of *Wonderland* several times, of course; its use here adds a Queenian resonance to even a plagiarized story. One cannot help but wonder if the scripter knew this, and added the *Alice* theme deliberately, feeling its inclusion somehow mitigated the sting of theft.) The central gimmick of the story—an actual, solid country inn that keeps disappearing—is lifted from "The Lamp of God," Queen's first short novel, from *The New Adventures of Ellery Queen*. The *Batman* version even goes so far as to duplicate not only the crime's solution, but the major clues supplied to solve it, though the motivation for the disappearance—so police cannot be led back to the scene of the crime after its guests are robbed—is different.

The second instance of Queen's pocket being picked by the comics appeared on July 18, 1943, in *The Spirit* comic section #164. *The Spirit*, created by Will Eisner, one of the most respected comics writers and artists in the history of the medium and still active today, established the feature in 1940 as a weekly Sunday newspaper section in the form of a comic book (much the same format as the *Gulf Funny Weekly*), telling the adventures of a masked crime-fighter in some of the most visually striking and best-written comics stories ever. The story in question, in which The Spirit deduces how a man can be accurately shot to death in total darkness, is a virtual scene-by-scene swipe of Queen's short story, "The Adventure of the House of Darkness," also from *New Adventures*. The scene of the crime in the *Spirit* story is even called "The House of Darkness." However, though the *Spirit* story is signed by Eisner, that week's installment is, to the trained eye, obviously the work of the Eisner studio, toiling to keep the feature alive while Eisner was serving in the Army during World War II, ignorant of the thievery perpetrated under his good name. (This script has been attributed to either Manly Wade Wellman or Bill Woolfolk, with pencils by artist Lou Fine. Given that Wellman would become a contributor to *Ellery Queen's Mystery Magazine*, circumstantial evidence seems to point to him, though one must keep in mind the musings of both Thoreau and Doyle on that subject.) Given the number of crime-related comics published in that era, and the fact that comics were for decades considered a "disposable medium," these two stories may be only the tip of a sizable iceberg.

Paradoxically, these plagiarized stories were better examples of how successfully Queen could translate to the graphic story medium than almost anything in the next two authorized series of Ellery Queen comics.

The Superior Comics *Ellery Queen* was published bimonthly for four issues from May to November of 1949. At least some of the covers and interior art were by long-time comics pros Jack Kamen (one of the con-

Ellery and the Inspector, *Ellery Queen* #3, September 1949, copyright 1949 by Ellery Queen

tributors to the famed E.C. line of horror comics such as *Tales From the Crypt*, which thrilled kids and gave parents fits) and Matt Baker. The *Guide* says LB. Cole also contributed to issue #1, and "Iger shop art" appeared in all issues. Though the stories, with names like "The Challenging Case of Faith, Hope and a Charlatan!" and "Rest(less) In Peace!", occasionally contain some clever gimmicks, and present the "Challenge To the Reader" before the solution is revealed, they are usually far from faithful to the mood of the E.Q. prose stories, and are to be collected only by completists. Issue #3, however, contains a rose amongst the weeds, a clever impossible crime story, "The Turbulent Tomb!" in which Ellery deduces how an isolated lighthouse keeper was killed in the middle of a raging storm.

E.Q.'s next four-color foray was for only two issues, Spring and Summer of 1952, from Ziff-Davis, the latter half of whom would later become publisher of *EQMM*. On both of the painted covers, by artist Norman Saunders, E.Q. is springing to the defense of mistreated females, with #2, according to Overstreet, qualifying as a genuine "bondage and torture" cover as E.Q. charges a brutish ne'er-do-well about to apply a heated poker to a lissome blonde.

The interiors were equally true to the spirit of "the logical successor to Sherlock Holmes." The art on such stories as "The Corpse That Killed" and "The Chain-Letter Murders" is a little dull when it comes to storytelling—the method by which the artist composes a comic book page to tell the story and convey information—but the drawing is better than that in the Superior comics. Two artists drew the four stories that made up the series, one of them signing himself "R. Kay." However, some of the Ziff-Davis stories break format in that they are not whodunits, as were all the prose E.Q. stories, but simply action-crime adventures, of the type blanketing the networks several times a week. The *Guide* indicates the series is a TV tie-in to the *Adventures of Ellery Queen* television show, starring Lee Bowman as Ellery, telecast on the ABC network in 1952; if true, it seems odd that Ziff-Davis did not do more to ride the TV show's coattails. The character of Ellery is not drawn to resemble the mustachioed Bowman, which may have more to do with lack of likeness rights than artistic intent.

The most successful series of Ellery Queen comics to date—if by "successful" one means faithful to the spirit of the source material—comes from the Dell *Four Color* series in issues 1165, 1243 and 1289, published in 1960 and 1961. The issues sport good but unremarkable painted covers. Each 32-page issue contains two 16-page stories, with the exception of #1243, which contains two 15-page stories and one 2-pager. Art on all stories was by the late Mike Sekowsky, best-remembered for his yeoman service on many hundreds of pages of *Justice League of America* for DC Comics in the Sixties. The scripts are a little stiff, but quite good for their time, utilizing the "Challenge" and containing a decided ghostbusting slant, as typified by such titles as: "The Mummy's Curse" and "The Witch's Victim." #1289 doubled up on the pseudo-supernatural theme, with "The Voodoo Victim" and "The Curse of Kane."

Sekowsky's storytelling was generally good, with his splendid use of blacks spicing up the page, guiding the eye and providing visual contrast. His E.Q. differs from all others in that he wears glasses, something the E.Q. of prose never did (though he did affect a pince-nez in the early days of his career).

In all of the above-mentioned series, Ellery is depicted as a handsome young man somewhere in his thirties. The Superior and Ziff-Davis series have E.Q.'s hair combed back from his forehead (as in the books), while in the *Crackajack*, *Gulf*, and Dell series E.Q.'s hair is parted on the side. In all the comics series he is accompanied by his long-suffering father, Inspector Richard Queen of Homicide, and Sergeant Thomas Velie who properly refers to E.Q. as "Maestro." Nikki Porter, who was created for the radio show as Ellery's secretary and on-again off-again love interest, was present in the *Crackajack*, *Gulf* and Superior series, but was missing from all others.

Credits in this article have dealt mainly with the artists of the stories, since art, by its nature, is more easily traced to its source by visual cues, while writers are identified by nuances of language or plot. Some interesting speculation is possible, however. As noted above, though Lee and Dannay probably did not supply scripts for the *Crackajack* stories, it may be that they edited or rewrote scripts to make sure their most valuable asset stayed in character. The Queen cousins probably (hopefully) had little to do with the lackluster Superior and Ziff-Davis series. The Dell series, however, may be another matter. Structure and pacing of the scripts are very much like those of the Queen prose canon, though this could be due to either contractual obligations and/or the overseeing eyes of Lee and Dannay, who may have wanted to make sure their creation was

. . . and soon has Ellery wondering if the
ancient curse on the Pharaoh's tomb might
have marked him for death!

Ellery Queen #1165, March-May 1961, copyright 1961 by Ellery Queen

The Maze Agency #9, February 1990, character depictions copyright 1989
by Ellery Queen, story copyright 1989 by Mike W. Barr

better served by the comics medium this time around. But at least one of
the Dell stories, "The Mummy's Curse," from #1165, uses the gimmick
of taking the first three letters of the alphabet as the suspects' initials
(Arnold, Burton and Coombs) to easily distinguish them. This mnemonic
device was used by Queen himself in some of his short stories for exactly
the same reason; its presence here may indicate that Lee and Dannay (or
just Dannay) had a hand in at least plotting the stories—or simply that the
scripts were from the typewriter of a Queen fan.

Ellery Queen would not appear in comics again for another twenty-
eight years, but the comic book industry—depicted none too accurately
—provided the background for an episode of the 1975 NBC *Ellery Queen*
series, starring Jim Hutton and David Wayne. "The Adventure of the
Comic Book Crusader," telecast October 2, 1975, with script by Robert
Van Scoyk, casts Ellery himself as a suspect in the murder of an unscrupulous comic book publisher who was proceeding with plans for a
series of unauthorized E.Q. comics, depicting Ellery as a broad-
shouldered, hard-swinging crime-fighter along the lines of Mike
Hammer. This is a far cry from the Ellery of Lee and Dannay, but not
a bad match with his comic book dopplegangers, who were sharp-
shooters, acrobats, expert skiers, scuba divers, or the master of whatever
skill was needed to make the story work.

Ellery Queen's most recent comics appearance was in *The Maze
Agency* #9, February 1990, from Innovation Publishing, in a story
pencilled by Adam Hughes, inked by Rick Magyar, and written by
myself. (In comics a "penciller" generally pencils in the story panels,
indicating figures, backgrounds and shading, while the "inker" is the
artist who goes over the penciller's work in India ink, aiding reproduction
and adding his own interpretation to the penciller's work.) A
professional comics scripter for some years, primarily of super-heroes, in
1988 I scratched a persistent "itch" with the creation of *The Maze Agency*,
a series of fair-play mysteries featuring private detective Jennifer Mays
and true-crime writer Gabriel Webb, who mix romance and ratiocination
in the manner of The Thin Man, Mr. & Mrs. North and Remington
Steele. I drafted my creations into service when wondering what I could
do to celebrate the sixtieth anniversary of E.Q.'s creation (though dated
1990, the issue was on sale in 1989). I had imagined E.Q. meeting
Jennifer and Gabe, first as nothing more than pleasant speculation, then
I realized my dream might be well within my grasp. If so, it would be

nothing more than a continuation of a tradition begun by the Queen cousins themselves. Lee and Dannay had been avid Sherlock Holmes fans in their formative years, and a later E.Q. novel, *A Study in Terror*, not only novelizes the 1965 Sherlock Holmes film of the same name, but includes a plotline in which Ellery Queen is able to match wits with the immortal sleuth of Baker Street. It was in that spirit of acknowledging influences, of attempting to repay an unrepayable debt, that I decided to obtain the rights to guest-star Ellery Queen in an issue of *The Maze Agency*. (Besides, having Jennifer Mays and Gabriel Webb meet E.Q. would be the next best thing to meeting him myself.)

It wasn't long before I had conceived the plot for what I called "The English Channeller Mystery." (E.Q. fans will note the title follows the pattern of the first nine Queen novels.) Since the E.Q. stories generally remained contemporary, it seemed fitting that Ellery, Jennifer and Gabe investigate a bizarre series of attempts on the life of an Englishwoman who claims to "channel" the spirit of a citizen of Atlantis who has been dead for ten thousand years. Eventually, this same spirit seems responsible for a murder. Can a man, dead ten thousand years, commit murder? Gabe and E.Q. can't accept that, but any other solution to the crime is impossible. As befitting the first new E.Q. story to be published in fourteen years (following the short story "The Reindeer Clue" in 1975, which was actually written by Edward D. Hoch), there is a false solution, a manipulative murderer, and a final scene that will not be unfamiliar to E.Q. devotees.

Having been an Ellery Queen fan over two decades by that time, it was both exhilarating and nervewracking to take the responsibility of writing a character I hold in such high esteem. I soon discovered Ellery, when kept in character, wouldn't perform just any trick like a trained dog; he would do only what was proper for his well-defined personality. The late CBS News correspondent Harry Reasoner once said that his meeting with Edward R. Murrow was like a parish priest meeting the Pope. Now I know how he felt. I can only hope that Mr. Lee and Mr. Dannay would have approved.

Fan mail was favorable to Ellery Queen's inclusion in *Maze #9*, with some fans writing that they began reading Ellery Queen as a result. This is the most gratifying result I could have asked for; hopefully future generations of Queen fans can look forward to more comic book appearances by Lee and Dannay's brainchild in the character's next seventy years.

ELLERY QUEEN: ONE OF THE MOST POPULAR MYSTERY WRITERS IN JAPAN

by Hidetoshi Mori

In Japan, Ellery Queen remains one of the most popular American mystery writers of any period. Ellery Queen (the author) is much more popular than Rex Stout, and also Ellery Queen (the detective, which we usually call "Ellery") is one of the best known, maybe only next to Sherlock Holmes or Hercule Poirot.

Let me show you some evidence of his popularity here. In the July 1999 issue of *EQ* (*Ellery Queen's Mystery Magazine*, Japanese edition), mystery writers, critics and readers chose the one-hundred best mysteries of all period. What do you think the best ten titles are? They are:

1. *The Adventures of Sherlock Holmes* (Sir Arthur Conan Doyle)
2. *The Tragedy of Y* (Ellery Queen, first published as Barnaby Ross)
3. *And Then There Were None* (Agatha Christie)
4. *The Innocence of Father Brown* (G. K. Chesterton)
5. *Phantom Lady* (William Irish)
6. *The Burning Court* (John Dickson Carr)
7. *The Long Goodbye* (Raymond Chandler)
8. *The Murder of Roger Ackroyd* (Agatha Christie)
9. *The Tragedy of X* (Ellery Queen, first published as Barnaby Ross)
9. *The Nine Tailors* (Dorothy L. Sayers)

In the best thirty mystery novels, three more Queen titles were chosen by Japanese readers: *The Egyptian Cross Mystery* (11th place), *The Greek Coffin Mystery* (15th) and *Calamity Town* (22nd). *Cat of Many Tails* which some American critics think his best work, was only in 40th place among Japanese fans.

You would be surprised to know that the Drury Lane series is still so popular in Japan, but *The Tragedy of Y* has always been regarded as a classic and one of the best whodunits from the Golden Age. People also prefer early Ellery Queen titles which have names of countries in their titles (*Roman*, *French*, *Dutch*, etc.) to his middle period masterpieces.

Before explaining the reason of this popularity, I need to tell you about the situation of the Japanese mystery scene. It is much different compared with other countries. From the 1960's to the early 80's, the Japanese public (mainly office workers) preferred realistic mysteries— mysteries in which there were no great detectives (sometimes no detections), and the crimes were realistic and emphasized some social issues. But the younger generation who were students at that time didn't read these realistic mysteries very much, as they were written by veteran writers and written mainly for office workers. Instead of reading realistic novels, the younger generation (including me) read Golden Age classics written by Agatha Christie, Freeman Wills Crofts, John Dickson Carr, S. S. Van Dine, and of course, Ellery Queen. In other words, our generation (which is now in early 40's or middle 30's) has grown up with these maestros. (Maybe some of you think differently about Van Dine, and I quite agree with you at the moment. But I enjoyed his books in my school days.)

This interest in Golden Age writers produced, in the late 1980's and early 1990's what we call *Sin-Honkaku* school (which means "New Who-dunit Writers"). The "whodunit" in this sense is, of course not equivalent to "cozy mysteries." It is similar to Golden Age classics—the great detectives arrive at the scene and solve some intricate puzzles like locked room mysteries or unbreakable alibis by using logical deductions. In other words, *Sin-Honkaku* writers came from the younger generations who used to be readers of Golden Age mysteries. They made their debuts when they were in middle 20's or early 30's and their age was not very far from the college students who became enthusiastic readers of these *Sin-Honkaku* writers. As these writers enjoyed Golden Age mysteries in their school or college days, especially written by Ellery Queen or John Dickson Carr, they attempted to write classic puzzlers with modern settings. So their stories contain intricate and clever puzzles, locked rooms and other impossible crimes, logical deductions, and sometimes even the "Challenge to the Reader."

And as these writers also write essays, articles and reviews and sometimes talk in front of their fans, they've often written or talked about Ellery Queen and John Dickson Carr; even sometimes, they've said that their literary idols are these writers. So the fans who had never heard of Ellery Queen or John Dickson Carr became interested in them, and read their masterpieces. What happened next? Yes, they discovered how wonderful these Golden Age maestros are! So, that is the main reason that Ellery Queen became popular once again. And as a Golden Age mystery and whodunit lover, I hope this situation will continue forever.

QUEEN'S GAMBIT:
THE LIFE AND TIMES OF ELLERY QUEEN

By Ted Hertel, Jr.

THE WORLD TRAVELER

In 1928 in an effort to claim a $7,500.00 first prize offered by *McClure's Magazine*, first cousins Frederic Dannay and Manfred B. Lee created author and detective, Ellery Queen, whom Lee later described as "the biggest prig to ever come down the pike." The premier author of detective fiction at that time was Willard Huntington Wright, who wrote the Philo Vance novels using the pseudonym S.S. Van Dine. Wright had revived the detective story in the United States, paving the way for what Howard Haycraft referred to as "the Golden Age."

Dannay and Lee patterned their protagonist on Vance and their contest novel on the books of Wright. Queen, the character, was a snobbish "thinking machine," almost without feeling or human emotions, spouting classical quotations. His affectations included carrying a walking stick and wearing pince-nez. Perhaps Dannay and Lee's most ingenious idea was naming the "author" of their collaboration Ellery Queen, as well as giving that same name to the principal character in the book in order to further solidify his name in the mind of the reader. But they carried the concept even further. In addition to being a sleuth Queen, the character, was also the author of a series of novels about Queen, the detective.

It took the authors only three months to complete the contest novel, *The Roman Hat Mystery*, an intricately plotted story of the murder of an attorney in a theater during the performance of a play. Although the cousins won the contest, *McClure's* went bankrupt and the prize money was given to a different author by the magazine's successor. However, their book was published by Stokes in spite of that apparent setback. This first book set the stage for the next eight mysteries in the series, as well. Like the Vance books on which they were patterned, these books also followed a set (but different) title format: *The* [Nationality] [Noun] *Mystery*. In fact for a time there was even speculation that Queen, the author, was actually Van Dine.

Without question these early stories were some of the finest examples of Golden Age mystery writing. The puzzles in this period were always presented in a "fair play" fashion, a significant departure from Van Dine's stories. They contained a "Challenge to the Reader," in which the authors literally halted the progress of the story, usually after a last piece of the puzzle was revealed. At that point, the reader was informed that all the clues were in place and, if the reader had paid attention, he or she should now be able to arrive at the mystery's solution along with the detective.

Rarely did this happen, of course, and this was one of the things that made these early tales so compelling. Only after Ellery explained things so clearly, usually over the course of the many pages of the solution, did the bizarre clues, the cryptic comments, and the seemingly innocuous, if unusual, incidents all fall into place, to the total surprise of the reader, who, "fair play" or not, generally had no idea what was actually going on during the course of the story.

The cousins wrote the second Queen novel, *The French Powder Mystery*, in 1930 and a third, *The Dutch Shoe Mystery*, in 1931. The stories proved so successful that they finally began to write full time, creating, plotting, outlining, and writing a new mystery in three months' time. These books reflected a strong sense of the 1930s. Further, they often used unusual settings that were as important and vital as any character in the story. A department store (and its display window) in *The French Powder*, a hospital (and its operating room) in *The Dutch Shoe Mystery*, a church graveyard (with a coffin containing two dead bodies) in *The Greek Coffin Mystery*, a grim West Virginia intersection and other locales (with their bloody, headless, crucified bodies nailed to crosses) in *The Egyptian Cross Mystery*, the rodeo (and its 20,000 witnesses to murder) of *The American Gun Mystery*, the mountain (with the raging forest fire that traps Ellery and his father) in *The Siamese Twin Mystery*, the New York hotel room (with everything backwards or reversed, including the clothing on a murder victim) in *The Chinese Orange Mystery*, and, finally, the lonely ocean peninsula (and the victim, naked except for hat and cape) in *The Spanish Cape Mystery*.

The other tale which should be mentioned in this period is the brilliant 1935 short novel "The Lamp of God," later collected in *The New Adventures of Ellery Queen*. Short though it may be, this story presented the agnostic Ellery with religious considerations that would play central roles in later works. According to Dannay's son, Richard, his father "was interested in religion, but was not religious." The same could be said of his and Lee's creation. Religion, however, was but one of several major social themes that would appear within the context of Queen's later mystery novels.

The mysteries in this period were often marked by one or more false solutions to the crime, either by Ellery or another, before Queen himself finally put all the clues together correctly. Even so, the incorrect resolutions were often convincing, solutions that could have been arrived at by even the casual reader. Such deductions came from the authors' clever misdirection, giving the reader a momentary sense of satisfaction with his or her own deductive abilities. However, inevitably, some not so obvious clue was discovered and added to the puzzle, requiring the entire solution to be re-examined. As usual Dannay and Lee were many steps ahead of the readers.

Another hallmark of the Queen series was the "dying clue," something which real life murder victims are seldom thoughtful enough to leave. Queen introduced this concept in 1933's *The Siamese Twin Mystery*. The owner of the house on the burning mountain is found shot in his study, clutching the torn half of a playing card in his hand. The dying clue played a large part in several Queen short stories of this early period, as well. For example, in "The Adventure of the Bearded Lady," the victim paints a beard on a woman's portrait before dying. In "The Adventure of the Glass-Domed Clock," an even more elaborate and time consuming clue is left in a murdered man's last minutes of life. These two short stories were reprinted in *The Adventures of Ellery Queen*. However, while introduced in these early stories, the dying clue all but vanished from Queen's works until the 1950s and 1960s, when it reappeared in full force.

These complex, deductive exercises were among the finest of all the Golden Age mystery stories. But the cousins' best work was yet to come. Unfortunately, before this would happen, Dannay and Lee made a side trip to California.

MR. QUEEN GOES TO HOLLYWOOD

Near the end of Queen's Golden Age period, Wright's influence on the mystery field and the cousins had waned. Wright, and his creation Philo Vance, were replaced in popularity by Hollywood and the so-called women's slick magazines. While some of Queen's early work was published in the slicks, it wasn't until after *The Spanish Cape Mystery* that its influence really took hold of the writing. The stories from 1936 to 1939 were marked with a reduction in the size of the cast of characters, a loss of the pure detective puzzle, and the decline of the fair play aspects of the novel, along with the elimination of the "Challenge to the Reader."

However, this era also laid the groundwork for Ellery's humanization. The stories grew lighter in tone as Ellery took himself less seriously. He began to interact on a more personal level with others besides his father. Meanwhile, those others also tended to act with emotion rather than as mere players on a chess board. In an apparent attempt to appeal to the "lowest common denominator" of the slicks, human interest stories were mixed in with the mysteries. This greatly diluted the puzzle aspect of the series.

The first book of the slicks period is *Halfway House*. The name change appropriately enough marks the shift. This was the final title to contain the Queen "Challenge." But the real change comes with the alteration of style. The puzzle is simpler, though well conceived. However, much of the book is devoted to the trial of the suspected murderess. Perhaps because of its closeness in time to the writing of the books of the Golden Age period, it remains one of the best stories of this time frame.

However, the same cannot be said for the next book in the series, *The Door Between*. The effects of the slick magazines were seen everywhere in this tragic tale of relationships and love triangles. Even Ellery's brilliant solution (in fact, two solutions) failed to save the story, mainly because it was almost pure guesswork rather than deduction, a fatality that had also harmed *The Siamese Twin Mystery*.

At this point in their career the authors shifted the focus of the books from the slicks to Hollywood. While still written with those women's magazine sales in mind, the next two books in the series were humorously savage attacks on Hollywood, movies and the exact place of screenwriters in the movie capital: namely, the bottom rung of the

ladder. *The Devil to Pay* and *The Four of Hearts* were based upon Dannay
and Lee's personal experiences writing for three different studios in
Hollywoodland. However, they never received any screen credit for their
efforts there and the books that grew out of that experience, especially
The Devil to Pay, were weak on characterization, plot and solution. The
books are fun to read with their look at Hollywood in the 1930s—and
the reader's realization that things there have not changed all that much.
But as mysteries, they simply are not up to Queenian standards.

The final book influenced by the slicks and most clearly by hopes of
a sale to Hollywood is *The Dragon's Teeth*, arguably the worst book of this
period. Although the setting returns to New York, nothing else has
really changed. The plot is weak and the solution, even once throughly
read, is short on both logic and the appropriate planting of clues
throughout. The emphasis for much of the book is on humor rather than
mystery. So while it is like some other books of this time, amusing to
read, it is very short on satisfaction of any other sort. It is filled with
legal errors that the cousins, having written as many mysteries as they
had, should have known to avoid. It is, quite simply, one of the weakest
entries in the entire Queen series.

Overall, the books of the Hollywood period, lack solid characterization, and are long on love and short on puzzle. As entertainment,
they are acceptable. As mysteries, however, they are, for the most part,
sorely lacking in the important aspects. As for Dannay and Lee, this
period was clearly their least successful. Had this been the end of their
contribution to the mystery field, they would probably be little
remembered today, even with their glittering Golden Age stories.

THE RISE OF SOCIAL CONSCIOUSNESS

Three years passed without a new Queen novel. When *Calamity Town*
arrived in 1942, it signaled the beginning of the greatest period of the
Queen canon. Ellery, himself already more humanized, had by this time
divested himself of his foppish affectations, as well. However, for the
most part, the lighter tone of the slicks period vanished, replaced by a
darker view of the world. No longer looking for sales to the slicks or to
Hollywood, the cousins had honed their writing skills to a fine point,
adding believable characterization to once again cleverly plotted
mysteries.

By the time of this novel police methods were becoming more sophisticated. The cousins had to find ways to remove Ellery from the ability of the police to rely on the scientific approach to crime solving, which would have enabled the authorities to solve the crime without benefit of Ellery's intellectual reasoning. So Dannay and Lee created Wrightsville, a small town in New England, where Ellery initially went to write books in solitude. But all was far from peaceful in small town America. Jealousy, envy, and hatred bubbled just beneath the surface, eventually resulting in tragedy, despair, and death, with perhaps just a glimmer of hope.

Queen had used isolated settings before, most notably on the burning mountain of *The Siamese Twin Mystery*; the lonely peninsula of *The Spanish Cape Mystery*; the little town of Corsica, New York, in "The Adventure of the Invisible Lover"; and the remote New England inn of "The Adventure of the Two-Headed Dog." The latter two stories were reprinted in *The Adventures of Ellery Queen*. Later novels, in particular *The King Is Dead*, with its private island location, would also use this ploy to separate Ellery from modern police methods, allowing him to make his reasoned intellectual deductions without that sort of "interference." However, with the creation of Wrightsville, the cousins had discovered the perfect locale for returning Ellery, time and again, to a different era of police science.

After a detour to the absurdist world of Mother Goose in *There Was an Old Woman*, an interesting but extremely bizarre blending of murder and nursery rhyme, Ellery once again returned to the town of Wrightsville. In *The Murderer Is a Fox* Ellery must investigate a twelve year old murder in order to prevent another one. This doubly hinders him in attempting a solution, since not only are the police un-sophisticated, but also memories have faded. While there is initially an incomplete solution, the final resolution is once again based on informed guesswork rather than a true analytical solution to the puzzle. In that regard only, it is as much a failure as *The Door Between* and *The Siamese Twin Mystery*.

Expanding on the religious themes first introduced in "The Lamp of God," *Ten Days' Wonder* is also set in the small town milieu of Wrightsville. The main cast is notably smaller than in prior novels, but this allowed the cousins to provide rich characterization for this examination of a family on the verge of destruction. The story is filled with religious imagery and symbolism, a true masterpiece of the mystery genre, indeed of literature, complete with psychological, philosophical and theological insight rarely attempted in the field. It is perhaps Queen's most complex, and most accomplished work, setting Dannay and Lee above most other mystery fiction authors.

At this point in the series Ellery has been to Wrightsville three times and generally has met with less than total success. He holds himself responsible for death in *Ten Days' Wonder*, as well as the unsatisfactory manner in which the case was resolved. Each of these three explorations of small town life puts a different family to the test. The problems that lie at the heart of those close relationships are central to the despondency which overtakes Ellery. He returns to New York, vowing never again to involve himself in such affairs.

But in *Cat of Many Tails* Ellery confronts murder on a scale seldom before witnessed by him. Seemingly unconnected victims throughout the city are strangled. In spite of his vow, Ellery returns to the hunt, only to once again fail to keep others from dying before the threads are untangled. This time, though, through conversation with a psychiatrist, Ellery is better able to understand the nature of mankind and its relation to tragedy, commitment, and hope. He learns that defeat is always possible, but that only through involvement in the world can he truly achieve success and rightfully take his place in it. Dannay has expressed that, for personal reasons, this was perhaps his favorite novel of the series. It is also Dannay and Lee writing at their very peak.

After so much introspection, it was inevitable that the cousins could not keep up such an intense pace. *Double, Double* finds Ellery returning to Wrightsville to investigate several deaths and a disappearance. As in *There Was an Old Woman*, a nursery rhyme forms the center of a killer's pattern, causing numerous problems both for Ellery and, in the structure of the novel, for the reader. But after the despair of *Ten Days' Wonder* and *Cat of Many Tails*, this comes as an almost refreshing break in style, in fact, a calm before the coming storm of the Korean War.

Queen's prior two rather weak Hollywood novels were written in the period of the women's slick magazines. But with *The Origin of Evil* Ellery returns to California for his best book set in that locale. Deeper and richer in plot and characterization, the novel is more cohesive in terms of the mystery itself than either of its Hollywood predecessors. The origin of evil clearly lies in Darwin's *Origin of the Species*, in the nature of man (and woman) to seek survival of the fittest, to tend toward evil in order to gain the upper hand. International politics, here in the form of the Korean War, are dealt with rather simplistically and unsatisfactorily. Fortunately, this element does not overshadow the central theme of the book and, while hindsight would require a different view of that war, does not detract from the power of Queen's writing.

However, international politics play a much more significant role in *The King Is Dead*. Once again Ellery, this time with his father, the Inspector, is removed from ready access to scientific methods of crime solving. They are kidnaped by agents of a wealthy and powerful munitions manufacturer, who is threatened with death. The Queens are taken to the manufacturer's private island, an amalgamation of concentration camp, industrial slavery and brute militarism. In spite of the fact they apparently know who the killer is and when he will strike, and that the arms dealer is locked in a sealed room where the murderer cannot reach him, Ellery and the Inspector are unable to prevent the crime. While attempting to solve the murder of the arms manufacturer, they must also confront and deal with the violent threat of totalitarian power. Although the plot has its weaknesses, the locked-room puzzle is both clever and fair.

In *The Scarlet Letters* Queen once again returns to the dying clue to provide an answer to the question of murder. A small, fully developed set of characters; an interesting Broadway setting; a rapidly dissolving marriage; and blackmail provide the background for, ultimately, murder. The problem with dying clues is that they can often be subject to many interpretations. Indeed, it might not be an actual clue at all, but a purely fortuitous act. So the detective needs to be able to read the victim's mind in order to solve the crime. He must think exactly as the deceased thought. In spite of the rather dubious nature of this form of clue, in particular the one used here—two bloody letters that Ellery actually helps the victim write!—no one did this type of clue and its solution better than Queen.

The novels in this classic period are generally without peer in the genre. Even the weakest among them are far from failures. Ellery explores, not always willingly, the dark underbelly of American life. Along the way he meets individuals worth saving, as well as those who should be destroyed before they do more harm. He finds corruption, insanity and tragedy in family life. He wages his own private battle for order against evil, not always successfully. Ellery confronts murderers and fascists, often paying a high price psychologically for his efforts. With these works Dannay and Lee achieved the pinnacle of their career as Queen. The cousins had gone from pure detection puzzles to richly drawn characters embroiled in the struggle for justice. These books stand among the best mysteries, and most insightful novels of the human condition, ever written.

THE FINISHING STROKE

By the mid-1950s Queen was nearing the end of his best period. Various clues within the next two novels, the last of the 1950s, lead the reader to believe the cousins were ready to close the book of Ellery's life after nearly thirty years. In 1956 they published *Inspector Queen's Own Case*, subtitled *November Song*. Inspector Richard Queen has reached mandatory retirement age, and finding himself with nothing to do, visits an old police friend in small town Connecticut. Ellery, being out of the country, makes no appearance in the novel, which is centered around Richard's relationship with a nurse he meets while there. Murder brings them together and more murder keeps them together. The book examines several issues from a gerontological point of view, including love, feelings of uselessness, and renewal of spirit and hope, thus proving that age need be little barrier to accomplishment. With Ellery not present to provide the deductions, however, the solution and the manner in which the case is resolved do not have the usual impact one has come to expect from Queen. But this is a minor quibble in an otherwise fine novel, even one in which Ellery is absent.

The last novel of this period was probably initially designed as the final novel about Ellery. *The Finishing Stroke* opens in 1905, the year that the cousins and Ellery himself were born. The story then shifts to 1929, the year of publication of *The Roman Hat Mystery*. But the Ellery of this book is the human, personable detective of the later periods, not the humorless "thinking machine" of the Golden Age period. In fact this Ellery has been stung by a review of *The Roman Hat Mystery*: "To be accused of mere competence was galling; to be called a 'philovancish bookworm' etched itself into his soul; to be charged with coyness revolted him." This nostalgic look back at the young Ellery Queen is clearly meant to be the conclusion of his long and illustrious career. The final section of the book opens, for the first time since *Halfway House*, twenty-two years earlier, with the "Challenge to the Reader," reprinted in part from *The Roman Hat Mystery*. The book then ends in 1957, twenty-seven years after the murder, with the final resolution of the crime. While probably far from the best of the canon, the authors' intent to come full circle, to connect the "two Ellerys," and to say good-bye to an old friend in a warm and touching manner is clearly seen. In this, Dannay and Lee succeeded splendidly.

Five years later, more books were to come. They were, unfortunately, mostly a repetition of themes covered previously, of relationships already explored and, with perhaps one exception, were far from the high standards set from 1929 through 1935 and 1942 until 1958. A number of the Queen novels in this final period, from 1963 to 1971, were ghostwritten, although the work was plotted by Dannay and overseen by the cousins. It is better to end this examination where the authors originally intended, with *The Finishing Stroke*, and with Ellery Queen, Frederic Dannay and Manfred Lee at the top of their game.

CONCLUSION

Anthony Boucher once commented that "Ellery Queen *is* the American detective story." But Queen was also much more than that. Queen, the detective, was a force for justice in the face of evil. Even though he grew and changed with the times, that facet remained above all. Queen, the author, recognized societal ills and sought, through the novels' underlying themes, to bring to readers more than just pure mystery stories. In *The Tragedy of Errors* Dannay planned to offer readers a look at the insanity of today's world. The authors' somber view of life expressed in *Calamity Town* and other works perhaps held true for Dannay a third of a century later, when the outline for that book was written. Even though the detective changed, perhaps the world around him had not after all.

The King is dead. Long live Queen.

CONTRIBUTORS

Robert Adey is a specialist on the literature of the locked-room mystery story, and author of *Locked Room Murders* (2nd edition, 1992) and co-editor of three anthologies of impossible crime stories. A retired official in Her Majesty's Customs, he has been Fan Guest of Honor at the Bouchercon.

Catherine Aird is the author of nearly a score of detective novels, mostly featuring Sloan and Crosby, and one volume of short stories. She is a past Chairman of the UK Crime Writers' Association and was the first winner of the CWA/Hertfordshire Libraries Golden Handcuffs Award.

Mike W. Barr's "First Story" appeared in the May 1973 *Ellery Queen's Mystery Magazine*; it was, fittingly, about murder at a comic book convention. He has sold hundred of pages of comics about such famous characters and series as Batman, Sherlock Holmes, The Shadow, Doc Savage, *Star Trek* and *Star Wars*. His creation, *Camelot 3000*, was the first comic book maxi-series and he is currently marketing a fantasy novel.

Jon L. Breen is the author of six mystery novels, two Edgar-winning reference works, over eighty short stories, and more articles and book reviews than he can count. He contributes "The Jury Box" to each issue of *Ellery Queen's Mystery Magazine* and is a professor of English at Rio Hondo College in California.

Douglas Dannay is the oldest son of Frederic Dannay and is living in new York with his wife Barbara. He has two children, Beth and Jeff, both living in Massachusetts, and six grandchildren.

Richard Dannay, a son of Frederic Dannay, is a copyright and publishing lawyer in New York City. He and his wife, Gloria Phares, are rare-book collectors. They have a daughter, Elyse, and a granddaughter Samantha.

Michael Gilbert's first mystery novel, *Close Quarters*, was published in

1947, and since then he has written almost thirty novels and nine short story collections. Considered one of the finest storytellers to emerge in the postwar era, he has been recognized as a Grand Master by the Mystery Writers of America, and is a recipient of the Cartier Diamond Dagger for Lifetime Achievement from the Crime Writers' Association. He is a Commander of the Order of the British Empire.

Ted Hertel, Jr. is a practicing attorney in Milwaukee, Wisconsin, and an adjunct professor at the University of Wisconsin Law School in Madison. He served as the Local Arrangements Chair of Eyecon '93 and as Conference Co-ordinator of Bouchercon '99. He is married to Maggie Ley and is a lifelong Ellery Queen fan.

Edward D. Hoch, past President of the Mystery Writers of America, has published more than eight hundred short stories and appeared in every issue of *Ellery Queen's Mystery Magazine* since May 1973. He was Guest of Honor at the 1991 Bouchercon, and his stories have been honored with the MWA Edgar Award and the Bouchercon Anthony Award.

Janet Hutchings came to *Ellery Queen's Mystery Magazine* as editor in 1991. She is also the editor of the *EQMM* short story anthologies *The Cutting Edge, Simply the Best Mysteries, The Deadliest Games, Murder Most British, Once Upon a Crime*, and *Once Upon a Crime II*. Prior to joining the magazine she held a variety of jobs in publishing, including mystery fiction editor for Walker & Company.

H.R.F. Keating has been writing crime fiction since 1959, most notably novels about the Bombay detective, Inspector Ghote. Since 1967, when he began writing for *The Times* in London, he has also written extensively about crime fiction. In succession to G.K. Chesterton, E.C. Bentley, Dorothy L. Sayers, Agatha Christie, and Julian Symons, Harry Keating is President of The Detection Club.

Rand B. Lee is a freelance writer and editor living with his blind husky, Moon-Pie, in Santa Fe, New Mexico. His short stories have appeared in *Isaac Asimov's Science Fiction Magazine, The Magazine of Fantasy and Science Fiction*, and *Amazing Stories*. His articles have appeared in *Horticulture, Organic Gardening*, and other magazines. His first book, *Pleasures of the*

Cottage Garden, was released last winter by Friedman/Fairfax Publishers, He is the youngest surviving son of Manfred B. Lee, co-author of the Ellery Queen stories.

Peter Lovesey has been writing long enough to have been reviewed (favorably) by John Dickson Carr in *Ellery Queen's Mystery Magazine* in the seventies. His twenty-one mysteries and three short story collections have brought him many international honors, including the *EQMM* Readers' Award and the Gold Dagger from the Crime Writers' Association.

Hidetoshi Mori is a mystery critic and translator specializing in Golden Age mysteries and impossible crimes. He has translated Douglas G. Greene's *John Dickson Carr: The Man Who Explained Miracles* into Japanese, and co-edited an anthology of locked-room stories with Robert Adey. He also recently won a critical award for his work.

Francis M. Nevins is a professor at St. Louis University School of Law, and author of five mystery novels and about forty short stories. He has edited more than fifteen mystery anthologies and has written several nonfiction books on the genre, two of which (*Royal Bloodline: Ellery Queen Author and Detective* and *Cornell Woolrich: First You Dream, Then You Die*) won Edgars from the Mystery Writers of America.

Bill Ruehlmann, author of *Saint with a Gun* (the first book-length study of the private-eye novel) and *Stalking the Feature Story*, is professor at Virginia Wesleyan College and book columnist for *The Virginian-Pilot* in Norfolk, Virginia. He encountered Sherlock Holmes in the fourth grade and has been a mystery fan ever since.

David Siegel was born during the height of the depression and grew up loving the world of radio entertainment. He has one of the largest collections of Golden Age of Radio audio as well as printed materials. He recently edited as collection of Gothic horror radio scripts, *The Witch's Tale*. Under the name Book Hunter Press, Dave and his wife write and publish a series of guides to used book stores.

Dr. Richard A. Smith, has practiced medicine in the Peace Corps and the

Indian Health Service; he is the winner of numerous awards including The William A. Jump Award for Public Administration, The Gérard B. Lambert Award for Innovations in Health Care ("for being slightly out of step with the majority of his colleagues"), The Rockefeller Public Service Award for Improving Health Care of the Underserved, and The Department of Health and Human Services Award for Pioneering the Physician Assistant and Nurse Practitioner Movement.

Steven Steinbock graduated from Hebrew Union College with an M.A. in Jewish Education, and he has served numerous synagogues and has written study guides, manuals, and textbooks for synagogue use. His mystery reviews and articles appear in various magazines and newspapers, and he is contributing editor of *Audiofile* magazine. He lives in Maine with his wife and two sons.

Bill Vande Water holds the Baker Street Irregulars investiture "An Enlarged Photograph" for his work in identifying BSI (and MWA) dinner photographs from the forties and fifties. He is photo editor for Jon Lellenberg's BSI history series and has been guilty of monographs in *Murder Ink, Baker Street Journal* and *The Serpentine Muse*.

Hillary Waugh is one of the major influences on the modern police procedural novel; his *Last Seen Wearing*, published in 1950, was calculated to resemble the investigation of a genuine crime. He received the Grand Master Award from the Mystery Writers of America in 1989.

James Yaffe is author of four novels and a collection of short stories about "Mom," the Bronx armchair mystery maven. He has written nine other novels, many stage and television scripts, and two non-fiction works, including *The American Jews*. He is professor of literature at Colorado College.

THE TRAGEDY OF ERRORS AND OTHERS

The Tragedy of Errors and Others by Ellery Queen, including contributions in honor of Ellery Queen's seventieth anniversary, is printed on 55-pound Glatfelter Supple Opaque recycled acid-free paper, from 12-point AmeriGaramond. The cover design is by Deborah Miller. The first edition comprises two hundred fifty copies sewn in cloth and approximately one thousand, two hundred copies in trade softcover. Each clothbound copy includes a separate pamphlet, reproducing (in reduced size) original manuscript and typescript pages of *The Tragedy of Errors*. The book was printed and bound by Thomson-Shore, Inc., Dexter, Michigan, and published in October 1999 by Crippen & Landru Publishers, Norfolk, Virginia.

CRIPPEN & LANDRU, PUBLISHERS

P. O. Box 9315
Norfolk, VA 23505
E-mail: CrippenL@Pilot.Infi.Net
Web: www.crippenlandru.com

Crippen & Landru publishes first edition short-story collections by important detective and mystery writers. Most books are issued in two editions: trade softcover, and signed, limited clothbound with either a typescript page from the author's files or an additional story in a separate pamphlet.

The Tragedy of Errors and Others is the twentieth book published by Crippen & Landru. Currently available are short-story collections by Marcia Muller, Edward D. Hoch, Patricia Moyes, James Yaffe, H.R.F. Keating, Margaret Maron, Michael Gilbert, Peter Lovesey, P.M. Carlson, Peter Robinson, Jeremiah Healy, Doug Allyn, and Ed Gorman. Forthcoming is a collection of the best Ellery Queen radio plays, as well as first editions by Marcia Muller, Edward D. Hoch, Clark Howard, Carolyn Wheat, Wendy Hornsby, Michael Collins, Max Allan Collins, Ron Goulart, Michael Z. Lewin, Joe Gores, and Christianna Brand

Crippen & Landru offers discounts to individuals and institutions who place Standing Order Subscriptions for its forthcoming publications. Please write or e-mail for details.